I0647495

POPULAR PUBLICATIONS   FACSIMILE EDITIONS

Terror Tales #9
(May 1935)

Starting in 1934, editor (and publisher) Harry Steeger unveiled *Terror Tales*: perhaps the flagship magazine in Popular Publications' so-called "Weird Menace" lineup of titles. Running for almost 50 issues, *Terror Tales* showcased some of the best suspense, mystery and terror stories to see print in the pulps. This facsimile of the May 1935 issue contains stories by Arthur Leo Zagat, George Edson, Nat Schachner, H.M. Appel, Paul Ernst, Arthur J. Burks, and Robert C. Blackmon.

Authors:

Arthur Leo Zagat, George Edson, Nat Schachner, H.M. Appel, Paul Ernst, Arthur J. Burks, Robert C. Blackmon

Illustrators:

John Newton Howitt, Amos Sewell

Contents originally appeared in the May 1935 issue of *Terror Tales* magazine. Copyright © 1935 by Popular Publications, Inc., and assigned to Steeger Properties, LLC. This edition copyright © 2024 by Steeger Properties, LLC. All rights reserved. "Terror Tales" is a trademark of Steeger Properties, LLC.

NOTE: We have attempted to restore the original page scans in this facsimile in order to provide an enjoyable reading experience. However, in some cases there can be text loss due to damage to the original pulp, tight bindings, or other reasons.

LONESOME?

Let me arrange a romantic correspondence for you. Find yourself a sweetheart thru America's foremost select social correspondence club. A friendship letter society for lonely ladies and gentlemen. Members everywhere; CONFIDENTIAL introductions by letter; efficient, dignified and continuous service. I have made thousands of lonely people happy—why not you? Write for FREE sealed particulars.
EVAN MOORE   P. O. BOX 988   JACKSONVILLE, FLORIDA

DIABETICS:

Read How I Had SUGAR RELIEF in 48 Hours
after years of suffering. Now I can eat, work and enjoy life. No costly or painful treatments. Sugar removed in easy natural way. Pleasant. Results amazing. Write for Specialist's Free Book.
ARTLEE REMEDY CO., Dept. 84, Box 1314, Chicago

GET YOUR MONEY'S WORTH!

Demand Magazines with the POPULAR SEAL— Your Guarantee of Full-Value, Thrilling Fiction!

Gallstone

Colic Pain, Stomach Distress, Pain in Right Side arising functional troubles Liver, Gallbladder, Indigestion, heavy load in stomach, tightness around waist, constipation, often quickly relieved with this Safe Home Treatment. Avoid operation if possible. Don't suffer longer. Send today for FREE trial. No obligation. Write Quick.
SOLVOTONE CO. K-2, 4393 Cottage Grove, Chicago

FREE TRIAL BOX

GET ACQUAINTED CLUB

Established Reliable Members everywhere (Many Wealthy)
If lonely, write for sealed particulars
P. O. BOX 1251   DENVER, COLORADO

Learn Radio in 10 WEEKS

I WILL FINANCE YOUR TRAINING IF YOU ARE SHORT OF MONEY

Prepare for jobs in Radio Broadcast, Talking Pictures, Television by 10 weeks of practical shop work in the great Coyne Radio Shops, on real machinery and equipment. You don't need advanced education or experience. Free Employment Service for life. Many earn while learning. Electric Refrigeration—Air Conditioning included. MAIL COUPON TODAY for free book which tells you how hundreds have become successful Radio Men after taking my training.
H. C. LEWIS, Pres., COYNE ELECTRICAL & RADIO SCHOOL
500 S. Paulina Street, Dept. 55-5H, Chicago, Illinois
Send Free Radio Book and facts. Tell how I can pay for my course on Easy Payment Plan after I graduate.

NAME
ADDRESS
TOWN   STATE

Kidneys Must Clean Out Acids

The only way your body can clean out Acids and poisonous wastes from your blood is thru 9 million tiny, delicate Kidney tubes or filters, but beware of cheap, drastic, irritating drugs. If functional Kidney or Bladder disorders make you suffer from Getting Up Nights, Nervousness, Leg Pains, Backache, Circles Under Eyes, Dizziness, Rheumatic Pains, Acidity, Burning, Smarting or Itching, don't take chances. Get the Doctor's guaranteed prescription called Cystex (Siss-Tex). Works fast, safe and sure. In 48 hours it must bring new vitality, and is guaranteed to fix you up in one week or money back on return of empty package. Cystex costs only 9c a day at druggists and the guarantee protects you.

BE A DETECTIVE

Work home or travel. Experience unnecessary.
DETECTIVE Particulars FREE. Write NOW to
GEORGE P. G. WAGNER, 2640 Broadway, N. Y.

NEW DISCOVERY Makes 100-400% PROFIT

OAKROMA, The marvel of the age: Scientifically compounded by processing finest mountain white oak and treating with imported flavors. Gives "aged-in-wood", natural color Bourbon, Rye or Scotch taste overnight, at 1-5 the cost of Bonded Goods.
OAKROMA SELLS ON SMELL!
Repeats on taste, Big Demand Everywhere. Homes, Offices, Clubs, Lodge Members, eager buyers. Oakroma plus a pint of druggist's alcohol, plus a pint of water—you have a quart of fine liquor with "aged in wood" taste, whiskey bouquet and mellowness. Write for "NO RISK TRIAL OFFER" FREE and Master Sales Plan.
HOME MFG. CO., Dept. 3465, 18 E. Kinzie, Chicago

Good LIQUOR at BIG SAVING

WALDE'S WONDER SALVE

Results are remarkable! It is more than a first aid, everyone should have it.
Sold with a money back guarantee. For—Infections, Boils, Burns, Old Sores, Fresh Cuts, Bruises, Sprains, Ulcers, Felons and Sore Eyes.
TRULY A WONDER PRODUCT
Order Now. 50c Prepaid
H. R. WALDE, Lake Wales, Fla., Dept. H

Try This on Your Hair 15 Days

- Your hair need not thin out, nor need you become bald.
- This different method stops thinning out hair, lifeless hair, itching, dandruff and threatened or increasing baldness, by strengthening and prolonging the life of the hair for both men and women. Send your name now before it's too late for the 15 days' FREE trial offer. Write JUEL DENN, 207 N. Michigan, Dept. 100, Chicago

CASH

For Old Gold Jewelry and Bridgework. There is money lying around in your old trunks and bureau drawers if you will only take action. Send us your old jewelry for free appraisal. If our price is not satisfactory to you we return it.
AMERICAN GOLD SCRAP CO.,   1617 FIFTH AVE., Government License No. P-12-2743   PITTSBURGH, PA.

U.S. GOVERNMENT JOBS!

START
$1260 to $2100 Year

Steady Work
Many early examinations expected.
Men - Women, 18 to 50
Mail Coupon today sure.

Franklin Institute, Dept. F-179, Rochester, N.Y.
Sirs: Rush to me without charge (1) 32-page book with list of U. S. Government steady jobs. (2) Tell me immediately how to get one of these jobs.
Name................................
Address................................

COUPON

1

Volume Three   May, 1935   Number One

Cover Painting by John Howitt
Story Illustrations by Amos Sewell

Published every month by Popular Publications, Inc., 2256 Grove Street, Chicago, Illinois. Editorial and executive offices, 205 East Forty-second Street, New York City. Harry Steeger, President and Secretary, Harold S. Goldsmith, Vice President and Treasurer. Entry as second-class matter pending at the post office at Chicago, Ill., under the Act of March 3, 1879. Title registration pending at U. S. Patent Office. Copyright, 1935, by Popular Publications, Inc. Single copy price 15c. Yearly subscriptions in U. S. A. $1.50. For advertising rates address Sam J. Perry, 205 E. 42nd St., New York, N.Y. When submitting manuscripts kindly enclose stamped self-addressed envelope for their return if found unavailable. The publishers cannot accept responsibility for return of unsolicited manuscripts, although care will be exercised in handling them.

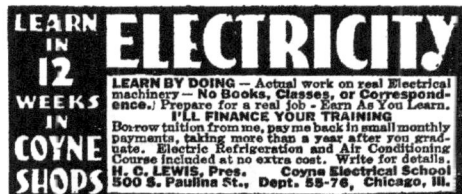

LEARN IN 12 WEEKS IN COYNE SHOPS ELECTRICITY

LEARN BY DOING — Actual work on real Electrical machinery — No Books, Classes, or Correspondence. Prepare for a real job - Earn As You Learn. **I'LL FINANCE YOUR TRAINING** Borrow tuition from me, pay me back in small monthly payments, taking more than a year after you graduate. Electric Refrigeration and Air Conditioning Course included at no extra cost. Write for details. H. C. LEWIS, Pres. Coyne Electrical School 500 S. Paulina St., Dept. 55-76, Chicago, Ill.

Be Your Own MUSIC Teacher

LEARN AT HOME

FOLLOW THIS MAN

Operator No. 38

Secret Service Operator No. 38 is on the job! Running down dangerous Counterfeit Gang. Tell-tale finger prints in murdered girl's room.

Free *The Confidential Report Operator No. 38 made to his chief. Write for it.*

Earn a Regular Monthly Salary

YOU can become a Finger Print Expert at home, in your spare time, at small cost. Write for confidential full report and details. Literature will NOT be sent to boys under 17 years of age.

INSTITUTE OF APPLIED SCIENCE
1920 Sunnyside Ave.
Dept. 73-85 Chicago, Ill.

to play by note, Piano, Violin, Ukulele, Tenor Banjo, Hawaiian Guitar, Piano Accordion, Saxophone, Clarinet or any other instrument. Wonderful new method teaches in half the time. Simple as A B C. No "numbers" or trick music. Cost averages only a few cents a day. Over 700,000 students.

FREE BOOK Write today for Free Booklet and Free Demonstration Lesson explaining this method in detail. Tell what your favorite instrument is and write name and address plainly.
U. S. SCHOOL OF MUSIC 3675 Brunswick Bldg., New York City

POPULAR MAGAZINES ARE IDENTIFIED By The POPULAR SEAL.

Buy Them!

REMINGTON PORTABLE

ONLY 10¢ A DAY

Free Typing Course

Buy this beautiful brand new Remington Portable No. 5 direct from the factory for only 10c a day! Standard 4-row keyboard, standard width carriage, margin release on keyboard, back spacer, automatic ribbon reverse—every essential feature found in standard typewriters! Carrying case and typing course free. Special 10-day free trial offer. You don't risk a cent! Write Remington Rand Inc., Dept. 193-5, 205 E. 42nd St., N. Y. C. Don't delay. ACT NOW!

10 DAY FREE TRIAL OFFER

Classified Advertising

Instruction

CUSTOMS, CLERKS, STENOS. Join CIVIL SERVICE. Men-Women, $1,800 up. Advancement, opportunities. Complete instruction, coaching, examinations course $1.00. BOX TWO, 24 West Twentieth Street, New York City.

GOVERNMENT JOBS. Start $105—$175 month. Men-Women, 18-50. Qualify now for coming examinations. Experience unnecessary. Full particulars—list positions, FREE. Write today. Franklin Institute, Dept. P-9, Rochester, N. Y.

Business Chances

SELL BY MAIL! BOOKS, NOVELTIES! BARGAINS! Big Profits. Particulars free. AL. ELFCO, 525 South Dearborn, Chicago.

Writing Services

MANUSCRIPTS SOLD. Collaboration. Coaching. FREE Booklet. "TRUTH ABOUT LITERARY ASSISTANCE," will save money and disappointment. Laurence D'Orsay, 122 Marion Bldg., Hollywood, California. Commission 10%. (Established 1915).

Personal

LONELY? Join reliable club. Sealed particulars free. Mary Lee, Box 445-M, Rolla, Missouri.

THE FRIENDSHIP CLUB aids you to make friends (with a view to matrimony). Members everywhere, strictly confidential. WRITE for sealed particulars. P. O. BOX 19, CHICAGO, ILLINOIS.

Patents

PATENTS SECURED. Reasonable terms. Book and advice free. L. F. Randolph, Dept. 573, Washington, D. C.

Frog Raising

BIG PROFITS RAISING JUMBO BULLFROGS. Inclose 10c for literature. American Frog Industries, South, Rayne, Louisiana.

Poem—Songwriters

WANTED: ORIGINAL POEMS, SONGS for immediate consideration. MMM Publishers, Dept. PP, Studio Bldg., Portland, Ore.

POEMS set to music. Published. McNeil, Bachelor of Music, 1582 W. 27 St., Los Angeles, California.

Motorcycles

SEND 15c for illustrated used Motorcycle catalog. Large stock. Bargains. Indian parts. Accessories. Indian Motorcycle Company, Kansas City, Mo.

Distributors Wanted

DON'T BE A JOB HUNTER—Start your own business on our capital. No hard times; no layoffs; always your own boss. Hundreds average $3,000 to $5,000 annual sales year after year. We supply stocks, equipment on credit. 200 home necessities. Selling experience unnecessary. Wonderful opportunity to own pleasant dignified, profitable business backed by worldwide industry. Write Rawleigh, Dept. E-U-PBL, Freeport, Ill.

3

CHAINS OF THE LIVING DEAD

A Feature-Length
Mystery-Terror Novel

What uncanny devil's crew roamed the bleak slopes of Superstition Mountain, clanking heavy chains? Was it madness that sent Laura Standish racing through the haunted night, begging for aid which no living man dared give her?

By

Arthur Leo Zagat

*(Author of "Crawling Madness,"
etc.)*

LAURA STANDISH blurted out her husband's name before she was fully awake. "Frank!" But there was no answer. Even before she realized just what it was that had awakened her, a chill, little quiver of dread brushed her spine.

The fire on the hearth, before which she had fallen asleep, was low and there was no other light in the huge, dark-ceilinged parlor. Good Lord! It was already night and Frank wasn't back yet! He was to have been gone only an hour, ample time to go down the hill to the General Store in the village and get some food for supper. She had been to tired after their long trip from the city to go with him, and he had seemed worried about leaving her here alone. Something must have. . .

A sound at the door brought Laura startled to her feet. He was here at last! Returning circulation needled her cramped legs so that she could not move. Frank had a key, but . . . .

The rasp of flesh against wood, out there in the gloomy foyer, was somehow furtive. Heat beat out from the glowing logs in the fireplace, yet Laura shivered with queasy cold. Suddenly she knew it was the very stealthiness of that groping hand—the menace implicit in its quietness—that had awakened her. And suddenly, she knew also that she was afraid.

Someone was trying to get in! And it was *not* Frank! For a moment, panic swept over her, and she cowered back against the fireplace, so close that the hem of her dress began to scorch. She was alone in this musty, old country house, and the deep pine woods separated her by a good mile from the village. From any ordinary prowler, she was comparatively safe. Frank had insisted on making sure, before he went, that all windows were safely locked. He had made her promise to shoot home the two heavy bolts on the big, front door.

But there was something eerie about the way whatever it was outside fumbled at the barrier, a strange quality of blindness, of mindlessness. If only Frank was here, with his capable shoulders and easy confident smile! But he was gone, had been, for hours. Overwhelming dread seized Laura Standish as she listened to the aimless groping, the queer slithering sounds, along the stout pine of the door.

Had the Thing outside caught Frank unawares as he was hurrying back to her? Was his dear body even now a cold and mutilated corpse somewhere in the depths of the woods? Did the intruder know that she was alone, a helpless, unprotected, lovely morsel?

She fought herself back to a semblance of sanity. She must not think such thoughts! She forced her trembling voice into just the right mold of casual inquiry. Perhaps, if the prowler knew she were not

afraid, if he thought there were others with her in the house . . . .

"Who is there?" she called.

Still there was no answer. The latch! Oh God, the latch! It was rising in its cradle, slowly, with infinite stealth. She stared at its inexorable movement with eyes that were frozen with terror. A new sound came—a snuffling, whining eagerness. It held no human quality in its muffled breathing; it was more like the whimper of an animal to whom human doors are insoluble puzzles.

Laura exhaled slowly. She had forgotten; the bolts in their sockets would hold. The Thing outside seemed to realize that too. The whimper became an angry snarl that pierced the double thickness of the porch. Then silence reigned for an instant, silence during which Laura, still backed against the fire, felt the blood pound madly in her veins. Had the snuffling monster given up the attempt, gone away to its lair?

C*R-R-RASH!* The heavy door quivered and bent inward. The stout iron bolts strained against their sockets. A screw started from its spiral bed, and sawdust fell in a tiny cloud to the floor.

Smash! Crack! Crash!

Again and again came the terrific thumps. The great, pine door groaned and sagged under the impact of the repeated blows. Each thud was a sledgehammer smashing home against Laura's skull. She could not move, she could not breathe in her terror. No human being could break down that heavy, reinforced barrier. Slam! Her stiffened lips worked soundlessly. A screw, inches long, clattered to the floor. One iron socket dangled uselessly on the precarious thread of a single fastening.

A choked scream tore at her throat. "Help! Frank! Help!" she cried in an agony of fear. Then dreadful realization clamored in her brain, saged her limbs to a feral crouch. Frank, her husband, could not hear. Perhaps never again would he . . . .!

She glared around with mounting madness. There was no hope, no escape for her. It was a small, summer cabin they had rented for the season, intent only on primitive seclusion and the cozy warmth of the two together alone. The ground floor was all one room—a timbered parlor with a gigantic native-stone fireplace for its kitchen. Overhead were two bedrooms, now empty and forlorn. There was no rear door through which she could flee, and her fingers twisting frantically at the window latches would bring the mysterious attacker down upon her.

Thick, ominous silence succeeded the smash of a heavy body against a weakening portal. The Thing had heard her cry for help, was waiting stealthily, flesh flattened against the rough pine. She could hear the slobbering wheeze of its breath, the whimpering sound in its throat.

Oh God! What dreadful monster was crouching out there, waiting for her to cry out again, resting before the final attempt that would bring the door and hinges and all crashing to the ground?

In the very extremity of her fear, Laura found new strength. She must *see* what it was that had come out of the night, that sought terrible entrance into the lonely cabin. She must see—before it was too late. Her limbs were no longer part of her. They moved her away from the dull-red embers of the hearth, across a long, interminable expanse of flooring, where the shadows ebbed and flowed with each flicker of the dying flames, toward the thick-curtained window that gave on the porch. One dreadful thought swelled and swelled inside her skull until the thin bone ached and reeled under its impact.

Why was the attacker slamming with unhuman strength against the door; why

had he not forced an easier entrance through a window?

She shrank desperately from the sinister implications of that thought; she spewed it out like an unclean thing. Outside, the whimper grew to an eager, slavering whine. It had heard her slow, tortured progress across the floor. *It was waiting for her to open the door!*

The thought rocked her consciousness, made her senses reel and swim. She tore at the heavy stuff of the curtain with terror-strong hands. It swung back to disclose a long, narrow panel of corpse-white luminance. A cold, dead moon struggled to pierce the dense, black shadows of the pines, the taller gloom of the hemlocks. A little beyond, where the old lumber road bent in an arc past the house, the victorious beams bunched in an irregular patch of leprous white.

But Laura saw only the crouching Thing on the porch. It was flattened against the tottering door as if it were listening, waiting. A slanting dart of moonlight spread shudderingly over its massive frame, bathed it in an eerie glow that paralyzed her limbs, exploded red horror in her brain.

And as if it had heard the moan that tore involuntarily from her pallid lips, the monster sprang away from the door, turned its head.

FOR one, long, terrible moment their eyes met, locked. Dear God, it was a man! But a man such as Laura had never seen before. No light of human reason showed in those glaring eyeballs, or softened the bestial madness of that ape-like face. Yellow froth dripped from the corners of the slobbering mouth, and the thick spume gurgled audibly in the throat. Worn, tattered pants and an even more tattered shirt of indistinguishable hue covered the barrel-thickness of the body.

Long, hairy arms dangled almost to the ground.

Laura tried to shrink back, but could not. Her hand gripped the curtain as if glued. Her muscles were beyond control. She knew now that the man outside was mad; stark, irretrievably mad. Prayers, pleas for mercy, could not penetrate that distorted brain. She was beyond all help, all human aid.

The madman whirled on bare, misshapen feet like a cat. His right hand, hidden in the shadows, swung into view. Great God in Heaven! The moon glinted with unholy glee on a broad band of greyish metal that encircled his powerful wrist, and sprayed in a shower of frozen light on the chain that dangled therefrom. The last link showed jagged, broken edges of metal where it had been snapped in two.

Laura felt herself fainting, yet she did not fall. She tried to tear her hand away from the revealing curtain, to run madly, anywhere, away from that awful sight. But a nightmare paralysis held her in icy embrace. The madman had been chained, like a wild beast, like a slave! He had broken away with superhuman strength to roam the wild woods, to find her, a hapless victim for his maniacal will!

The creature thrust his manacled hand toward the window in a strange gesture. The links rattled hideously. He opened his thick lips and a curious whimpering, like that of a beaten dog, spewed from his mouth. As if—almost as if he were imploring her to open the door, to let him in.

Terror flared in Laura's eyes. She dared not, she must not. It was the cunning born of a diseased mind, luring her to destruction. The maniac seemed to sense her loathing, to read her great fear aright. A change came over his bestial face. His lips snarled back to show yellowed teeth; he lunged against the already battered portal. There was a great rend-

ing sound. The loosened bolt flew with a doomful thud to the floor. Only one shaky bolt remained between her and his raging lust.

He heaved back again, shoulder arched for the final blow. Laura came to desperate life. Little sobs whimpered in her throat, cataracts of ceaseless blood made turbulent noise in her ears. Her unlocked fingers flew to the catch on the window, tugged frantically at its rusty iron. If only she could twist the stubborn metal, swing up the window in one swift heave, and catapult her slender body through the opening just as the madman rushed in the door, perhaps . . .

The maniac hunched forward, heedless of her puny efforts. His darkened mind could not associate the window with entrance or exit. In seconds, he would be through, upon her shrinking body. And still the window catch, imbedded with all of Frank's lean strength, refused to give. With sudden, awful clarity she knew it would not open.

The flame of hideous triumph glowed on the madman's brute face. His shoulder bent against the portal. It tottered, split. The night air swirled through the crack with beating wings. Laura shrieked, and lifted her small white fist to smash out the pane of glass.

Clank! Thud—thud! Clank!

WILD hope swept like a consuming blaze through Laura's shaking form. She was saved! That thudding noise was from the old lumber road. It was the sound of many men, slogging along through the rutted dirt. She would shout, she would shriek, she would pour all her desperate terror into one last cry. They would come running, those unseen, blessed men; they would rescue her from this obscene Thing outside. Perhaps even —her bursting heart bounded even more madly than before—Frank was with them, hurrying them back to save his Laura.

See, already the monster had heard, was afraid! He whirled away from the sagging, half-open door. He darted back into the shadows, a crouched, dim-seen animal. Whimpers of fear rumbled in his hairy throat.

Fierce joy surged through her veins. She thrust back the heavy shrouded curtain. She raised her clenched fist to slam against the glass; she opened her mouth to cry for help.

But the cry choked back in her throat with a sudden tautness of muscles; her hand fell like a leaden weight to her side. A horrible thought had seared her brain and clogged her veins with ice. *Clank! Clank!* Much louder now, nearer, coming down the mountain. *Clank! Clank!* Beating out a steady, slogging rhythm, a strange, Satanic music. One—two—one —two! March, march. Clash of metal on metal. One foot up; other foot down! Clank—clank!

Laura caught at the window sill to keep from falling. Her scalp was a squeezing cap of horror; her lungs fought for breath. She knew now what caused that eerie sound. *It was the chains of manacled men, marching Things coming down the mountain after her.* Coming to help their fellow monster, coming to cut off all hope of her escape!

On and on they came, still invisible, still shrouded by the dark-massed pines, chains clanking, metal ringing in horrible unison. The madman in the shadows stirred, whined, and was gone into the night like a ghost called back to its grave. But she knew why he went. He was joining that hideous rout of his fellows, summoning them with slobbering whimpers to the attack.

She stood at the window like immovable stone, left hand still frozen to the curtain hem. Her brain shrieked madly:

"Run, while there is yet time. Out the door, into the woods, anywhere before *they* come for you!" But her muscles were tight knots of flesh, and her skin, a leaded coffin.

Now it was too late. The ominous clank of the chains burst upon her frozen senses with a wild, triumphant chant. Out there, where the road bent in an arc, and the moonlight lay in a splotch of scabby, leprous white on the grey dirt, a figure moved. For one moment it stopped and lifted its head, laved in the cold, dead spotlight of Hell's own theater.

GREAT God in Heaven! The face that turned toward the house, as if it saw her fear-rigid at the window, was the face similar to that of the madman who had just slunk away from her porch. The glare was gone from this one's eyes, the snarl from his flabby lips. His huge, knotted shoulders bowed forward in abject servitude, as if crushed under unutterable weights. The links of the manacle encircling his wrist stretched back into the blackness from which he had stepped. A new band of metal enclosed the thickness of his ankle.

For a moment he hesitated, brutish face vacant with the quenched embers of madness. Then, a strange hissing sound from the rear, and he jerked forward his head, hunched shoulders, and stepped into the blackness of eternity.

Clank—thud—clank! Laura's heart was pounding so she had not sensed the momentary cessation of that Devil's march. The dual chains writhed across the dead white patch of moon like disembodied serpents, endless, gleaming with unholy luster. All her faculties were concentrated on that small spot of light. What was coming next, what dreadful portent to snap the bonds of her reason?

The links jerked taut. Another figure lurched forward into the moon, blinked, raised his head. Black, mindless eyes bored into her very soul, shrivelled it to nothingness. Mad, mad, every one of them! Madmen, chained to each other like wild beasts, marching along the road like slaves to some dreadful auction block! Hate distorted his stubbled countenance; mad lust leered at her from under a mop of uncut hair. His chains clanked startlingly, he lurched toward the house with sudden motion. He had seen the terrified girl at the window.

Again that sinister, hissing sound. He jerked backward, the links stiff as ramrods. Unutterable terror flared like sheet lightning over his hideous, lecherous face. His head bent low, his shaggy form strained forward. The chains resumed their rhythmic clanking, and darkness swallowed him whole.

Clank, clink, clank! Oh God, was there no end? More chains writhing through the moon-flooded spot; another bowed and mindless figure, stumbling through the patch, blind and weary, not pausing in his staggering pace, not lifting his head. Black night enfolded him too. And still another figure moved into the light, shaking his head from side to side, leaping upward with little grotesque hops, jerked downward by the restraining metal, mouth wide in horrible, soundless chuckle. He was even more dreadful in his mindless mirth than the others.

And still the double chains writhed backward into the night. An endless, marching army of the damned, hell's creatures clanking their way from blackness to blackness. Laura could stand it no longer. Her throat was a strangling fire, her body a shivering lump of ice. Madness plucked at her own brain, leered at her with eyes like those of the manacled Things, invited her with loathsome whispers to join that procession of the doomed.

With the last grim shreds of her rea-son she held back the shrieks, held back from rushing out into the night. The road bent in a sharp curve around the house. The clanking madmen now enfolded her, hemmed her in on three sides. Behind was the grim, precipitous upthrust of Superstition Mountain. Soon they would turn, creep forward through the murk, spring upon her with horrid slaverings.

Her heart rapped out a last desperate tattoo, then stopped altogether. Everything stopped; every process of her being. The room, the night, the earth, the universe, froze like a run-down clock. This was death, or worse. . . .

CHAPTER TWO

Terror That Walked By Night!

OUT in that little spotlight of the damned, another figure had moved —another unit in that endless, terrible procession. He was thinner than the others, and his clothes, ripped and torn though they were, held still a semblance of civilization. His lean, etched head was lowered, and the chains clanked dismally from his wrist and ankle.

The moonlight gloated over his form, slithered over every slender line. He jerked his head upward, dug his heel in the dirt for a sudden stop. The chains tightened and clashed with harsh, metallic noises. His eyes, wide, dark, blank-seeming, were fixed on the house, on the very window where Laura stood, turned to nightmare marble.

The universe stopped, then crashed into headlong ruin. *That staring face— smeared with filth, hollow with the sagging stupor of the idiot—was the face of Frank, her husband!*

For one long second, her heart was a small, still ball; for one eternal second, her mind was blank and dark as the faces of the madmen, as even Frank's was.

Then heart and lungs and brain seethed and roared with whelming floods. She whimpered in her throat like an animal in pain. It was impossible; it was not true! It was a delusion, a frightful dream come to torment her! What was Frank, her adored Frank, doing in that dreadful company? No! no! He was still down in the village, buying supplies. Something had happened to delay him; he had met someone he knew. They were talking, unmindful of the time.

That was it. Certainly this was all a bad dream from which she would wake soon—shuddering and gasping with strange, remembered terrors—and Frank, his dear face aglow as ever with live intelligence and with tenderness for his wife, would be shaking her gently by the shoulder.

She hugged that thought, turned it and twisted it in her half-mad mind. Madness, madness! *She* was mad; not they outside. It was all only a trick of the fiendish moon, done to plague her. Oh Lord, please don't let them torment me like this; please drive them away!

But the figure of Frank refused to fade into mist as had the others; his sightless eyes clutched at the window, yet did not seem to see. Then she knew it was true, that it was real. The curtain ripped away in her down-gripping hands; she lunged against the window, eyes wide, mouth grim with a force beyond all fear. Her husband was out there, chained like a wild beast, broken to a mindless wretch. But he was hers, *hers!* She must get to him, she must rescue him, tend him carefully. Nothing else mattered. The window was the quickest, shortest way.

Glass crashed under her beating fist. The jagged shards pierced her delicate fingers, gashed them cruelly. But she did not even feel the pain. She raised her bleeding hand to smash out the rest.

Frank's head came higher. Was that a flicker of light, a mere spark of moon in his eyes, or was it warning? She had no chance to know.

Out of the blackness of the road behind leaped a figure. His form was shrouded in a mantle of swirling black; his head was a startling mask of white. The moon beat in vain against the grey baldness of his head, the white bushiness of his eyebrows, the snarl that contorted his bloodless features. His right arm was uplifted, and a long, snaky whip swept downward with a hissing sound.

The lash whistled on Frank's bent back, bit deep in shuddering agony. A quiver raced across his dirt-encrusted countenance; then it was wiped clean of all expression, vacuous with the dreadful emptiness of the mad.

Frank stumbled, lurched forward, head bowed down like the others. He moved out from the ghastly spotlight, into the hellish darkness of the trees, with never a backward glance. After him strode the jailer, whip hissing and writhing, his face, turned momentarily toward Laura, a leering object of evil. Then he too vanished into the murk.

Laura must have shrieked then. Woods and shattered window and the moon above joined in a devil's dance. Round and round and round—blur of whips and mouthing maniacs and insistent rhythm of clanking chains. Farther and farther —fading away; then closer—closer, strangely transmuted into a hissing and crackling like . . .

SHE opened her eyes, looked wildly around. Where was she? The room was a thing of groping shadows. The logs on the hearth were dull, red embers. At one end, a last charred stick had fallen, flared into fantastic flame, crackled, and died again. It was that which had brought her out of her faint.

Faint? Laura struggled unsteadily to

her feet, looked with dull wonder at her bleeding arm, pressed it to her aching head. What had happened, why had she fallen down? The night wind blew across her cheek. Good Lord, she must have let the door open, or Frank . . .

"Frank!" The name forced its way out in a tearing crescendo of remembered terror. "Frank!" It all came back in a nightmare sweat that drenched her limbs. "Frank! Frank!" she screamed again, and plunged for the sagging door. With undreamt-of strength she ripped open the last, loose bolt, sent the crazy barrier crashing to the ground. Out on the porch she ran, calling again and again: "Frank!"

But the anguished name was lost in the muttering forest, in the unrelieved blackness of the night. The moon had dropped behind Superstition Mountain, and the glacial stars mocked her desperation. The road was a dim thread of darkling stuff, and the leprous patch was gone.

Silence pressed down upon her with weighted shrouds. No sound of chains, of thudding feet, of hissing whip. The chained madmen had gone their clanking way, and with them, Frank. Frank, who had seemed mad as they, bound to them in hideous life and death!

Oh God, she mustn't go mad. That was what they wanted, that hellish crew and still more hellish jailer. Perhaps, out there, in the Stygian gloom, they still lurked, moving forward with each rustle of the masking night breeze, coming to drag her down with them.

Her eyes were balls of fire, her ears a straining tension. The night closed in on her with stealthy whispers. Alone in a forest of evil, where mindless Things gloated and lusted for her. If only Frank . . . She sobbed aloud, and the sound was like plunging knives. *Frank was out there too!*

She must save her husband. Fear dropped from her like an outworn garment. Her brain cleared. She must get help to rescue him, to rid Squam Village of the marching horror. One mile down the winding dirt road lay the village, one long mile of unrelieved darkness and shapes and sounds and Things in chains.

The skin crawled over her flesh, but she forced herself down the steps, across the little clearing, into the road. If only she had a flashlight! But the batteries had gone dead in the old one, and Frank had expected to buy new ones in the village.

On and on she went, groping her way along, smashing into trees, tripping over unseen roots, hearing the loud thud of blood in her ears, hearkening to the scuttering noises of the woods, panting, gasping for breath, jerking with unimaginable terror when a ghostly branch whipped across her face. She must have been delirious half the time; her blurred senses gave no clear impression of that dreadful flight. But indomitable will, the flame of her love for her husband, forced her on and on.

The invisible road dipped sharply. Below her, nesting in a hollow, was the tiny village of Squam. It was an oasis in a wide-flung desert of pine and towering hemlocks. A single light glowed ahead, in the very center of a clump of huddled shapes. Its feeble, yellow flame struggled wanly through an oblong of dirt-encrusted window; its tiny flicker died in hopeless struggle with the encroaching darkness.

But the glare of a thousand arcs, the brilliant illumination of the Great White Way, could not have been more welcome to Laura just then. Tears streamed down her pallid cheeks as she flogged her tottering limbs toward that glimmer of hope.

SHE swayed uncertainly across the threshold of the General Store, Squam's only business mart and focal center. Here, amid boxes of crackers and open barrels of sugar, between fly-specked counter and shelves bulging with faded calico bolts and unsold axes, hugging the pot-bellied stove in winter and spitting dexterous gobs of tobacco juice against its cold, grey sides in summer, congregated nightly the menfolk of Squam.

Here, under the rheumy eyes of old Matt Kroll, owner and tutelary genius, were settled the profoundest political problems of the nation as well as the proper bait to use for pickerel in the nearby lakes.

A single lantern swayed drunkenly from a cobwebbed rafter. The air was drowsy with cheap tobacco and the odor of much-worn clothes. A half-dozen men sprawled negligently over as many boxes, their forms indistinct in the wavering yellow smoke.

Old Matt was saying in his high, querulous voice, edged with anger at some unexpected opposition: "I tell you, Lem. I seen 'em with my own eyes, down in the Holler, a-marchin' under the moon an'—"

Laura caught at the door jamb and fought for breath. These men would help her, they would find Frank for her. They were natives, born and raised in the woods; they would track down the man with the whip and his hellish rout.

Lem saw her first. He clucked out a warning that made Matt break off abruptly. Lem was the town cobbler and village atheist. He and Matt were forever arguing over the old wives' tales that clustered around Superstition Mountain. But now the sneer wiped off his dark, bony face, and fear leaped into his snapping, black eyes. Matt suspended his last word in midair, and his jaw gaped as if he had seen a ghost.

The other men, workers in the lumber camps, turned negligent, stubbly faces toward the girl framed in the doorway, and froze as they were.

"Miss' Standish, heh, heh!" Matt cackled with obvious effort. "Why, it sure is good tuh see yuh. I wuz jes' telling the boys . . ."

Some inner reserve of strength pushed Laura into the center of the room. Matt wavered and stopped. No one noticed. All eyes were intent on the panting girl. A deathlike silence enveloped her.

"My husband, Mr. Standish," she gasped. "He—he's . . . !"

There was secret terror in the furtive glances they gave each other. Lem averted his eyes, broke in hastily: "Why sure, Missus Standish. He was here 'bout three hours ago. Got hisself some groceries and went on home. Didn't he now, Matt?"

Matt's shrunken face was suddenly more shrunken than before. He mumbled over toothless gums what might have been confirmation.

"But he never reached home!" Laura cried desperately. "He—never—reached home!" she repeated with a dreadful sob.

No one moved; no one stirred. Even the lifting layers of smoke seemed frozen in the air. Eye sought eye stealthily, thin lips licked secretively. Silence eddied about Laura like a hostile sea.

Lem's swarthy face was a dirty grey. "Heh, heh!" he chuckled with forced heartiness. "Mister Standish musta taken the long way back. P'raps he stopped at Bottomless Pond t' catch hisself a mess o' bass fer supper. Bought hisself a fishin' rod from old Matt, didn't he now?"

There was a chorus of eager grunts. Laura looked wildly around at their dim-seen faces. They knew something; something dreadful. They were hiding it from her.

"You don't understand!" she cried imploringly. "I—saw Frank. He was—"

She fought against rigid throat muscles at the memory. "He was in chains, manacled—with madmen. Oh God!" she hid her eyes shudderingly. "They marched and clanked, and a Thing with a whip beat them on." She took her hands away and screamed out. "Frank will go mad! They will kill him! You must—you *must* save him."

A BOX fell over with a startling crash. They jittered to their feet, babbling hoarsely. Their hands trembled and their jaws twitched with uncontrollable nerves. Their stubbly faces were grey with fear.

"You're crazy, gal," Lem snarled through stiffened lips. "You've been dreaming, an'· seein' things in yuhr sleep. Bet Mister Standish is home right now, wonderin' whut's become of yuh."

Two lumberjacks in the rear, great hulking fellows, shuffled furtively toward the rear of the store, where a door led out to the back road. Shoulders hunched, they slunk out into the night.

Old Matt, the storekeeper, opened his mouth, gulped, but no words issued. "Lem's right," a lanky woodsman muttered, and eased unobtrusively toward the door.

Scorn, searing anger, effaced all other emotions in Laura. These men were afraid, that was it, deathly afraid of something. They would not help—they dared not help! They were trying to make her out as mad, subject to hallucinations. *She had not seen?* God, if only she hadn't! See how they were scattering like chaff, slinking away into the night, like cowardly rabbits.

"I did *not* dream," she blazed, "and you—and you—and you—" she stabbed an accusing finger at each cowering man in turn, "know it as well as I. You are afraid—cowards, all of you!" Then her scorn broke down, and she was a frightened, sobbing girl again. "Please," she implored, and choked over the words, "help my Frank! They have made a mad Thing out of him; they are whipping him with terrible whips. Please!"

They looked at each other uneasily. Terror was bright in their eyes. The gangling woodsman had already edged toward the entrance, and he moved suddenly into the blackness. There was an oath, an exclamation, a squeal of terror from the escaping man as he rebounded back into the room. Feet clumped angrily.

"Good Lord, Wally, what's the matter with you?" someone said gruffly. Wally shrank against the shelves, trembling like a leaf. Two men entered with hearty, banging strides, like a breath of fresh air into that brooding, fetid room. Laura gave vent to a gasp of relief. Here were men who would understand, who would believe. More, they would act; they would force these others into shamed movement.

"Thank God you've come, Sheriff!" she cried.

"Hello!" The tall, spare man with the greying hair and grim, weathered face stopped short with an air of surprise. "What are you doing out this time o' the night, Mrs. Standish?"

His companion, a stout, rubicund individual with a bright gold watch chain across his ample stomach, and a shabby stethoscope peeping out of his vest pocket, looked quickly at Laura's drawn, bloodless face, then at the staring, silent men in the store. He was the village physician, Dr. Alva Carey. He had stopped several times at their cottage to pass the time of the day.

"What's happened, Laura?" he asked sharply.

Everything was a haze to her. Precious minutes were passing, while Frank . . . . She sobbed out: "You—you *must* believe me. Madmen, with a monster who whips them on, have caught my husband. They have chained him; they are driving him mad. Doctor, Sheriff, you *must—must* save him!"

Split second of hesitation in which time seemed to stand still. Would they think her mad too, as those others pretended; would they . . . ?

DR. ALVA CAREY cleared his throat. That little sound crashed upon Laura with the dreadful effect of a thousand tons. Oh God, he did not believe!

"I'd suggest," he said with careful casualness, "a little sleeping draught tonight, Laura." He fished in his capacious pocket, pulled out a fold of brown paper, extended it to her.

She dashed it violently out of his hand. It dropped to the floor, burst open, and white, crystalline powder sprinkled over the dirty, pine boards. Fools, fools, all of them! She caught hold of the Sheriff's rusty black coat with desperate, imploring gesture.

"Sheriff, I demand you do your duty. I tell you I saw them with my own eyes, marching in chains right in front of my own house. I saw—Frank. He stopped, looked at me. Then that frightful monster whipped him on. If you don't hurry, it'll be too late. Too late!"

Sheriff Tom Beasley looked down at the panting, swaying girl. His lips tightened. There was perceptible hesitation in his manner.

"Well, Mrs. Standish," he drawled, "if you put it that way, I s'ppose there's nothing else for me to do, but go hunting through the woods. But that there tale o' yours, as Dr. Carey kin tell you, is one of the oldest stories we got round these here parts. That's how Superstition Mountain, back of your place, got its name."

Dr. Carey nodded absently. "That's right, Laura," he muttered. But his man-

ner was fidgety, as if he were anxious to get away.

"But you'll go, won't you, Sheriff?" she implored.

Sheriff Beasley sighed audibly, tightened his belt, looked with longing eyes at the ancient stove, plentifully decorated with tobacco juice, spat, and said:

"Right this minute, ma'am. I'll get out right now an' comb the woods. My advice to you, though, is tuh go back home, and see if maybe your husband's there by this time." The Sheriff turned to the silent few who were left in the store. "Any o' you boys want tuh help me?" he inquired genially. "I'll swear ye in as deputies."

No one answered. As one man, the lumberjacks drifted to the door, vanished hastily into the night. Lem brought up the rear. His dark, glowing eyes were full on Laura as he passed, then he too was gone.

Dr. Carey fidgeted, looked at his watch. "Good Lord!" he muttered. "I've got a call to make. 'Bye, Laura, and don't worry. Frank'll be all right. Bet he's waiting for you now." Then he was out, hastily. The next moment the rattle-bang of his Ford made thundering echoes along the road.

Sheriff Beasley looked at Matt Kroll, the storekeeper, who seemed as if frozen behind his counter, and chuckled morosely.

"Lots o' help a peace officer gets in Squam, eh, Matt?" He turned to Laura. "Now don't you go worryin'," he advised. "I know these woods like a book. An' if they's any bunch like you say in there, I'll get 'em." His grim lips were a straight, compressed line, and his lean, sinewy hand patted the holster that protruded underneath the rusty black of his coat. A tarnished star gleamed dully on his shirt. But Laura detected scepticism in his frosty, blue eye, saw the imperceptible wink he tipped old Matt.

Then he clumped through the door, down the sagging steps. His boots made dull, thudding noise in the night and died away to a faint shuffle.

CHAPTER THREE

Handprints of Horror

LAURA pressed her hand to burning temples. No one believed her, not even the Sheriff. Yet—faint hope—he had promised help. He was efficient, he knew the woods. Perhaps . . . .

A dull ache pervaded her being. Somehow, she knew that Beasley would never find Frank. That skull-faced man with the whip, driving his chained maniacs along—no human being could find him. A little moan parted her gelid lips.

Old Matt Kroll stirred. His shrunken visage was a faint blur behind the counter. "What ye aim to do now, Miss' Standish?" His voice was high and querulous.

Laura started. She had forgotten he was still there. Suddenly she was afraid of this store of flickering, yellow shadows, of the weazened storekeeper whose rheumy eyes blinked like those of a cat.

"I—I am going back home," she gasped. "Perhaps my husband has returned. Perhaps it was all—" She was near the door, poised for flight. She stopped, lifted a bewildered hand to her forehead. Was it possible that it was all a dreadful dream; that she had never seen . . . ?

Matt pressed the counter with stiff fingers. Driving terror cracked his voice. "Don't ye do that, Miss' Standish! Fer God's sake, don't ye go back t' that place. Stay here in the village. I'll put ye up in my place, only don't go back. It— it's . . . ."

He broke off, clamped his trembling lips tight. He had said too much. But Laura shook her head wearily. "I must," she said very low. "If Frank is there, he'll need me. I—thanks—"

She fled out into the cool air, driving her aching limbs through the murky dark again. Matt's quavering accents followed her, hoarse with warning, with fear. "Don't go! Wait, I want to—"

But the dense, marching trees swallowed his words. Up and up she climbed, up to the base of Superstition Mountain where their cottage nestled—the secluded, lonely house in which they had planned to spend such a lovely summer. Laura's lips drew back in a bitter groan even as she flogged her way through the impenetrable darkness. Each tree was a thing of menace, behind which lurked a maniac with glaring eyes; each whisper of wind in the branches the crackling hiss of the whip; each rock that loosened beneath her pounding feet clashed with the sound of chains.

But one driving purpose held her from going mad, from falling headlong, a gibbering, screaming thing, in the crowding forest. Frank was home—waiting for her, wondering where she was, worrying! All the men in the store had said so. Dr. Carey was sure of it. They ought to know; they knew this place and all its tales. She must have imagined it, of course. Something that she had heard in the village and forgotten, had troubled her dreams in front of the waning fire. She had slept, hadn't she? She pumped air into her gasping lungs. It was all very natural. She hadn't awakened until much later, with the dream thick upon her, and she had rushed out like a madman. How Frank would laugh and scold her in that gentle way of his! How the village folk would gossip and whisper about her nerves behind her back. She could never face them again. But—and dread cramped her limbs again—they had *known*. She had seen it in their faces, in the way they had slunk from her presence as if she were a plague. She lashed on in the Stygian gloom, heedless of ripping branches, and stumbling feet. What terrible conspiracy of silence had been wrapped around her; what awful thing was being hidden from her?

They *knew* what had happened to her husband. They knew, and the blood had drained from their faces, had locked their lips in frozen fear!

The faint starshine disclosed the clearing ahead, the place where the chained madmen—and Frank—had clanked on their way to Hell. Nothing was there now, nothing but slinking shadows and a blob of trees. She turned up the path, with feet that suddenly dragged. Her heart was a pounding triphammer. Anticipation squeezed her skull. Soon she would know. . . .

THE house loomed like an unquiet shadow. A faint flicker of red peeped out at her, died into the merest glimmer. Her heart stopped pumping; she swayed, forced herself erect again. It was true then. She had not dreamt. The door lay on the porch just as it had fallen, and that little whisper of flame was the dying hearth-fire in the living room.

She moved forward like an automaton. Nothing mattered now. Frank was in chains, a maniac, held in thrall for some frightful purpose. There was nothing for her to live for—nothing!

Without knowing what she did, she entered the living room. A dim glow of red stained the bottom of the fireplace. Soon it would be gone, and the advancing shadows would claim the place for their own. She shivered and life flooded her veins again.

Oh God, what would she do, alone here, surrounded by creeping shapes, encompassed in darkness? She must have a fire, a great, roaring, blazing fire, to chase the grinning maniacs back to their lairs, to keep her from going mad through the long, dreadful hours before daylight. There was a stack of wood in the alcove recess the other side of the hearth. Frank had chopped it, and sawn it into neat lengths only that morning. How faint and far away it all seemed!

Good Lord? What was that? She stopped dead in her tracks, whirled around to face the door. She wanted to scream and could not; icy fingers slithered along her spine.

Something was coming up the path, dragging, shuffling, as if . . . . Dread encased her in a gelid sheath, held her in a death-like grip. Up the stairs to the porch the Thing dragged leaden feet, its breath, loud in the stillness, was like a whine. For a moment it hesitated, and the panting grew heavier. Then, slowly, very slowly, it dragged across the creeping boards. Laura felt as if she were in a press that ground her bones to powder and crushed her frozen flesh into a million splinters. Shrieks tore her throat yet could not issue.

Something dim and shadowy bulked in the doorway. It swayed, straightened, turned its blurry head from side to side. Then, pad—pad . . . it was coming in!

The bonds of terror broke. Her body flooded with roaring flame. Shriek after shriek burst from her throat. The figure jerked to a halt, then raced forward.

"Laura!"

Laura shrank away. Had terror turned her brain, made her insane? But there was nothing unreal about the arms that gripped her tight, the tremulous flow of endearing expressions, tendernesses known only to the two of them. It was Frank who held her close, so close that the thumping of her heart was one with the equally loud pounding of his own; it was Frank whose mouth sought hungrily for hers. The ecstacy, the reaction, was too much for her. With a little moan she sank limp in his arms.

IT must have been only a minute after that she awoke dizzily. Fresh wood on the hearth had just caught, and the yellow-blue flames were licking greedily up the sizzling pitch that exuded from the pine. Frank was bending over her, his face in the shadows.

"Frank darling, what a dreadful nightmare I had. Can you imagine—I thought you were chained to madmen, that you too were. . . ? But it's all over now. You're back, you're really back!" She extended aching arms. "Kiss me, dearest."

Why did he stiffen against her questing arms? Why did he keep his face averted in the shadows? A terrible fear flared through her bursting veins. She lashed upward to her feet from the couch on which she had been extended; she caught the hand that hung limply at his side. The contact sent a chill to her heart; it was so icy cold.

Terror seized her again. She dragged him by main force to the fire, kicked with backward heel at the logs on the grate. They flared into a blaze of sparks. The shadows ebbed away from her, from her husband. He tried to disengage himself, to jump back into the fleeing darkness, but she gripped him with desperate strength.

"Frank!" The anguish of her voice beat about him like surf on a rocky shore. His face! Oh God, *his face!*

It was blank and grey in the stormy red of the fire. It was cold and hard and bruised, but the bruises had been washed with painstaking care. In that first moment, his eyes, those eyes that had always glowed with tender love at the sight of his wife, had held a secret glare, a wild, fearful light she had never seen before.

But even as she shrieked, something else struggled in their depths; something excited, that tried to mask itself into a poor replica of that former tenderness. A wan smile flitted over his grey countenance that chilled her blood even more than the earlier blankness. Frank was trying to conceal himself from her, to mask from her wifely eyes the hell that raged beneath.

"Laura," he muttered, "don't be afraid. Everything—will—be all right!" How terribly strange and stiff his voice sounded; with what effort he spoke!

She shrank away from him. "Then it was true, all of it!" she gasped.

"I don't know what you mean," he said thickly. "Nothing's true. You've been dreaming."

Oh God, he too thought that! Or was he pretending, as he would if he were really—mad? For the first time in her life, she felt fear in the presence of her husband. What had those monsters done to him?

She stared frenziedly at his clothes. They were no longer in disarray, as they had been—out there. They had been brushed, smoothed out; but a sleeve was rent—a tear showed on trouser leg. His coat was close about him, as if to hide some dreadful thing beneath.

"Tell me the truth!" She came close, caught his shoulders, glared into his eyes. He tried to pull away, but she held him fiercely. "Tell me—everything! I am your wife. I won't desert you, Frank. I'll care for you, I'll nurse you—" her voice broke, "back to health. Only tell me!"

"There's nothing to tell," he said vaguely, and his gaze slithered past her. "But I must be getting back; there are things I must do. But you," and for the first time the warmth of human emotion crept into his voice, "you must not stay here, Laura. You must go to the village at once, to Dr. Carey. Stay there until you hear from me again. And for God's sake, in the name of our love, of all that we meant to each other, do not ask me any more questions now, and do not stir from Dr. Carey's house until you hear from me. Do you understand? No matter what else you hear or see!"

HIS voice was urgent, imploring now. He gripped her slender arms with fingers that were chilled with cold. His eyes swung to hers; in their depths was driving desperation, but—thank God!—no trace of madness. Laura swayed happily. Her husband was sane, sane as she was! The whole thing had been a confused nightmare! She had mistaken someone else who resembled him in that furtive, shimmering moonlight. He wanted to protect her; he knew there were unclean Things on the mountain. She would not ask questions.

"All right, Frank," she murmured, "I'll do as you say."

Again she saw that strange gleam in his eyes. He dropped his hold, tugged at his coat pocket. His arm came out, holding a small flashlight.

"Here!" he said with queer, strained voice once more. "I got it in the village for you. You'll need it to show you the road."

She reached for it dully. His long, lean hand was out, extended, holding the black cylinder with scrubbed fingers. The sleeve of his coat fell back a bit. No shirt cuff showed. His wrist protruded, bare and white. *Bare and . . . !*

THE flashlight dropped with a clatter to the floor. She had seen! Oh God, she had seen! Everything was true, *everything!* The house rocked before her fainting vision, her husband's face swung in a hideous, distorted arc. A whimper of fear wheezed in her throat.

Frank caught her haunted gaze, followed it stupidly to its focus on his exposed wrist. A broad red mark encircled his flesh, a sinister band against the dead-white pallor of his arm. *A metal manacle had dug deep into that skin and shrinking flesh; a manacle which had been recently removed.*

His eyes came up smoldering, then flared with strange lights. His lips worked madly; he mouthed thick, indistinguishable words. Laura shrank back from the man who was her husband. Terror fought with the great love she had borne him. In a delirious ash, she saw everything. Frank had come back to her —a madman! He was no longer the man she had loved. He had come back, transformed, bestial, crafty with the perverted cunning of the insane, to entice her into the woods, where his fellow creatures could pounce upon her, could . . . !

She flung up a warding hand. Her horror-warped mind burst into a flare of rocketing lights. Toneless shrieks tore her frame to shreds.

Her husband took a step forward, hands clawing out. She stumbled back, back until her heel thudded against solid wall. Then, suddenly, he stopped, listened with tense fixity. Outside, from far away, came a faint, terrible sound. The unmistakable hiss of a whip slashing through the night.

Frank seemed to hesitate. His clouded gaze swung irresolutely from his whimpering wife to the door. The whip cracked again, nearer, louder. One quick, startled glance and he was racing toward the door, racing as if—oh God!—his master was calling him!

The bonds of fear fell from Laura. One desperate thought hammered at her brain. He was going back, back to that troupe of the damned, back to the Hell from which he had come. He was leaving her forever!

She started away from the wall; she stumbled across the expanse of floor.

Tears blinded her eyes, weariness locked her limbs to nightmare slowness.

"Frank, come back to me! Frank, don't go; don't leave me!" she wailed. But he did not hear; he could not hear. Out there in the woods, black with the blackness of Hell, came swift, rustling sounds. Then a sudden crash, followed by a silence thick with unknown terror.

Laura stumbled out on the porch, tripped, fell headlong to hard, unyielding boards. Somewhere, far off, before she drifted into oblivion, a Thing raised its voice in eerie, gloating chuckle. . . .

AN ape-like maniac pressed close over her rigid body. Laura could feel the glare in his red-rimmed eyes, the fetor of his breath. His hands slithered clammily under her shoulder; something hard and unutterably cold pressed against her ribs. A chain rattled loud in her ear.

With a faint shriek, she opened her eyes. Dim in the starlight, a figure bulked heavily over her. Even as fear parted her lips, it moved away; the small, hard object lifted. The chain gleamed yellow against a rounded background.

Dr. Alva Carey clucked soothingly as he crammed his stethoscope back into his vest pocket, jingled his watch chain. "You gave me quite a turn, Laura—finding you stretched out unconscious like that. But you're all right."

Slowly Laura's fuddled senses focussed on reality again. For a moment she stared upward at the rubicund, kindly-seeming face of the rotund doctor. There was something in his eyes that he tried to hide; something that belied the cheerfulness of his smile. She tottered to her feet. Fear beat with thudding wings against her ribs. What was masked behind that smile? What had he been about to do before she wakened?

Dr. Carey moved toward her. How carefully casual was his voice. "Frank come back yet?" he asked.

Frank! Laura glared wildly around. Great God, had she forgotten? The broken door leered vacantly back at her; the woods were a darkling, sinister stretch; Superstition Mountain reared its vast, inaccessible bulk directly to the rear—a gigantic, truncated mass of stone against a frost-blue sky.

She wrung her bleeding hands. "He—he's gone again," she wailed. "He was here, mad, like the rest. Then—then, the whip cracked, calling for him, and he went. I must have fainted." All former fears were forgotten in the agony of that terrible recital. Frank, her husband, was gone forever—a maniac! She caught hold of the doctor's sleeve with imploring, desperate gesture. "Dr. Carey," she cried, "you must find him; you must save him."

The doctor pulled away. His eyes were hard, blue pebbles and they refused to meet her anguished ones. They stole surreptitiously to the flattened top of the mountain, flicked away again. "I'll see what I can do," he muttered evasively. "In the meantime," he continued, and for the first time he stared directly at the girl, "I want you——"

She shrank away as he moved closer. She was suddenly afraid of this doctor who had mocked at her story in the village, who had appeared without explanation at this place in the heart of the woods, and who looked at her so strangely. . . .

He reached out to lay his hand on her arm. Laura jerked blindly away, whirled to run, when both froze in their tracks as if turned to stone. Far off—so far it seemed to emanate from the distant sky—came a long-drawn-out howl. It was the howl of a man in the last agony of pain; it was the bitter cry of a human being whom torture had bereft of reason. It was the voice of Frank Standish!

Close on its heels came a fainter sound, muffled but unmistakable and sinister in its implications. The sharp hiss of a whip lashing across a bared, slashed back. Hiss, crack, swish! But no further answering noise from a tortured throat. Then all was silence again, as if the shuddering sky had closed its portals against such dreadful deeds.

LAURA'S flesh crawled on her skeleton; red lightning thundered in her skull. With an inarticulate moan she tottered forward, stumbled, and fell. Dr. Carey stood momentarily motionless on the porch. The starshine shimmered with ghastly pallor on his rounded form. His ruddy smoothness had become grim and hard and grey. His eyes were fuliginous flares. His lips writhed in grey distortion. "So they've started!" he snarled.

The next instant, he was pounding down the steps, over the clearing, up the rutted lumber road toward the mountain. Over his shoulder he yelled a queer, harsh voice: "Stay where you are, Laura! Don't you dare leave the place!" Then all sound ceased, and the woods became alive with stealth and the noiseless gropings of eerie Things.

Laura rose unsteadily to her feet. Her limbs were water-weak; her skin, a prickling sheath of horror. But one consuming thought blazed in her brain. It seared all fears—all dread for her own safety—to shrivelled, tenuous wisps.

Frank had cried out like a mindless animal; Frank was in the clutch of a Devil who drove the creatures he had made mad with whip and clanking chains. She, and she alone, must save her husband!

But where was he? From what distant lair in that ominous, far-spreading forest had that tortured wail emanated? She clenched her lips until the blood came. Despair overwhelmed her. The woods billowed like a waveless ocean, vast, interminable. No further sound drifted to her straining ears. That strange, roaring noise she heard was the pounding of her own blood.

Suddenly she stiffened. Superstition Mountain! The great, truncated block of primeval stone slashed the star-studded brambles, scrambling through rubble and sky like a grotesque Titan. Its treeless, granite flanks scowled down upon her with lowering laughter. Dr. Carey had flicked his surreptitious glance at its ominous bulk, had looked hastily away when he thought she saw. At Frank's last anguished shriek, he had raced up the old lumber road—the twin, dirt tracks that dwindled to a trail and died abruptly at the grim upthrust of the barrier wall.

Dim, half heard stories swarmed her fevered brain, crawled into every nook and cranny of her mind. Stories she had heard on the few occasions she had gone with Frank to the village to get their mail, to buy supplies. Stories that had been mumbled around the inevitable pot-bellied stove in the General Store, of strange lights that gleamed on certain moonless nights on the sawed-off top of Superstition Mountain, where no human being had ever climbed. In the dim, long past, hardier men than those who now inhabited the faded village of Squam had tried to scale those sheer, granite walls. None had ever returned; no trace of their bodies had ever been found.

It was they, claimed the villagers with bated breath, who, neither dead nor alive, were doomed to a dreadful eternity on the inaccessible top of the mountain. Their thin shrieks were heard on still nights as they bent under the lash of the Devil who drove them on his hellish business. They —and others who had gone into the woods since then and never returned. Death came from causes unknown, from drowning in Bottomless Pond, from the wildcats that still lurked in the farther forest, from accidental discharge of their own guns.

But the natives of Squam knew better, and cowered at night under blankets when the lightnings played over that grim, stony mass and the crackling thunders were dreadfully like the crack of a snaking whip.

Frank had laughed at those stories raucously, and she herself, intent on her purchases from old Matt Kroll, had smiled at with half-absent thoughts. Only Lem, the cobbler atheist, and Dr. Carey, of the village folk, had not believed, and Lem alone had aired his opinions with harsh contempt.

CHAPTER FOUR

Trail of Despair

LAURA'S body became rigid with sudden driving purpose. She clattered over the fallen door into the parlor. The fire in the hearth had died to dull, grey ashes; the boards creaked loudly underneath. But her seeking foot crunched against the flashlight Frank had dropped. She groped for it, found it. A flick of a frozen finger and a thin pencil of white light stabbed through the murk.

Out into the moonless night again, flogging her numbed limbs along under the whip of her will. Hurry! Hurry! The elongated oval of luminance pierced like a pointing sword before her. She raced across the open patch, thudded with slim, high-heeled shoes over the rough, uneven ruts of the road.

The woods raced with her. The trees bent down over the trail, plucked at her with slithering branches. The ground heaved and rocked unevenly with her insane flight. Unseen shapes padded stealthily through the black masses on either side, closing in on her with furtive gait. The stars gleamed wanly overhead and shed no radiance. The beam bored a tunnel of whiteness through the solid blackness, and tilted up and up. The road was climbing.

The road became the trail and then a thread of forgotten hooves. The trees were giving way to stunted firs, to tangled underbrush. Superstition Mountain hulked ominously above.

On and on she drove, the breath wheezing in her lungs, her heart a squeezing gout of blood. She held her eyes desperately ahead, focussed on the beam that bobbed before her. She dared not look behind. That insistent sound was merely the thump of her own heart, the pounding in her own ears. But even as she clamored it to herself, she knew that it was not true.

Someone, something, was following her up the trail, was even now increasing its pace!

God, they were coming for her! The Things that were chained, the horde which had claimed her husband! They were coming to drag her, shrieking insanely, to their Master—he of the lash and horrible, white head.

Faster and faster she fled, heedless of twining saplings up the first slope of the mountain. Behind her, loud with doom, were pantings that were not her own—gusty sounds that did not issue from her throat. It seemed as if they were calling her, trying to slow down her pistoning limbs.

Her fingers froze to the flash. Her lungs were bellows without any air. The Thing behind was gaining. Soon it would be upon her, would . . . !

Insanity poured its gibbering turmoil into her brain. Laura did not know she was running and sobbing wildly now, did not know that even the trail was gone, that the mountain was a sky-climbing wall just ahead. One maniacal desire hammered at the confines of her skull. She must see this Thing that pursued her through the night, she must laugh shrill and loud in its face. Face? Perhaps it had no face; perhaps it was an insubstantial horror, an excrescence out of Hell. No matter. The desire to laugh, to shrill out her answering mockery, became an overwhelming madness.

She thrust her corpse-rigid head back over her shoulder. Her features glared with impending insanity. In her delirium, she did not realize that her back was against granite now, pressing into it with numb, icy flesh. She did not see the silent shape that rose like mist of the underworld out of the solid blackness of the mountain, that moved toward her without a sound, with shadowy tentacles outspread. . . .

* * *

All her shattering faculties were strained on the Thing behind, still clambering and puffing up the grade. She whipped her electric torch suddenly downward, back over the trackless waste she had just climbed.

The white pencil of flame flashed on a scrambling figure that jerked backward in startled fear. It held for a split instant on a swarthy, bony face, on eyes that gleamed like live, dark coals. The pursuer opened his mouth, and hoarse, strangled sounds spewed forth. Then his eyes flicked to one side of her. They went wide with desperate, grinding terror. With a great bound, he heaved out of the oval of radiance, into the blackness of the encompassing bushes. Shrill cries accompanied his sliding, plunging retreat down the rubble-covered mountainside.

Laura thrust back her head and laughed. There was madness in that laughter; there were fiery worms seething in her brain. But her limbs shook and her teeth unlocked.

It had been Lem—the cobbler of Squam, the village atheist—who had followed her, who had fled before the slash of the electric torch! She was safe now, safe to seek her husband, to get him away from the devils of the mountain.

The thought of Frank chased the crawling things from her skull, brought her back to sanity. She turned to force her way upward again. As she swung around, a shadowy shape flowed over her.

Suddenly she was enveloped in clinging, clammy folds. Her screams strangled in her throat, her flailing hands beat vainly against insubstantial softness. Something sickeningly sweet seeped into her consciousness. Her thoughts drifted slowly away. She tried to reach out for them, to hold them tight. Her mind tottered, fell into a bottomless pit of blackness. From far up, almost from the sky itself, came a low, snarling chuckle.

THERE was something wrong with this place. It was true it was night and her eyes were still closed in sleep. But this was not her bedroom on the upper floor of the summer cottage. Laura stirred uneasily, moaned in her drugged daze. She thrust out a lethargic arm as she always did when she dreamt and the things she dreamed were frightening. The feel of Frank's firm, warm flesh, the little ridge of muscle along his shoulder blade, always comforted her, always soothed her trembling nightmare fears back to the sweet drowse of untroubled sleep.

But now nothing met her questing fingers, nothing but chill, dank air and hard, damp stone. The dull ache in her head exploded into hurtling shards; the clinging, sickening embrace fled from her limbs. Her pain-heavy lids swung open; her bewildered eyes fluttered like frightened birds. A scream ached in her throat, jittered thinly through her lips. She pulled leaden limbs upright from the rocky floor on which she had been sprawled.

She had not been dreaming! It was no nightmare that vanished with a touch, with the first level streamer of light through the east-facing window. Terror flooded her being anew, locked her throat tight. She glared wildly around. Where was she? Where had that shapeless Thing which rose out of the depths of Hell transported her? Was she dead and buried beneath whelming earth in a vaulted grave?

All around, enclosing her like a living tomb, was rock and solid, curving stone. Shiny black it was, spangled with innumerable pinpoints of fire that lit up the whole round of the chamber with a ghastly, eerie light. Alive and gloating they seemed, those pinpoints, like baleful eyes mocking her whichever may she turned. The strange radiance bathed her shrinking form in a yellowish aura of flame. It seemed to flow through her silken dress, to tingle with prickling fingers against her skin. It seemed to slither into her quaking flesh, to munch with greedy, invisible mouths at her very bones.

Suddenly she was afraid; unreasoningly, instinctively afraid of the ghastly, probing light which emanated from the walls. More afraid even than she had been of the madman who had heaved against her door, of the stumbling, manacled Things who had been whipped through the woods. Her whole body felt unclean, her skin crawled under the impact of those strange, unholy flares. The strength seemed to ebb from her body, from her bones. They could not longer support her.

Laura swayed blindly toward the nearer wall. Her smarting eyes lowered, blinking against the weird luminance. She jerked backward with a choked cry. Horror stiffened her spine. held her rigid and unmoving.

There, at her very feet, lay a row of ghastly, frightful Things. Things that had once been men, and now were un-

mentionable decay. Nude corpses from which the clothes had long since rotted, glowing in the pale, yellow glare with a terrible greenish putrescence of their own.

The hard, virescent flesh was pitted and gouged—as if fanged, unhuman monsters had munched their hideous meals; the eyes were holes. that yawned in fleshless, grinning skulls; the jaw bones were crusted with dull, grey powder.

Corpses of men, dead for years, on whom the flesh had grown green and hard and pitted; corpses who had been carefully laid out in a grinning, dreadful row for her to see!

Laura's skull squeezed like the metal cap on a condemned man's head; rivers of ice pounded through her veins, crashed sickeningly within her heart. Merciful Heaven! These were the men of long ago who had dared scale the prohibited heights of Superstition Mountain, who had paid for their temerity with their lives. What demons out of Hell had done this to them? What fiends had thrust them in this gruesome chamber where the very walls flayed them with unholy light? Light that pitted and burned and seared —and held from natural decay. . . .

SUDDENLY Laura knew that this was to be her fate; that she too was doomed to scrutiny from the myriad, baleful eyes hidden in the shiny, black walls. She knew that she too would soon be a gouged and green-glowing Thing, immured for all eternity with these others.

Great, tearing shrieks ripped from her pallid lips, shrieks that mounted and soared to the bursting point of madness. She dashed insanely from side to side, beating on the light-studded walls with bleeding hands. Her stumbling feet kicked against a phosphorescent corpse. They sank deep into mouldy powder; ghastly dust that rose in a suffocating cloud. The solid-seeming Thing her shoe had touched had disintegrated into nothingness.

She jumped back, pressed her burning eyeballs with frantic fingers. Insanity knocked with peremptory summons at her brain. Her limbs twitched and her lips were a frozen orifice through which terror and madness went rocketing.

A thump penetrated somehow to her shrieking senses. What was that? She whirled just in time to see a yawning hole in the wall, to see two figures come clumping through.

Now surely, she was mad, even as Frank had been. Shrill laughter, more terrible than any scream, burbled from her lips. An insane husband and a maniac wife! What a perfect couple to roam the world together! She must find Frank and tell him of the jest. It rocked her sides and tore at her bones. Frank! She must go to him, tell him. . . !

If she were not mad, how could she have imagined these figures who stood motionless before her? First, a tomb of rock with a million glaring eyes; then corpses that flamed with a cold green fire, and crumbled into powder at her touch. Now these. . . !

They were huge, shapeless Things with grey, amorphous sides and fingerless appendages—monstrous beasts that stared at her unblinkingly out of round, glassy eyes set in grey globes that served for heads. Motionless, sinister, appalling! Like metal monsters they seemed to Laura's half-mad mind, spawned in the bowels of the earth; soulless beings obedient only to the will of Satan.

They stirred simultaneously into clanking movement. Their huge, hoof-like feet lifted, thumped down with metallic sound. Their dangling arms, grey and scaly, spread wide to engulf her.

The screeching laughter died in Laura's throat. A cold wind stirred her hot, dry skin, shivered down her spine. The madness fled and terror took its place. The monsters were coming for her!

Whimpering, she shrank back from their gelid embrace. On and on they came, with doomful, inexorable tread, the thump of their grey-shod feet loud in her ears. Back, ever back, forcing her closer and closer to the chrome-spangled rock, while the row of silent, green-tinged corpses grinned up at her with pock-marked laughter. Back, back, while her yielding feet stumbled and slid, and whimpers of fear grew to hopeless shrieks.

The monsters did not seem to hear; their glazed eyes did not waver. Laura felt smooth rock press against her back. She had reached the limits of the cavern. Pain lanced suddenly through her flesh; a thousand stinging arrows of fire. She swerved desperately away, just as a grey-skinned monster plucked with fingerless, shapeless hand for her body.

She stopped short, whirled again. The other loomed in her path, blocking with metal body and terrifying head all escape. Moaning, she darted back and forth in short, frenzied runs while the gruesome pair slowly and undeniably closed in, as if intent to crush her frail body between their unyielding forms.

An arm extended clumsily, swung around her slender waist. A baleful, unwinking sphere bent over her. Within that glassy eye, Laura sensed malignant hate, destroying lust. The touch of that whipping arm was icy hard to her quivering body. . . .

WITH a last despairing scream Laura rebounded from the gelid contact. Blind, mad with terror, she lunged forward, low, like a wrestler. Her soft flesh smashed against a steel-hard leg, caromed off in a sprawling dive that carried her under a down-clutching arm. She was free for the moment.

But the monsters were already turning, slowly, clumsily. Strangled snarls of rage sounded in what might have been throats. They were coming for her again. . . .

Laura pushed her trembling limbs erect. Where, in this place of horror, was there safety from the underworld Things? She shrank again from their thudding approach. This time they would get her; this time she could not escape!

The breath seemed frozen in her lungs, her legs were flowing water. She could not continue to fight. For the last time, she glared wildly around at the circumscribing rock with its unholy sparkle.

A grey monster lunged forward, just missing Laura as she leaped. But she had seen, and hope flared like a beacon light in her brain. Off to one side yawned round blackness. It was the opening in the stony wall through which the subterranean denizens had penetrated. What lay beyond she did not know; what dreadful horrors awaited her she did not pause to think. It was her only chance; and even now, as she hesitated, the farther creature seemed to read her thoughts. He quickened his clumsy gait; in another second, his metal form would be between her and the beckoning cavity.

She pivoted on her heel and ran madly for the opening. Muffled howls crashed in her ear drums; then blackness swallowed her whole. Her feet raced across the stony ground, forced her panting form up and up what seemed an endless tunnel. Behind her, the thick murk was loud with the pounding noise of pursuit. Laura sped on, caroming off invisible walls, bruising her tender flesh against sudden projections, slipping, stumbling, sobbing, squeezing her tortured lungs for the last reserve ounce of energy.

Then suddenly, the pursuing sounds ceased, and she was alone, in solid darkness. She leaned against a damp, cold wall, all strength gone. For what seemed hours, she swayed against the supporting rock, waiting for her pounding heart to slow to normal action; for her blood to stop its mad mill-race through her veins.

And all the while, her every sense was straining, listening for sounds or signs that the monsters had caught up to her. But the strange, breathless silence continued. . . .

Were those grey denizens lurking back in the tunnel, blocking escape in that direction? Were they chuckling, even now, in those muffled, snarling tones of theirs, knowing that worse lay ahead for her; that soon she would rebound, desperately, madly, to welcome even their horror rather than what was at the end of the tunnel? But mercifully, she did not know. . . .

Slowly her limbs resumed their functioning; slowly her brain clicked back to a semblance of coherent thought. She must think clearly if she were ever to get out of this frightful place.

Where was she? The enshrouding rock returned no answer, but she knew. The shadowy Thing had attacked her at the base of Superstition Mountain; when she awoke from her drugged unconsciousness, she was in a cavern; now she was in a tunnel of solid stone. That meant that somehow she had been carried into the very bowels of the granite upthrust; that even now, millions of tons of solid rock pressed down upon her.

Laura repressed the shudder of fear that rippled over her. Evil things were happening within Superstition Mountain, macaber beings swarmed in its womb who seemed not of earth or its denizens. And Frank, her husband? A pang pierced her heart. Where was he; what was being done to him in his mind-clouded state? What dreadful use was being made of him—of those other chained, bestial madmen who had clanked with bowed, brutish heads down the lumber path?

She started up again, aching for her husband. She must find him. Somewhere ahead, in the darkling upward swing of this mountain bore, lay the secret—and Frank! She must be brave; she must not give way to that shrieking madness again. Either she would win, or—well—life meant nothing without the man she loved. . . .

CHAPTER FIVE

Temple of Torment

LAURA put out her hand to find the wall. Its icy cold sent a shiver up her arm. She moved carefully along, feeling her way, trying to make no noise. But her heels clicked terrifyingly loud on the stone. For what seemed endless hours, she stumbled ever up and round and round in an ascending spiral.

In God's name when would this end? Suddenly she froze to the supporting wall. She pressed against its frosty surface as if she would push herself through the very rock. Nightmare terror encased her in a moveless shroud; retching nausea heaved at her stomach.

Somewhere, far ahead, came a dread, familiar sound. The clank, clank of chains dragging against stone. The manacled maniacs were coming for her!

Oh God, she could not stand this any longer! Behind her were the metal creatures, waiting for her in the cave of a thousand horrors. In front were madmen with brutish faces and gloating, red-lusting eyes. She was trapped, she had no way to turn, to run.

The clanking grew louder. The rock magnified the sound, the tunnel air caught it and threw it with unholy glee from wall to wall. *Pad, pad* went the naked feet.

Laura pressed tighter to the rock. A tiny flicker of hope pierced her frenzy. The steady, padding march was that of a single pair of misshapen feet. Perhaps, in the blanketing dark, he would not see her; perhaps he would pass her by unknowing.

She steeled herself for the supreme effort. He was closer now. She could hear the sharp rattle of chains, the banging sound they made as they struck against the rock. Bare feet pressed the stone with a sinister, sucking sound. Low, snuffling whimpers preceded him as he shuffled ceaselessly along, closer and closer. Already she could smell the peculiar fetor of the bestial mad, an effluvia that turned her stomach and made her faint with its foulness.

Here he was, snuffling and whining like an ailing dog. The noise of his groping approach was overwhelming Laura bit her lips to keep back the terror that welled within her; she bruised her flesh in a mad attempt to make herself one with the wall. She held her breath until her lungs were suffocating and bright lights danced before her eyes.

Oh God, please make him go on; please make him miss me! He was almost abreast now; his fetid breath was a foul exhalation. Thank God, he was moving ahead! Thank God!

Laura gulped in air and froze again. He had stopped. In the pitchy blackness, nothing could be seen. But all sound had ceased, even the whimpering noises in his throat. The silence pressed down on Laura's skull with unbearable weights. He had heard that sudden intake of breath.

She dared not move, dared not make the faintest noise. Somewhere in the tar-barrel murk crouched the madman, waiting with perverted cunning for her to betray herself. A hideous game of hide and seek in which she was the mouse.

Death-like stillness, more terrible than any noise, grew hideously. An enveloping glare of unseen eyes; the stale, rank odor of an animal's den tainted the air. Laura swayed faintly. She fought to hold herself erect, to control the shuddering of her body.

A grim, premonitory clank came to her. The maniac was tired of waiting. His chains dragged, and his bare feet made shuffling sound. Along the wall came the slithering noise of a sliding, pressing hand. *He was coming back for her!*

Every nerve shrieked madly for her to run. But he knew this tunnel and she did not. She could never escape. Her only chance was to stay—motionless, soundless, hoping. Oh God! Flashes of burning heat and unutterable cold swept over her quivering form. She was suffocating, bursting with an agony of fear. The slobbering of his brutish lips was loud in her ears.

Something brushed against her side. A long, choked scream tore from her throat at that contact; she flogged her fainting body away; she tried to run. Too late! A great, hairy arm whipped out, caught her in a grip of steel. A hoarse, avid cackle came out of the darkness. The next instant, her thrashing form was lifted into the air. An overpowering stench enfolded her, and she was being carried swiftly—where. . . ?

HOW long that dreadful journey took Laura was never able to tell. Mercifully, her mind was misted, unravelled by the very horror of her situation. It was the sudden cessation of movement—the murmur of strange voices—that roused her from her torpor.

Her captor had crouched against the wall; the thick gurgling in his throat had ceased. His filthy fingers dug deep into her form. Feet were moving up the tunnel.

A harsh voice raised in anger. The echoes made it hollow, artificial. "You damned fools!" it said. "You let her

get away. If she finds her way out——"

"It wasn't our fault, Boss," someone else whined placatingly. "It's those suits what did it. A fellow can't even turn properly in one o' them there things."

"Don't be worryin'," a third coarse voice spoke up. "She ain't got a chance t' get out. We'll find her fast enough, and then——" He chuckled, but there was no mirth in that chuckle.

"God help you if you don't," growled the one they called the Boss. He sounded nervous.

They were passing close by now, feet thudding in unison. Laura opened her mouth to scream, to cry out for help. They were at least human beings; perhaps there was mercy in their souls. There could be none in her captor.

But the madman sensed her movement. A great paw clamped down on her mouth, stifling the sound in her throat, choking her with vile odors.

Then the noise was further up, fainter and fainter, until it blanked out. Not until then did the maniac move. The retching noise in his throat was horribly like a paean of triumph. He moved swiftly again, heedless of clanking ends of chains, as if he knew he had nothing now to fear.

Laura gave herself up wholly for lost. The escaped madman was taking her to his secret lair, and then . . . ?

Light glimmered ahead. It was yellow and dim, but it grew stronger as they progressed. Laura opened her pain-haunted eyes. The tunnel was widening. Then they were in a great, irregular cavern. Blinding lights flashed into her face, lights that stabbed and burned her body. Once more, she felt as if the bones were rotting within her shriveling flesh.

The jagged walls were alive with a million yellow sparkles, just as the smaller cave beneath. The black, gleaming rock was cut and hewn, and mounds of fragments and broken chunks flamed with a wild, unholy luster at regularly spaced intervals. It was a place of evil, of stifling, almost unbreathable atmosphere.

Her captor growled like a wolf whose hackles bristled against an unknown enemy. He seemed to sense the frightful burden of this blazing cavern, and hastened his shambling walk almost to a run. The chains clanked dismally behind him. Once more, his paw clamped over Laura's mouth, shutting off all sound.

Again the cavern narrowed, became another tunnel. The terrible luminescence was left behind, but another and ruddier radiance cast its flare ahead. Cool, night air flowed with reviving vigor over her pain-wracked body; helped mitigate the stupefying effluvia of the beast-man who pressed her close to his filth-stiffened shirt.

Somehow, she knew that here was the end of the journey; here would come the tremendous dénouement to this night of terror and horror. What dreadful scene was she, a captive to a mindless beast, about to witness?

He was going slowly, cautiously now. His chains made barely perceptible noise. The tunnel took a bend. A rude, plank door blocked the opening to the outer world, but the planks were rough and so nailed as to leave wide gaps between.

The mindless being crouched before a crack. His hairy paw tightened on Laura so that her breath was a choking gasp. The growl in his throat was a low rumble of hate. Fighting for air to fill her lungs, helpless in a grip of iron, Laura nevertheless peered out into the night with him.

Before her stretched level rock, the truncated top of Superstition Mountain. The night pressed down with cold, dead stars on the desolate stone. The winds swept in from the sinister emptiness of space.

A blood-red fire leaped and mouthed tongues of flame at the whistling blast. Shadowy figures silhouetted blackly against its ruddiness, vanished into encompassing darkness, and reappeared again like disembodied creatures of the void.

But it was not this that held Laura's wide, horror-filled gaze, and brought the shrieks gurgling against the broad, restraining paw. It was the smooth, round pit that yawned in the solid rock, almost beneath her very eyes.

FLAMES spilled gory shadows into that dreadful hole, and tossed in a bloody scarlet on the upraised faces that swirled within. Faces loomed there: snarling and bestial, more animal than the ape, more cruel in their mindlessness than the wolf. Foam dripped from their protruding, slobbering lips; howls of rage mingled with gruesome cackling and horrible laughter. Great hairy arms swung threateningly up at the figures who moved restlessly about the fire. The blood-red light glinted on manacled wrists and long, pendant chains. One upthrust, naked arm held a long white bone, horribly like the thigh bone of a human being. The creature who brandished it was chuckling, and as he snarled his eerie laughter, he thrust the gruesome relic into his mouth, and crunched on it with sickening sound.

Laura moaned and gagged. Her stomach churned with queasy motion. These were the maniacs who had been driven down the lumber road in chairs. These, and others like them. From this pit had her captor somehow twice escaped. From this pit, in which they were manacled and staked like bears for some dreadful sport.

Suddenly she twisted with superhuman strength in the madman's arms. She flung free for a moment, and a great shriek of desperation burst from her lips before the smothering hand could grip her down again.

She had seen—in that leaping, twisting, rattling, howling mob of the living dead— Frank, her husband! His lean face was stubbled with dirt and unshaven beard, his cheeks were hollow with straining madness—and he leaped and danced and howled wilder and louder than all the rest.

"Frank!" She screamed in the last extremity of agony at the sight of him.

Instantly, the platform of rock was a swirl of movement. The shadowed figures around the fire leaped toward the sound. The madmen whipped up their clamor to a hideous pitch. Frank, the man who only that morning had kissed her with understanding affection, seemed to hesitate a split second. Then he too went on with his interminable leaping and howling. He had not even turned his head.

Laura's captor whipped his great arm about her throat with a bestial snarl. She gasped and tried to struggle, but the cruel pressure cut off all air. Searing pain lanced her neck; blackness enveloped her.

Then, suddenly, the pressure relaxed. The maniac whimpered with fear, threw her crashing to the ground, and ran with a huge clangor of chains back the way he he had come.

"Get the girl!" a hollow voice ordered. "Never mind the other. He will keep."

She was being lifted, carried out into the open. The cool night air cut across her fainting senses, the rushing wind stung her back to life. She opened her eyes slowly, closed them again with a long, shuddering moan. Three men stood over her, etched in the flare of the whipping flames.

Three men! Two she had never seen before, though vaguely she sensed that they had been the monsters of metal in the cave of yellow horror beneath. Now they were clad in white, shapeless pants and semi-sleeve shirts. They grinned at her with evil mockery and the little worms of lust crawled in their narrowed eyes. One was broad and thick and heavy-set, with the bullet head and brutal look of a battered pugilist. The other was like a swooping vulture, with huge, enormous nose, black, bent brows, and misshapen, flapping ears.

But it was the third man who had forced the moan from her pallid lips and thrust icy fingers down her spine. Yet he seemed more kindly—as he was more ancient—than his brutish companions. A black shroud swathed his spare form. A wrinkled, bony mask of white emerged in startling contrast from the midnight robe. The top of his skull was a hairless, grey expanse. White, bushy eyebrows projected incredibly over shadowed eyes. His mouth was thin and bloodless and his cheeks were of a queer, grey pallor.

This was the man with the whip, who had driven his manacled slaves along the road, who had slashed Frank across the back when he had stopped in dumb vacuity before the house where his wife had crouched, shivering with terror.

THE Boss motioned with his head. At once his two companions sprang to Laura, jerked her roughly to her feet. She swayed and could not stand. That bony face before her seemed alive with the wisdom of age, but something in those deep, shadowed eyes sent her heart hammering madly against her ribs. There was more of mercy in those driveling maniacs in the pit than in this tall, spare, benevolent-seeming creature!

"What do you want of me?" she gasped. "What have you done to my— husband?" The word almost choked her. Frank in that pit of mindless men, dancing and leaping and shrieking . . . Oh God!

For a moment, the Boss stared motionlessly at the frightened girl. She tried to face him bravely but the thought of Frank made her wilt into a human pendulum, swung on the powerful arms of his minions.

"Ah, yes, your husband!" he said finally. His thin lips writhed into a fleshless smile, but the rest of his face did not move. His voice was like a rumbling echo, deep and hollow. "He will be useful to me. Already he is more a madman than the others. It took very little of the precious serum to blast his reason loose from his mind. Look at him, my dear, and see how he recognizes you!"

They swung her around on dragging feet to face the pit. The smooth, funnel-like depression became a bedlam of noise and clamor. The maniacs leaped high against their chains at the sight of her, raging lust inflamed their bestial countenances, dragged delirious howls from their maddened throats. And—dear God in Heaven, let me die now, she prayed—her husband leaped and yelled with the rest. His eyes glared at her without recognition, and his chains were a frenzy of clangor as they dragged him back from his jumpings.

"There you are, my dear," the Boss cackled. "He is indeed a prize. I'm sure he'll be the best worker I have."

Something snapped within Laura. She tore loose from the restraining arms, she jumped screaming and clawing for the beast who taunted her.

"You vile, filthy creature!" she shrieked. "You've made animals of men; you've made a living Hell for my husband. But you—you shall die!"

Her clawing fingers raked for his face. He jumped back with an oath of rage. His lean fingers plucked under his shroud, came out with a short, scimitar-like blade. She hurled herself forward again, ready to transfix herself upon the knife, if only she could reach that devilish countenance.

But the two henchmen were upon her.

They caught her plunging form by the arms, wrenched backward until they almost tore them out of their sockets. Sobbing, gasping, whimpering, Laura glared with half-mad eyes at the Boss.

There was unutterable evil about his lips and in the blazing depths of his eyes. He fingered his blade meaningly. For one moment, it seemed as if he would drive it into her loud-clamoring heart. Then his eyes flicked past her to the pit, where the madmen were yammering more horribly than ever. His lips curled sinisterly.

"That would be the cream of the jest," he said thinly. He thrust back his head and laughed. That bloodless laugh sent chills down Laura's back, shriveled her heart to a small, motionless ball.

"Exactly," he nodded with self-satisfaction. "It will be great sport. I should have thought of that before. Now, listen to me, you little she-devil. Listen and faint with very terror. Know what I am doing before you—*die!*"

THE significant pause before that final word, dreadful enough by itself, whipped the madness from her brain, brought in its place crawling maggots of fear.

"I have found in the depths of Superstition Mountain rich deposits of radium ore, the richest in the world. It was I who discovered the tunnels and caverns that lead all the way to the top where we now are standing. But the mountain belongs to some one else. He would not sell. So I am mining the ore in spite of him." He laughed horribly.

"Radium is terribly dangerous," he continued. "It burns the flesh away, it rots the bones. My men and myself use leaden helmets and lead-impregnated clothes when we descend into the caverns where the pitchblende lode is to be found. But they are clumsy, and it is impossible to work in them. Besides, I needed more hands for the work, and I dared not trust any one else. So I thought of a scheme."

He paused while Laura almost fainted with loathing, with dread of what he was going to say.

"If I could make men into maniacs, mindless creatures to obey my will, it would serve a double purpose. They would not know the danger and would mine the ore for me. Nor could they betray the secret, if they broke away and escaped. I obtained a certain serum, known only to an ancient Indian medicine man, that was guaranteed to drive men mad if given in doses at definite intervals. It worked!" How the beast gloated over his fiendish scheme!

"Already they have mined enough to make me a millionaire. But I want more. I want to be the richest, most powerful man in the world. And I shall!" An insane light glared in his eyes. "Another month of toil with this fresh supply of wretches and there will be enough."

"But the poor creatures you have tortured," Laura burst out. "What happens to them?"

He was unutterably evil now. "They —die! A month of toil in the mine and they gangrene and rot away, flesh and bones and all, from the radium emanations. It is not a pleasant death. They scream and beg for death to come, but it delays." He thrust his snarling lips close to the panting girl. "Your husband will scream louder than the rest."

Iron bands compressed around Laura's skull. "You damnable fiend!" she panted, struggling in the iron grip of the thugs.

The Boss leered down at her. "But you haven't heard the rest of my plan. It concerns *you!*"

"Kill me!" she gasped. "I—don't—care —any more."

"*I* shall not kill you," he said slowly, leaning forward to observe the full effect of his dreadful words! "Your *husband*

shall kill you—he and his lovely mates. *I shall throw you into the pit with them!*"

CHAPTER SIX

Slaves of Madness

FOR a moment, her squeezing brain did not understand. Then red ruin exploded in her skull. It could not be, it was impossible! No human being—not even the Foul Fiend himself—could have conceived such a frightful torture. To be torn apart, limb from limb, by howling, slobbering maniacs; to be broken and twisted and wrenched into blood-soaked shreds of flesh by Frank, no longer the man of her love, but a ravening, lusting madman! Almighty God! Can You allow such things to be?

She felt herself jerked forward. Her feet dragged desperately against the bare, flat rock, seeking footholds. Her head lolled to one side. The thugs were forcing her to the pit.

There, at the very edge, they paused. Behind them towered the Boss, his grey baldness bloody with the light of the fire. He pointed downward toward the mad crew with his knife.

"Throw her in!"

For one desperate moment, she hung on the brink. She screamed, she begged, she implored for mercy. But Hell itself was not more cold, more merciless, than these fiends in human form, than those lusting, mindless creatures of the pit.

They leaped like slavering dogs against their manacles, tongues lolling from drolling lips at the sight of her. And Frank leaped higher than the rest. His eyes were blank and staring; his voice was a senseless screech.

"Look how her husband welcomes her," the Boss chuckled hideously. "Let us not stand in the way of such true love. Throw her down into his arms."

"No! No!" Laura moaned in frenzy. She threw back her head and the scream of snapping reason tore her throat to pieces. Her feet slid along the smooth rock. She was being forced inexorably over. A last desperate attempt at a toehold, and she was going . . . going. . . . !

The last thing she saw was the eager clutch of her husband's unmanacled arm, and then she went down the smooth side, sliding and tumbling.

Hands gripped at her, tore with frenzied claws at her clothes, ripped them into fluttering strips. Mad fingers raked down her smooth, soft sides, wrenched at arms and legs. Pain lanced through every nerve and quivering muscle. Hot, snarling breaths beat with fetid effluvia about her face; unhuman faces leered into hers and dropped suddenly out of sight.

Fists and arms and legs and clanking chains whirled round and round her tortured form in a kaleidoscope of distributing parts. Shrieks of pain rose from the mindless wretches, yells of rage, and howls of agony. Suddenly she was alone, crouched, fainting and bleeding, at the farther end of the pit.

In front of her was a mass of heaving, flailing maniacs. Fists lashed out and crunched home against bone and smearing flesh. Oh God, she moaned to herself, they are fighting over me! Soon it will be over and the victors will come. . . . !

But there was something wrong. The Boss, who had grinned fiendishly down upon the struggle, now shouted orders. His henchmen moved carefully around the edge, trying to get to her. The Boss ran to the fire, raced back with his huge, black whip. He snaked it crackling through the air. But the madmen paid no heed.

With a snarl, he aimed the lashing leather at the head of one who seemed the very head and center of the riot. He ducked, and it wound itself like a coiling python

around the neck of a maniac who was in the very act of striking him down with manacled arm. He screamed horribly, gurgled, and dropped out of sight under the trampling mass.

The madman who had ducked, lashed out again with two unencumbered fists. A brutish face disappeared, and bone cracked audibly on another. He turned his sweaty, thin-etched features toward Laura.

SHE jumped from her terrified crouch. It was Frank, and he was grinning. That old-time grin she knew so well. His eyes flicked understanding warning; then a rush of infuriated manics bore down upon him. He submerged like a racing boat under tons of water. There was a violent, swirling commotion, over which the Boss teetered vainly, holding his whip poised. His face was hideous with rage, yet he dared not strike indiscriminately. Already had he killed one of his precious, mindless workers.

Laura shrieked high above the uproar. Frank was not mad! He was sane, sane as she was! But it was no use. The others were upon him, they would tear him to pieces even as they would her when they were through. She jumped madly forward, just as a straining hand reached for her shoulder from above—and missed!

She clawed, kicked, pulled at the ravening throng. They were killing Frank, they were . . . !

The snarling, yelping pack heaved upward and outward in all directions. Frank's bloody head emerged like a yacht shouldering the waves apart. He was bleeding from innumerable gashes, but still he grinned. He caught sight of Laura, slammed his way to her side.

"Okay, darling!" he panted. "If only we can duck those fellows above——"

The Boss let out a blasting roar of rage. He slashed out with his great black whip, straight for Frank's head.

"Look out!" Laura screamed, dragging her husband down. The lash whistled sharply through the air, inches above his face. The scattered madmen bunched and came on, throwing themselves to the limits of their chains.

But the Boss was a snarling, raging beast, mad even as they. He smashed downward again, leaning far over the pit in his eagerness to catch this man who had pretended to be mad and was spoiling all his careful plans.

The heavy whip snaked out, caught him off balance. For a long moment, he teetered on the very brink, while his henchmen rushed with alarmed cries to catch him. But it was too late!

With a wild, eerie screech he slipped down the smooth rock sides, into the very midst of the blood-lusting men he had made into madmen. A huge, hairy arm reached out, grabbed him by the body, bore him under. His long, thin hand worked madly at his clumsy shroud. A pistol gleamed underneath; he had tugged it half out when the avalanche swept over him. Then nothing showed but a snarling, yelping eddy of brawny bodies.

The thugs on the edge of the pit drew back in horror. Guns appeared in their hands. Again and again they fired into the squirming, swarming mass.

Frank caught Laura, dragged her to the extreme end, where the fire-reflection did not penetrate. Desperately he tried to hoist himself up, but there was no purchase. He slipped and went down again.

"Sorry, Laura," he breathed heavily. "But I'm afraid it's no go. They'll finish off those poor devils and then come for us."

She smiled bravely back, trying not to let him see the ache in her heart. She had found her husband again, and now they were both lost.

The sharp crack of the guns punctured the screams of the dying. Then there were no further yells, and the firing ceased. For one dreadful moment, there was silence.

AS they crouched deeper into the shadows, away from the flickering ruddiness of the flames, they saw the motionless mass of legs and arms and distorted torsoes of those who had been driven to horrible madness, and who now were dead.

"They're better off, poor things," Laura whispered. "But we——?"

"The Boss's men will get us," Frank said grimly. Laura clung to his dear, wounded body with aching love. Fear clutched her heart. There was no escape.

See, there they were, coming to look for them, to make sure everything was over. Feet boomed hollowly on the rock. "Seems like they're all dead," said one.

"Whew!" shuddered the other. "I seen terrible stuff in my day, but nothin' like this. An' the Boss—he's gone. What're we gonna do?"

"Do?" echoed the first thug sarcastically. "Man, it's a cinch! Now we got all that stuff fer ourselves. We'll slip it out tonight, and we'll get those thousand grands the Boss was always beefin' about."

"Say!" cried the other in alarm. "Nix. We dassn't touch it. Remember what it did t' the first batch o' loonies?"

"Su-ure, that's right! Mebbe some of those bozos in the pit ain't dead yet. We'll use 'em."

Two figures loomed over the hole, guns snouting. Frank and Laura pressed against the sides, held themselves moveless. But they had been seen.

"Come out, you there!" one shouted exultantly.

"No, no!" Laura whimpered. "I'd rather die now than——"

Frank cried defiantly. "We won't do your hellish work!"

"Okay, feller," the thug grinned. The

fiery shadows made him a horned devil out of Hell. "Say yuhr prayers, then. I'll kill yuh and grab the girl." He raised his gun deliberately, took aim.

Laura shrieked and threw herself before her husband. "You'll have to kill me too!"

The thug licked his lips at the sight of her slenderness under the remaining shreds of garments. "Not on your life, girlie. Hey, Jerry!" he raised his voice. "You shoot him, but don't hit the girl. We need her."

"It's no use," Frank said gently. "Break away, Laura darling. Let them shoot. But get to the body of the Boss. He had a gun. Use it on yourself if necessary."

"Okay, let 'im have it."

Frank squared his shoulders, while Laura dropped in a faint. Two shots rang out. For a split second, he stood in a daze. Why hadn't those bullets torn through his body? Then he saw the two gunmen totter and go crashing to the rock.

There were shouts, cries and the thudding of many feet. Then Frank too drifted into the black sea of oblivion.

WHEN Laura awoke it was to find herself in Frank's arms, swathed in bandages. His face was pale and drawn, and one arm was in a sling, but his grin was warming. Dr. Carey was bending over her, busy with the last bandage.

"There, you're all right now," he said. His rubicund face was shiny and flushed in the firelight. Lem, the village cobbler, glowered at his side. Other men of the village crowded in the background, muttering and whispering excitedly.

"We'll split the cache of radium between us," Frank was insisting. "I've got your contract to sell the mountain, of course, but you didn't know at the time what it was worth."

The doctor hesitated, smiled. "All right, if you feel that way."

Laura snuggled closer. "I—I don't understand," she said, bewildered.

Frank grinned. "I closed the deal in the village. I didn't tell you, but that was why I made a flying trip to New York. I had a sample of ore I picked up at the base of the mountain that I wanted analyzed. Looked like pitchblende to me, and that was what the chemist said. Where there is pitchblende, there is sometimes radium. I took the chance. But someone else had discovered the secret before me, and tried to buy the place."

"I wouldn't sell to him," Dr. Carey interrupted. "He had cheated me in a deal years before and I swore then never to do business with him again."

Frank's jaw hardened. "So he concocted this scheme—the vilest, most devilish since the world began. He caught me with his drove of madmen as I was coming back from the village. Evidently some of them had died, and he needed new recruits. He jabbed the needle into me. I fought off the effect, but pretended I was just as mad as the rest. Up here, I learned his plans but then I could do nothing. I waited for my chance and it never came. I had slipped my manacles, but left them on with the spring open. Then, darling, you came." Frank's eyes clouded. "I'll never want to go through that again. We have Dr. Carey to thank for coming in the nick of time. How did you find out about this?"

The doctor smiled modestly. "I had been suspicious about disappearances around here for some time. I found a trampled trail that led to the rubbly base above the road. I watched there after Laura told me you were gone too, but saw nothing. I hurried over to your house, heard the rest of Laura's story, and went back for a more thorough search. Then I saw Laura running up the mountain, with Lem after her. I had warned Lem to watch her while I was gone. Lem got scared and ran back, but from my hiding place I saw Laura seized by a shrouded being who was—er—the man called the Boss. He seemed to disappear into the ground."

Dr. Carey took a breath and went on. "I hurried back to the village, raised the folk, and came back as fast as I could. But tell me, Frank—if you managed to break away from the chain-gang once in the woods, why did you return?"

Frank grinned sheepishly. "I wanted to warn Laura away, and yet not get a posse on my trail. You see, I hadn't learned a thing then as to what it was all about. I was afraid they'd get away, so I stuck along."

Laura squeezed his arm reproachfully. "But who," she asked suddenly, "was the devil who called himself the Boss?"

"Come," Frank said, lifting her to her feet. They hobbled painfully to the fire.

On the ground were rows of bodies. The madmen stared peacefully up at the stars, all their induced insanity wiped clean from their faces. But the solitary figure that lay to one side was twisted in demoniac hate. The high, bald head was punctured and thrown to one side. The bushy brows were half-ripped off and reddened with blood. Beneath the disguise were the unmistakable features of Sheriff Tom Beasley!

Laura shivered with cold as Frank led her gently away. . . .

THE END

Next Month—

TWO BIG NOVELS!

—By—

Nat Schachner and Hugh B. Cave

—Plus—

TWO EERIE, THRILLING TERROR NOVELETTES

—By—

Arthur J. Burks and John Knox

And Gripping Shorts by

Wyatt Blassingame—H. M. Appel—Robert Newman

All Complete in the June Issue

TERROR
TALES

Out April 25th

PORTRAIT OF EVIL

By George Edson
(Author of "The Cross of Blood," etc.)

Slowly, malevolently, that ruthless Presence first guided John Murdock's helpless hand, then seized upon body and brain, enslaving them. What unspeakable destiny—which neither God nor human could thwart—was to be his?

T HERE was no sane, no explainable reason why I should always have had some creeping sense of terror in that room. Yet I did have it. Even then, as I sat there at the desk and vainly attempted to concentrate on my work, I knew I was trembling. I knew my breath had again begun to come in unnatural jerks, that clammy perspiration again oozed slowly from my pores, bathing my forehead in a damp sweat of nameless unanalyzable fear.

Then I realized that something was pulling at my eyes—some insidious and irresistible force. Against every attempt not to, my head turned, lifted. I found my gaze fixed on the huge portrait hanging on the wall. It was a portrait of Philip Brant, the man who had built and lived in this house until his death a year ago; a portrait in which he was posed at the very desk I now occupied. I had disliked the thing from the first sight of it. But having merely rented the house for a few months, I hadn't felt privileged to shift any of its furnishings.

Yes, I had disliked that portrait from the first. Yet it had never made me feel, before, what I felt in this moment—an awful, nameless *dread*.

For the twisted lines on that lean face seemed no longer just lines of paint; they were creases in human skin. The lips, drawn into a mocking sneer, were human lips. The gleam in those dark eyes could only be inspired by evil thoughts in a human brain behind it.

I caught hold of myself. How ridiculous! It was only a picture. The artist had been clever, very clever; but he had done no more than daub. . . .

I stiffened. A chill swept over my body, a soundless scream tore from my lips, then I was actually horrified into numbness.

My gaze had slid down to the hand in the portrait—the thin hand holding a pen to a sheet of paper which rested on that pictured desk where now I sat. And the hand seemed to move. I'll swear to it—it *did* move. It was writing words on the sheet of paper.

Horror? Terror? Even then I didn't feel the full shock of those mingled emotions. Not then, while I watched the hand in the portrait move. Not until the next second, when I realized something else.

First I realized that I was sitting in exactly the same position as that in which Philip Brant had posed. Next that I also held a pen in my hand. Finally—and this was when stark terror struck me—that my own hand moved in time with his *and that I couldn't stop it!*

I tried. Tried to yank my hand away from the desk, to push my chair back, to jump to my feet. God, how I tried! But my body seemed to be gripped in an intangible vise, my muscles were under a control other than my own. I couldn't even drag my gaze away from the moving hand in that portrait—until it finally went slower and then became still.

After that the force which had drawn my eyes to the portrait shifted, pulled my gaze down to the real sheet of paper, on the real desk. That paper had been blank. It was blank no longer. On it were words scrawled in my own handwriting.

Fearfully, scarcely breathing, I read them:

"A man has not known life until he has killed."

I DON'T know how long I sat there, nor how many times I read that damned sentence. I don't know why I did what I did. I still wanted to jump up, rush out of the room. I wanted to shout, to call someone who would tell me I had been having nothing more than a nightmare.

But I didn't do any of those things. I picked up the sheet of paper, crumpled it, put it in an ashtray. Then I lit a match.

It was while I watched the paper burn that I first vaguely recognized some strange yet recognizable division which had taken place within me. I seemed to be not one man but two. My conscious brain was as clear and sane as ever. But somehow I knew that it no longer had any power, no longer could control my body.

In control over my body was another force—a force of evil.

A moment later I began to find out just *how* evil. Without any conscious impulse I lifted my head and again glanced at the portrait on the wall. Did those thin, bloodless lips move? God! My brain shouted that they couldn't—yet my eyes *saw* them. They moved to form silent words of command.

What the command was my conscious brain didn't know at once. Yet my body seemed to understand, for I turned, walked across to the door and through, into the next room.

Hilda, the maid, was busy dusting over in a corner and had her back to me. I went toward her. With a terrible shock the sane part of me grasped what I was going to do; it even attempted to make my voice cry a warning. A faint mumbling sound did gurgle from my throat. But the poor woman was a little deaf and didn't hear.

Frantically my mind struggled against the hellish power which drove my body. But it struggled in vain; the power seemed to be invincible.

Step by deadly step I crept toward the helpless woman. My eyes—I could feel the burning fires of unnatural lust in them—fixed themselves on her neck. I felt my lips curl back, baring my teeth. My hands swung up and out; my fingers stiffened.

I was almost upon her. Only three steps farther. Two. . . .

My mouth was dry, hot. My heart pounded. I should have been sick from the revulsion in my brain, but I wasn't— I was an aching mass of bestial desire.

One more step. . . .

And then it happened. I thought at the time that my struggling mind, perhaps with some divine aid, had finally succeeded in saving me. Later I knew that I hadn't been saved—merely granted a short reprieve because Hilda wasn't the proper victim. I didn't clutch her throat and throttle life from her. I halted, dropped my arms to my sides.

She must have heard me then, or sensed my presence, for she uttered a startled gasp, spun and stared at me. Something she saw in my eyes made her cringe against the table she had been dusting.

"Professor Murdock!" Her voice shook as if with some chill apprehension. "What —what's happened? You look so— strange. Are you—"

"I'm all right." I was surprised that my words sounded so calm. "You needn't be upset, Hilda."

Then I felt my face twist into a smile. Father in Heaven, a smile after what I had nearly done! And before—though of course I couldn't foresee the horrors of the future—what I was going to do! But the smile simply came, as if placed on my features without my willing it.

Even so, it didn't quite reassure Hilda. She stammered: "I—I forgot something in the kitchen." Then she edged around me, and abruptly scurried from the room.

FOR a moment I stood motionless. Finally a quiver ran over my body; I sensed a sudden release of tension, some slight recovery of power over my faculties.

Twisting, I stumbled across to the hall. I wanted to get out of that house, go somewhere to think. I grabbed my hat, ran to the front door, yanked it open. Julia, my wife, and Marian, our little daughter of six were just coming up the walk.

I tried to draw back before they saw me, but couldn't.

"Daddy!" Marian skipped ahead to be swung up in my arms. "We've just——" She broke off quite suddenly.

My wife stared at me. "Why John, what's the matter? You're as pale as a ghost!"

"Nothing much. Little headache." I hurried past them. "I'm going for a short walk before supper."

I knew they both stood there and watched me in puzzled surprise as I hastened off. Julia even called to me once. But I pretended not to have heard, did not turn back.

I walked four or five miles, aimlessly, yet keeping away from any settled parts of the village. I didn't want to meet anyone. Striding along, I thought of what had just happened to me, sought for a possible explanation. Overwork? Nerves? No, I was up against a thing much greater—and far more insidious!

There seemed to be only two explanations. Either I was going insane or had been in the control of some sinister psychic force.

I remembered the strange sensation of which I had, several times, been aware in that house. The first time was on the day we had arrived to take up our residence. My wife and Marian had gone out to explore the grounds; I had been alone in the study. And I had suddenly had an eerie feeling of a presence near me—a malevolent presence in the very room.

That had also been the first time I'd really noticed the portrait on the wall. My eyes, on that occasion as today, had been drawn to it. But then it had only seemed a diabolically clever painting of an unpleasant man. I had laughed off the sensation that I wasn't alone.

The feeling had returned, however, on various other occasions. Now I recollected that in each instance I had been in the study and that my eyes had been drawn to the portrait.

PHILIP BRANT, the builder of the house and the man of the portrait, had been no favorite in this country village where he had lived. That was evident from the general reticence concerning him. The villagers seemed to have feared him. The still seemed to fear him —dead.

Why? A nameless dread clutched at my heart as I asked myself that question. Why did they fear a corpse which had been mouldering in its grave for a year?

Abruptly I remembered what Tim Dolan, the old fellow who cared for the grounds and who had worked for Philip Brant, had said. Tim had told me the little I know of Brant: that he had been wealthy, had come from somewhere in the south, had brought with him a young wife and a baby daughter. He had been an unfriendly sort of man and hadn't mingled with the natives. When the child was five or six she had wandered off into the woods, according to the story, and had never been found. The child's mother, crazed by her loss, had plunged the length of the cellar stairs and broken her neck. From the peculiar way in which Tim had spoken when telling me all that, I had gathered that he believed she had thrown herself down those stairs on purpose.

But it was what Tim had said afterwards that I now remembered so clearly:

"Then Brant got even queerer," he had told me. "Locked himself up, he did, and for days at a stretch wouldn't see no one except me. Me and that damned idol he kept on his desk. He used to talk to it. He had it buried with him. He claimed he'd never really die while it guarded him. . . ."

At the time, I had passed the story off as meaning that Brant had been demented by his double sorrow, then, in the course of hard work I had forgotten all about the idol. I hadn't at all connected it and

Brant's fantastic statement with the occasional weird sensation of an unseen presence in the house.

Never really die! Now I shivered. Had Philip Brant told the truth?

Suddenly another question, a terrible question, blasted at me. I had never before given much credence to tales of psychic phenomena; the whole business had seemed improbable. But suppose my body and subconscious mind had really been under the control of Philip Brant this afternoon? A thing that had happened once could happen again. And then the fiendish bidding might drive me on beyond where I had stopped today.

Why might I not, if there were a next time, attack my own wife and child?

GOD, the torture I went through at the thought! Murder the two whom I loved so dearly? Murder them to please the hellish whim of a man who had died and yet not died?

My very heart cried out in anguish. Certainly, certainly I could save them—I who lived only for them! I could—I must save them!

And then the inevitable solution came to me. If I no longer lived. . . .

But must I die? I didn't want to leave them, couldn't leave them. It wasn't that I was afraid. That is, I wouldn't have hesitated to give my life, and even suffer hell in the giving. Yet it didn't seem as if I had the courage to part from them forever. Perhaps that was cowardice. I don't know.

How much grief would have been spared had I killed myself then and never taken the chance I took!

Instead, however, I decided that only flight was necessary. The evil spirit which had controlled me must, I thought, be associated with the house and the damned portrait; I had never felt the presence anywhere save in the study.

I just wouldn't go back. I'd telephone Julia, tell her to bring the child and meet me somewhere. We would leave the village on the very first train. Surely the cursed thing which had seized me this afternoon couldn't reach out and. . . .

A tearing sob racked my body. Couldn't reach out? It had! At this very moment I felt it clutch me, felt myself divide!

The mental agony which assailed me in that moment was almost unbearable. Madness, utter and awful madness, threatened to deprive me of my mind—the one faculty the hellish thing couldn't seem to conquer.

I had thrown away my opportunity. During this last short period of normalcy I could have destroyed my physical body and saved my loved ones. But now—now only the devil in hell knew what would happen!

I went back to the house. I didn't want to go, yet walked swiftly, as if eager to get there. Part of me, the part in the grip of the unseen power, was eager.

Why? The possible answers to that question made ravening terror gnaw at my conscious brain.

* * *

Never shall I forget that night of horror.

I found my wife and daughter in the living room, and I went in to join them. My brain struggled desperately to make my body move in any other direction and then to make my voice give them a warning. But that part of me was already powerless.

"John . . . I'm so glad you've come home." My wife hurried toward me. "How's your head? Don't you think we'd better phone——"

"No doctors for me, dear." Those words—I swear it before God—were not *my* words. They fell from my lips and in my voice but they were not mine. "My headache's gone. I'm fine. Please don't worry."

"Oh, I'm so glad," she sighed. "But you must take a rest, John. You've been working too hard on that book."

Wouldn't she stop coming toward me? I felt my arms lift from my sides. Wouldn't she stop before she walked right into them, right into the grasp of my already lusting hands?

"I know." And my face smiled. "I'll take a rest."

She didn't stop. My brain pounded with terror as my hands touched her shoulders, stole up toward her neck. They were . . .

Ah, thank God! They didn't tighten. One of them slid around to the back of her head, pulled it forward until her lips met mine. And that was all.

My little daughter skipped to me. She said: "Daddy, give me a bear hug now that you feel all well again."

Once more, while I swung her small body in the air, cold terror held me in its nerve-rending grasp.

But I didn't hurt her. I gave her the bear hug, then let her down and fondled her head.

I tried to tell Julia about the thing after we had put Marian to bed. I couldn't. Then I tried to hold back when it came time for *us* to go upstairs. I couldn't do that, either. I was powerless to avert what I knew was coming.

And thus I went up and into our room, with the woman I loved. God in Heaven, how I feared for her! How I wanted to tell her to flee—flee from the monster that was myself!

WE HAD twin beds. For several minutes we talked idly across the space between, then Julia dropped off to sleep.

I lay flat on my back, staring up into darkness. Gruesome thoughts filled my mind. Dread of what I might do in the very next instant probed to the depths of my soul. I tried to keep my eyes open. I *had* to stay awake—so that I could get up and kill myself if this second fit passed.

But it didn't. And finally, sheer mental exhaustion robbed me of the power to stay awake any longer. . . .

*   *   *

I came out of deep slumber with a start. My body was taut, quivering; my throat and mouth dry. The blood in my veins was like liquid fire. My head turned, and my eyes strained through the darkness trying to fix on the motionless form of my wife. Slowly I pushed down the covers of my bed.

Terror lashed at my brain. What was I going to do? Was I . . . ? Holy Father, stop me! Stop me!

I pulled myself up to a sitting position, swung my feet down to the floor, rose. Crouching, I glided across the narrow space to the other bed. A faint ray of moonlight filtered through the window and caressed Julia's dear face. She was smiling as if from a pleasant dream. And while she still smiled my hands moved down toward her throat.

Dear Lord, stop me! Stop me from doing this horrible thing! Stop me, annihilate me—send me to *any* destruction before I——

But no divine help seemed to come. My twitching fingers touched my wife's soft white skin. I could feel my chest heave with awful, debased desire, could hear my panting breath.

And then, just as abruptly as I had halted this afternoon, I halted now. I drew my hands away from that darling throat and straightened.

At first relief whirled in my brain. But as swiftly it faded. For I had pivoted and walked across to the door. Had opened it, stepped out into the corridor, turned to the right.

I was gliding toward Marian's room.

My brain sent up silent prayers, mad threats, curses to heaven, even as I stopped before the child's door. For a moment I seemed to hesitate. But finally I twisted and moved on toward the stairs.

Even as I was driven on to what I knew must end in some horror, I gave thanks to God. My loved ones were to be spared. In darkness I descended the stairs and went back to the study. I switched on a lamp, crossed the room, stopped before the portrait of Philip Brant.

My thanks died. The man's dark eyes seemed to mock me, seemed to tell me that I bore only false hopes. Again the lips seemed to move. I understood that they must be uttering a command to the part of me which he controlled. I turned when the lips settled once more into that fixed sneer, edged myself over to the desk, sat down at it. I took up my pen.

My eyes were still riveted on that evil face. They were drawn to the thin hand as they had been in the afternoon. The hand seemed to move. And *my* hand moved. In a moment my eyes were pulled down to the paper to read the words I had written:

"The greatest ecstasy comes from knowing what one is to do and waiting. Have patience. All of life will be yours very soon."

All of life would be mine very soon! And the other words I had written were that a man did not know all of life until he had killed! I realized that I was, as I had feared, going to commit murder while in this hellish state. I had stopped before murdering Hilda, before murdering my wife, before murdering my little child. Who, then, was going to be the victim?

AGAIN I crumpled the paper on which I had written, and burned it. With calm deliberation I put three or four matches in the pocket of my pajamas, rose

to my feet, walked out of the study. I turned toward the kitchen.

As I moved, I had some dim idea that I could make myself understand the strange division within me, reason why I had twice been compelled to write. Though I had never before believed in the existence of spirits, I had been sufficiently interested in the abstract idea to read theories about it. I had read that a spirit could only gain control over a person's subconscious mind—and, through that, the body. The person's conscious mind or brain remained untouched in itself, though robbed of its power.

Philip Brant's spirit—for I was now fully convinced that his spirit did rule my body—could make my subconscious mind understand his commands. He had compelled me to write in order to transmit words to my conscious brain. . . .

By now I had reached the end of the hall. But I didn't go into the kitchen. I twisted away from it and opened the door to the cellar. It was down these same cellar stairs that Philip Brant's wife had either fallen by accident or thrown herself on purpose.

Would that I could have met death at the bottom of them as she had! There was, however, no such release for me—I snapped on the lights and descended in safety.

With deliberate steps I started to move across the cellar. Evidently my subconscious mind had implicit instructions about what I was to do.

In one corner stood a collection of implements used by Tim around the grounds. My hands chose a spade and a short iron bar. Carrying them, I swung about, stalked along one wall. Presently I stopped. I put down the spade and focused my eyes on one large rock near the base of the wall.

A thin crack, noticeable only under close scrutiny, separated the edges of the rock from the mortar clinging to the other stones around it. My hands fitted the point of the iron bar into a little hole already chipped from mortar. I used the bar as a lever and pried the huge rock out until I could grip one end. Then, hooking my fingers around that end, I tugged with all my strength. The huge rock moved.

Dank air swirled out of the black cavity behind it. A putrid stench of decay assailed my nostrils. At another time that stench would have nauseated me; now I smelled it with no reaction except knowledge of its existence.

My body, my hands worked with haste. I dropped to my knees, flung aside the iron bar, grabbed the spade. I crawled head first into that black, horrible cavity.

That it was more than a tiny hole I learned when I pushed to my feet in the darkness and straightened without bumping any ceiling. I drew out one of my matches, struck it, pivoted, and held the flame to a candle fixed on a jutting edge of rock.

LIGHT from the sputtering flame showed me a square chamber perhaps six feet each way. The three dirt walls were braced with timbers which served also as uprights for planks forming a ceiling which connected with the stone wall of the cellar.

Wonder filled my brain. Obviously this was a secret chamber. But what was its purpose?

I was soon to know. A vague suspicion stole into my mind even before I did know —and that one sane part of me steeled itself for horror.

My body understood its task. My hands gripped the spade more tightly, plunged it into the damp earth. The point hit something. I cleared away several shovelfuls of dirt and realized that I was digging up a box.

The box was oblong and not very large. As soon as I had cleared off enough dirt I lifted it, set it under the candle. With the spade I pried off the top.

God! The gruesome picture of what I saw. . . . It will never leave my mind while I live!

In the box were the remains of a tiny human form—a child. The flesh had decomposed. Bits of dried skin and mouldering shreds of cloth clung to a few of the bones. The shriveled scalp had peeled away from the head. The head itself, or skull of a head, was twisted to one side. A section above the temple had been crushed as if by a vicious blow.

Now I realized the hideous thing Philip Brant had done. This was his child who had supposedly wandered off into the woods. She hadn't wandered off into any woods. He had murdered her.

* * *

For a moment, outraged fury at a man who could slay his own child, in cold blood, inflamed my mind. But then came insidious questions. Why had his diabolical spirit driven me down here to defile her poor grave? Had it, lacking substance of its own, merely used my body to dig up the crude coffin over which he could gloat and perhaps receive some further perverted thrill? Or had it wanted to horrify me?

Sudden terror froze my soul. Had it taken this ghastly way of showing me what I was going to do?

I'm afraid the rest of my tale will sound a little incoherent, for what happened during the next few minutes caused my brain at last to succumb to madness.

I dropped the spade beside the pitiful coffin. Then I crouched, wormed back through the hole into the cellar, hurried up the stairs. Along the hall, and up again, to the second floor. Down the corridor to the door of the room in which my own child lay sleeping.

Merciful God! Was I going to take her? Was I going to carry her down there to that tomb? Could nothing help her, stop me? *Nothing . . . ?*

Outside, thunder rumbled as I pushed open the door into my child's room. In the short while since I had left my bed a storm had arisen. I crossed to her trundle bed. Lightning flashed, showing me the sweet face which had always smiled so joyfully at sight of her daddy, showed me the soft golden curls on the pillow, the small hand tucked under her chin. It was a picture to make any father fall to his knees and thank heaven. Instead, I shoved my arms around her, lifted her, and glided out of the room.

Another crash of thunder came as I descended the stairs. The house shook; bright blue light streaked through the windows, illumined the hall. It was as if God had sent this sudden storm to express his wrath at me for succumbing to a spirit of the devil. I wondered why he hadn't sent one of his bolts to strike me dead. . . .

MARIAN awoke just as we reached the bottom of the cellar stairs. She uttered a quick cry of fright, then recognized me and smiled.

"Where are you taking me, Daddy?"

"This is a new game we're playing," that voice which was mine, yet not mine, said. A laugh rattled from my throat. "Yes . . . a new game."

"What is it, Daddy? What do we do?"

"Wait," my voice answered. "You'll see very soon."

My brain screeched a frenzied protest when I went to the corner where Tim kept his tools and picked out a rusty axe. Dear God! No! No! It was too horrible . . . !

But my left hand tightened around the handle. Carrying both it and my child, I turned toward that foully stinking chamber that had been used for a tomb.

Marian must have smelled the odor of decay—or she may have seen something in my eyes. Her slight form stiffened. She wailed: "Daddy, what are you going to do?"

"Quiet!" The word was a harsh snarl. I could feel my body quiver, feel maniacal desire surge over it.

"Daddy!" She squirmed in wild fright. "Daddy . . . please!"

I gripped her harder and jammed my left forearm over her mouth. Her cries became stifled moans. I suffered a thousand hells of mental anguish at the sound of them, at the sight of her terrified eyes. But my steps toward that tomb didn't waver.

And suddenly she stopped moaning, went limp. From the shock of fear alone, she had fainted.

Oh God! Those next moments! I shoved her through to the chamber, crawled in after her. I dragged her to the middle and smoothed her hair back from her forehead. I clutched the axe with both hands. I raised it. . . .

"John!"

Only the sound of that scream stayed my swing. Floating down from an upper floor, I knew it for the voice of my wife. She must have discovered that Marian and I were missing.

What would I do?

For three or four seconds my body remained motionless, my arms still holding the axe poised for the blow. Finally my subconscious mind decided. I stepped away from the form at my feet, dropped the axe to the ground. I wriggled through into the cellar. Julia appeared at the top of the stairs just as I reached the bottom.

Her face was pale, frightened. She cried: "John, Marian isn't in . . ."

She stopped. Staring at me, she stood as if paralyzed.

Then I realized the second hideous thing Philip Brant had done. His wife had neither fallen down these cellar stairs by accident, nor thrown herself down them. He had murdered *her also*.

He had murdered both his daughter and his wife! *And now his fiendish spirit was driving me to re-enact the horror!*

I was more than halfway up the stairs. Still Julia stood numbly waiting. I heard a feeble whimper from below me. Marian had regained consciousness.

My fingers twitched. My whole body throbbed. Father in Heaven, do something to stop me! Kill me! Kill me before I murder the two people I love!

Two more steps. . . .

A blast of thunder rocked the house.

A flash of flame blinded me. My head seemed to split, my lungs to burst. Then everything went black. . . .

I CAME to with rain lashing my face. Opening my eyes, I saw a gigantic mass of fire. It was the house. I was out on the rear lawn. But Julia! Marian!

I tried to push to my feet. A hand caught my shoulder, pulled me back to the ground. Then I saw Julia's face.

"Marian!" I gasped.

She pointed. I twisted my head, saw my child on the other side of me. I uttered a silent prayer of thanks. God had struck to save them from me.

But me! I wasn't dead! I knew that the spirit had momentarily released me, yet it might . . . Oh God, let me die! Then it can't return!

"John, you were wonderful." Julia was talking, tenderly. "You were stunned by that lightning, almost unconscious—but you got us out of that house in time. And you're going to be all right. The doctor came with the firemen and told me you would be."

Now I could hear the shouts of the firemen, glimpse their forms against the blaze. The house was an inferno—except for the study. The flames didn't seem to penetrate that.

But suddenly they did. One of the windows broke; a yellow tongue licked through the opening. And I heard—I swear it—I heard a scream of mortal agony. A scream that lasted for seconds, before it finally trailed off into a shuddering moan, and then silence.

Somehow I knew, then, that there was a connection between the hellish spirit which had controlled me, and the evil portrait of Philip Brant. I knew that my loved ones were safe. The portrait, through which the spirit had manifested itself and created those weird illusions, had burned. Once and for all, that spirit had lost its power.

I groped for my child's hand and relaxed in my wife's arms.

SHAVING COMFORT
— hits all-time low in price

● You'll rub your finger-tips across your chin and smile with pleasure after your first shave with Probak Jr. For here's a razor blade that's made for easy work on tough beards — brings true shaving comfort down to the lowest price level. This record-breaking double-edge blade is ground, honed and stropped automatically — assuring unvarying high quality. Save money and shave with ease. Ask your dealer for Probak Jr.

"The Weirdest Stories Ever Told"!

10¢ DIME MYSTERY MAGAZINE

Complete, Blood-Speeding Mystery-Terror Novel

JEWEL OF MADNESS

By Arthur J. Burks

—Three Weirdly Gripping Novelettes—

SLAVES OF THE PAIN GOD

by Norvell Page

My Lady of Death
By James Duncan

Shadow of the Plague
By Chandler H. Whipple

—Plus Short Stories of Soul-Freezing Terror by—

Ray Cummings

Paul Ernst ● John Knox

All in the Great April Issue

ON SALE NOW!

THE DEVIL'S BREWERS

By Nat Schachner

(Author of "Death Teaches School," etc.)

THE party was over! It was over the moment Lucy Alcott shrieked. A second before, the wide, formal lawn had been alive with light and movement. Guests sipped their tea at round, intimate tables and chattered gayly against the weaving tapestry of a small string orchestra. Huge Japanese lanterns swayed overhead and cast a warm, golden glow on the smooth expanse.

But now the lawn was emptied of movement; the tea cooled unnoticed in forgotten cups, and the musicians had frozen into fearstruck immobility. Even the vari-colored lanterns seemed shrouded in a murky pall through which light barely filtered.

Lucy Alcott did not see the crowding people, nor hear the sharp intakes of breath of the men, the thin screams of the women. Horror held her rigid as in a vise, forced her eyes wide-staring upon the pallid corpse at her feet. *She* had made the discovery, had seen the pitiful high-heeled shoes where they stuck out of the clump of birches bordering the bend of the road.

It seemed to her frozen senses an etern-

The citizens of Ellendale, behind locked doors and shuttered windows, guarded their daughters jealously and whispered of the shriveled, bloodless maiden-corpses. For it was rumored that blood —the clean, swift-flowing blood of virgin maids—was the priceless ingredient of the liqueur brewed by red-robed men on the bleak slopes of Devil's Mountain!

ity ago that she had wandered over the lawn, starry-eyed with happiness at this birthday party which Dave Cooper, Ellendale's young lawyer, had tendered her. Even now, the thought of his keen, alert face—the adorable way in which his eyebrows raised in quizzical wonderment at her, the unruly cowlick of hair which always refused to stay in place—pierced like a warm gush of sunlight through shrieking darkness.

The dead girl stared with drained, sightless eyes up at the shuddering, huddled guests. She was nude, except for the slippers on her small feet and the coarse sacking that barely covered her shrunken torso. Even in the half-shadows, her body seemed oddly grey and empty. A deep, bloodless gash gaped across her twisted neck.

A babble of voices broke the first stark silence.

"My God!" a woman shrilled, "it's Flora Wells!"

As if Lucy hadn't known! Flora, who had been her friend and playmate from childhood, whose non-appearance at her party had brought the first vague dread to her that the unseen menace had struck again at Ellendale.

"And look," someone else gasped, pointing with shaking finger. "There's no blood in her body. She's been bled white—like the others!"

A mutter of horror went rippling through the cowering guests. Lucy moaned, reached blindly for the solid security of Dave's shoulder. She had not dared think that, even to herself. For three months, doom had stalked the streets of Ellendale, striking with dreadful secrecy at its victims. Flora Wells was the third —the third of those slim, virginal, lovely girls whose laughter had been stilled in their throats—whose life-blood had been drained from their shrunken arteries. For what dreadful purpose? *Why were the bodies found, without a single smear of blood on their pallid nudities, with wide, gaping wounds in their throats, as if—as if they had been hung, head downward, and the flooding gore carefully collected in waiting basins?*

Lucy clung desperately to Dave. She hardly felt the comforting pat of his strong fingers on her quivering cheeks. "I'm so afraid, Dave dear," she moaned. "Please, please, let us go away from Ellendale— now—before anything happens to me."

She felt him go rigid under her blind-gripping arm. His strained face bent sharply down to her. There was a strange look in his eyes, as if steel shutters had swung in place over his inmost thoughts.

"Nonsense!" he objected quickly. "You're just overwrought at poor Flora's death. Nothing will happen to you. I've got to stay in Ellendale; you know that."

SOMETHING warm and glowing shrivelled into a small, cold ball within her. Dave had never spoken to her in that sharp, quick tone before. Why was there no tenderness in his eyes—those eyes that used to thrill her with the depth of their ardor? Why did he suddenly seem a stranger to her?

Faintly, so faintly it seemed like a whisper from another world, someone was saying: "Queer! Three of them found in that same clump of birches, on David Cooper's property!"

The rustling voice slithered into her bosom like a striking serpent. It congealed around her heart with deadly venom. Her whirling thoughts affrighted her. Now she knew why her feet had led irresistibly to this very spot, why she had peered with half-expectant eyes into the dreadful shadows where the light of the lanterns had not penetrated.

A man loomed suddenly before them; dissociated from the formless mass of the guests. In the dim glow from the mockery of the still-bobbing lanterns, he seemed an avenging spirit. He stared at the poor, bloodless girl on the ground with bitter, slitted eyes. Lucy felt a vast feeling of pity for Tom Steele. Poor fellow! His life had been completely futile. An invalid mother had claimed all his youth; held him in sterile bachelorhood. Now that she was gone, age had overtaken him, greyed his once black hair, stooped his powerful shoulders. His distillery absorbed more and more of his attention. But to Lucy, it had seemed that the fresh young beauty of Flora had awakened a more than kindly interest in him. And now she lay dead before him.

"This damnable thing must stop," he said hoarsely. "A monster lurks in our midst, a monster who strikes down the loveliest of our maidens, who sucks their veins empty of blood. There is a fiendish reason behind these murders. We must find that reason, we must hunt down the devils; we must kill them without mercy!"

An eerie whisper rose in the tightening air. It seemed a mere exhalation rather than a voice.

"Dave Cooper!"

"Oh!" Lucy gasped faintly. Her hand shuddered off the arm of the man to whom she was engaged. It was not true, she said wildly to herself. Dave, her beloved Dave, could not be the hideous pervert who stalked the streets of Ellendale secretly at night, who .... Why then had she shuddered away from him, why did he make no move to resent that accusing whisper? She peered stealthily into his face, for signs of anger, of furious contempt. But he did not seem to have heard. His face was a rigid mask, his eyes blank on some far-off sight.

Steele swung on the shrinking huddle of people.

"Dave Cooper had nothing to do with this," he lashed out heatedly. "Whoever says so, lies!"

No one answered. No one stepped forward. Steele had thundered the slander down. Good old Tom! Lucy felt a flush of gratitude for his prompt defense of the man she loved. She had not expected it of the distiller. But why was Dave so silent; why, even now, did he make no move to thank Steele for his chivalrous defense; *why, in God's name, did his veiled glance contain so much dislike, hatred even?*

Steele lifted his hand. "The blood of these girls! There's the answer. Who needs this blood? For what foul purpose?"

Each of the guests held his eyes aloof from the secret terror in his neighbor's. Each thought of his own young daughter, with firm, warm flesh and the racing blood of youth in her veins, and panic swept in a great shuddering gasp through their ranks. Tom Steele knew; he knew the echoing whispers that had murmured up and down the streets of Ellendale since the first dreadful corpse had been discovered; he knew as well as they did what was muttered behind masking hands and tight-locked doors.

Irresistibly, against their wills, their eyes went sidelong in the direction of his pointing finger.

Bong—bong—bong!

The bell flooded the valley in which Ellendale nestled with a great diapason of sound. Slowly, sullenly, the brazen clangor beat out the hour, while all life seemed frozen in a nightmare paralysis at that reiterated knell.

Lucy's blood congealed, and her heart raced furiously to pump the sluggish fluid through her veins. Flora's ghastly death, the strange, aloof manner of the man she loved, the wild talk of Tom Steele, his pointing finger, and now, pat with his unuttered accusation, the bell! Oh God, she did not want to be hysterical, but a terrible, unreasoning certainty grew on her. *She, Lucy Alcott, was marked for destruction!*

She tried to keep her head from turning with the others, but a power beyond her will forced it around and upward in mechanical movement.

Bong—bong—bong!

WOULD it never stop, that dreadful, booming bell? Her eyes lifted. Across the road, the valley unended abruptly in the satanic configurations of Devil's Mountain. Half way up, perched like a bird of ill omen over a doomed village, grey and hideous like a vampire bat with outspread wings, were the long, dim battlements of the House of Hermes.

The House of Hermes! Even as a child, Lucy had run as fast as small feet could carry her when darkness swooped unexpectedly upon her homecoming in this particular section of the valley. Many were the tales that were bandied around the firesides on the long, shuddering winter evenings concerning this strange sect that had descended mysteriously upon the valley some thirty years before and built that frowning, fortress-like retreat.

Bong—bong—bong! Nine o'clock! Lucy felt herself counting those long, slow strokes with breathless intensity. No sound came from the other guests of the tragic, birthday party. Steele's pointing hand seemed frozen into eternal rigidity; Dave, pale and grim, looked a far-off stranger. And the bloodless corpse of the dead girl lay exposed to a merciless sky.

Ah, there it was coming! Lucy clenched her little hands in dreadful anticipation. The scream she barely managed to choke back hurt the swelling muscles of her throat. It was silly, she knew, but she could not help it. Every night at nine o'clock this happened. It had never affected her quite this way before. But now. . . . !

She turned blindly to Dave, plucking at his sleeve for comfort. But he did not seem to sense her presence. His face was a grim, set mask that she had never seen before. This was not the man she had loved with all the warmth of her nature. She shrank away from him with a little moan, and still he did not hear or see.

As the last stroke of the great bell died away with dreadful reverberations, the moon, full and dead of face, was transfixed on the topmost spire of Devil's Mountain. Its waning light made a dull, leaden ribbon of the grey battlement of the House of Hermes; it lingered with a fearful fascination on the figure that had suddenly appeared in the single embrasure.

A long, blood-red robe enveloped his powerful body. Distance dwarfed his head to a pallid blob of indistinct features, from which a blur of uncut beard fell in a hairy mop over chin and robe. He faced the valley like a tiny, malignant doll, his scarlet arms outspread over the huddled village of Ellendale.

Faintly, as the echoes shuddered away, his voice shrilled out in an indistinct gibberish that no one in Ellendale had yet been able to decipher. Once, years before, Lucy, lost on the mountainside, had heard that dreadful gabble close at hand, had seen the huge-thewed body of Golas, the Head of the House of Hermes, as he thundered out what seemed a hymn of hate, a fierce blaspheming against a cowering world.

On and on it went, this travesty of the night-blessing of the *muezzin* in the minarets dedicated to Allah. Lucy, locked in rigid terror, felt her scalp freeze to the very marrow of her brain. God, would it never stop? This dreadful, incomprehensible prayer that seemed like a curse, that now, with Flora dead at her feet, was directed at her own poor body. Already she felt the blood drain in gushing torrents from her throat, already she felt. . . .

CHAPTER TWO

Messengers of Madness

THE moon sank beneath the jagged rim of the mountain, the dun, grey walls of the House of Hermes merged into the sombre black of the slope, and the scarlet flare of the sectarian blanked into nothingness. His screeching, ghastly voice died as abruptly.

Silence lay like a crouching panther over the valley, waiting . . . waiting . . . . Someone stirred uneasily, exhaled an explosive gasp of long-withheld breath. Lucy felt her limbs again, sensed the warm blood go rushing through her veins. They were suddenly too heavy for her to carry; she sagged and swayed with a little moan.

Dave caught at her slim body with an ejaculation. Anxiety leaped into his frozen eyes.

"Good Lord, Lucy, are you ill?" A little shiver of happiness coursed through her. Thank God, he was normal again. She had been imagining things. Of course! The dreadful body from which everyone had ebbed away, the strain, the sudden apparition of the strange recluse—all had sapped her strength, given rise to horrible fantasies.

She smiled wanly at his perturbed features, saw with curious clarity that upstanding cowlick she always ached to smooth down.

"It's nothing, Dave darling," she said. "Just a passing faintness."

Already the guests were scattering, slinking off with hasty, muttered goodnights, eyes carefully averted from the dead thing that had been Flora Wells.

Dave pushed Lucy quickly into a chair. "Just a moment," he called back over his shoulder. "I'll get you something. . . ." Then he was swallowed up in the house.

The night pressed down with leaden weights on Lucy's aching eyeballs. Only Tom Steele was left of that birthday party which had started off so bravely with lights and music and laughter. Only Tom —and the huddled corpse.

Steele dragged his somber eyes away from the grey, ominous line that etched the House of Hermes against the black hillside. Fear, warning even, leaped into them at the sight of Lucy. His age-lined face showed startlingly distinct in the shadowed amber of the lanterns. Only a few were still lit, and the candles within guttered and flared unevenly.

"Lucy," he whispered hoarsely, "be very careful. I am afraid for you." His face writhed painfully. "I—I cared a bit for Flora, and she is dead. Now I am lonely again. . . ." He gulped, stopped, looked around fearfully, and went on hurriedly.

"That *liqueur* the House of Hermes is making—what is in it? What gives it that strange flavor that everyone is crazy about? I am a distiller; and I tell you, Lucy, it's something never before used. It's——" He brought his head closer to Lucy's. She knew what he was about to say, what had been hinted around in evasive undertones since Elsie Dunn, the first of the blood-drained victims, had been found. Yet, now, knowing what was coming, why did every nerve-end quiver in shrieking protest, every muscle twist into involuntary knots against the open utterance of the secret horror that oppressed them all?

"It's——" Steel commenced, and stopped.

"Coming, Lucy!" That was Dave's voice. His feet thudded loudly on the verandah.

THE distiller cast her a strange, warning glance. "Not a word of this to anyone—yet," he whispered. "Especially not to Dave. There are certain things I must find out before I can explain further. Good night, Lucy, and be careful."

Then he was gone, swallowed up in the tar-barrel murk of the line of trees.

Dave Cooper was running now, his feet making padding sounds across the lawn. He held something in his hand.

"Lucy darling," he cried with panting anxiety. "How do you feel?"

She collapsed with a long, shuddering sigh in her chair. Her limbs, a moment before rigid with ice, were now weak as flowing water. What had Tom Steele meant? Why shouldn't Dave know? Then, unreasonably, the deep concern etched into his finely chiselled features made her happy. She loved him, loved this young lawyer who had crept like a flame into her hitherto secluded life.

"It—it was——" she started weakly.

"Never mind," he said peremptorily, with just that touch of masculine bruskness she loved. "Don't speak, but drink this. It's the natural reaction to—Flora."

His eyes jerked to the maimed thing on the lawn, swerved back to her. Solicitude, anxiety, showed candidly in their shadowed grey depths.

Her shoulder clung to the supporting arc of his pulsing arm. She raised herself to the glass he offered her lips. It held a beaded liquor, bright red—red as the robe of Golas, red as blood.

Her lips closed over the bubble-thin rim of the glass.

"It will do you good, darling," he urged. "It's *Sang de la Fille.*"

Lucy's lips, parted to absorb the fiery fluid, jerked away.

Sang de la Fille! The new *liqueur* that had swept the world. The beady drink with that strange, lingering flavor which had already driven all other *liqueurs* off the market. The product of the cryptic cult who called themselves the House of Hermes: shaggy, bearded men who performed secret rites in the underground depths of the grey, stone structure they had builded themselves in Ellendale; whose leader was Golas. "The *liqueur* of the secret formula, of the inimitable ingredient," read the scarlet label on the squat, round bottle.

Sang de la Fille! Blood of the maiden! The sinister meaning of that name struck her with stunning force. She had never thought of that before. Why had no one . . .? But of course they had! Tom Steele and others who whispered among themselves. Tom had been about to tell her, to warn her, when Dave's reappearance had struck him dumb.

IN Lucy's fevered mind arose a vision of madmen, deep in the bowels of the mountain, huddled over a hideous, bubbling brew in a vat, adding with gloating chuckles the last ingredient, the . . . . The vision blotted out and others swarmed with flickering shadows in her brain. Elsie, then Ruth, now Flora, cold and shrunken. Later, would it be Lucy Alcott?

Dave said: "Drink it, dear!"

There was impatience in his voice. He tilted the glass, to force the fluid against her pallid lips. Lucy laughed madly, silently. It made crashing thunder in her ears, that unuttered sound. So Dave Cooper was anxious for her to drink that devil's brew! He was trying to force it upon her, was he? That light in his eyes as he bent over her—which seemed concern, commiseration—was nothing of the sort. It was a secret gloating, like that of the band of Hermes as they bent over the stirring of their nauseous concoction.

She remembered now. David Cooper, the stranger in town of a year ago, who had opened his law office and struggled for months until, suddenly, he had money, plenty of it. Why? Where did he get it? Only a few of the villagers were his clients, and they had little business. Yes, she remembered now. *It was just after The House of Hermes had announced Sang de la Fille, the liqueur with the different taste.*

She understood—everything! A fierce fire burned in her veins. Horror of that staring face, which seemed so kind, so lovable, swept over her. Elsie, Ruth, Flora, now Lucy Alcott! If she drank that blood-red drink, she was doomed.

With a wild cry she dashed the brimming glass from her lips. It spilled in a bloody spray over the greedy lawn; it splashed in dreadful sisterhood over the drained corpse. The glass smashed into a tree and splintered into a thousand jagged shards.

Dave cried out in alarm. "For God's sake, Lucy, are you mad?"

Lucy bent back her head and shrilled laughter, shrilled until the tears rolled down her cheeks. Mad! Not she! *She knew now; knew everything!* Back in the small dim recesses of her brain was a tiny doubt. He *did* look so genuinely bewildered, so startled. But the doubt sank in a weltering flood of hysteria. She stopped abruptly. She crouched away, her breath coming in quick little gasps.

Dave started for her, arms outstretched. "Lucy dear," he said, "you are ill. Let me take care of you and call a doctor."

In another step he would have her. For one queer instant, she swayed, forgetful of everything, tugged by the thrill in his voice, the pain on his face. Then she glimpsed the lifeless corpse of Flora Wells. Its nude pallor, its grey-white skin, whirled her around on small, fleeing feet as if it were a turntable.

Down the road she fled blindly, away from the direction of her home, beating out a desperate tattoo on the black asphalt with her high-heeled shoes. Behind her came shouts, calls, imploring cries to stop. Dave was coming after her.

WITH sly cunning, knowing even in the red haze of her thoughts that she was being cunning, Lucy slipped into the close-pressing fields, crouched with withheld breath in the impenetrable dark, heard the mad clatter of Dave's feet as he rushed past her hiding place. Only when the pounding thud had died away in the distance did she rise from her crouch and retrace her steps, past Dave's home—the home she had once thought would be her own—up the road to her own cottage, where she lived alone with an aunt.

Already her madness was passing. The moon had sunk behind the mountain and the blackness was a palpable shroud. The grey line of the House of Hermes loomed almost overhead, leering down at her with avid, eyeless gaze. The breeze fanned her fevered cheek, slowly unloosed the strange hysteria that had overtaken her.

Lucy flushed in the dark. What had she done, how had she acted toward Dave? She had been mad, she realized that now. He would never forgive her, would never. . . .

What was that? Something was moving stealthily along the road, paralleling her clicking heels. Fear crawled with spiny legs down her back. It was nothing, she told herself desperately; it was only the rustling of the breeze in the grass. But she knew it was not that. She pulled her quivering limbs to a halt, listened. All she heard was the pounding of the blood in her ears. She went ahead, and the stealthy gliding kept even pace with her.

No, no! she shrieked to herself. There was no one out there in the Stygian darkness; nothing but her own fearful imaginings. Oh God! If only Dave were here, if only Tom Steele were walking by her side, encouraging her trembling limbs. . . .

She started to run. Her heart tore at the thin covering of her ribs; the breath wheezed and sobbed in her throat. Beyond the next bend of the road, as it curved around the mountain's flank, was home— the little cottage which spelled safety, surcease from terror.

There was no mistaking that pursuing sound now. The Thing was coming after her. She flogged her failing limbs to renewed effort. Oh God, it was no use! She was doomed! The corpses of the other girls, grey-shrunken, drawn of all blood, flared in her fevered brain with horrid beckonings, inviting her with dreadful mockery to join their mummified estate.

Slowly the unseen menace crept up on

her. Now its hot breath seared the nape of her neck with scorching exhalations. A great scream burst from her laboring lungs. It went racketing down the valley, ascended with pitiful appeal to the leering House of Hermes, and choked off abruptly.

A huge, powerful hand crept out of the dark, clamped with terrific force over her pallid mouth. Her wire-taut, struggling body crushed within the shrouding folds of a billowing garment, went limp under relentless pressure. Complete darkness overwhelmed her.

Before she sank into oblivion, Lucy felt a sharp jab in her left arm, like the stinging sensation of a needle prick. Someone chuckled—a low, grating chuckle—then she knew no more . . . .

CHAPTER THREE

The Pointing Finger of Doom

SOMEHOW—Lucy was never to understand just how—she awoke to find herself weaving with sagging, drunken feet along the valley road. The sharp pain in her left arm still persisted; it stung as if with the venom of a million bees. The warm, night breeze fanned her dizzy brow, dried the terror-dew upon her cheek. Her skull was a throbbing fire; her arm hurt; her legs could barely support her.

Slowly, very slowly, realization came to her, and with it renewed fear. Merciful God, what had happened to her? What being still lurked in that groping murk, waiting with fiendish grin to attack her again? Lucy staggered on with moaning, laboring breath. She *must* get to her home. She repeated it over and over, forcing it through clenched teeth, willing her body forward against the strange suction of the night. Unseen hands plucked at her dress; eerie voices shrilled mockeries in her ear;

strange, monstrous faces mopped and mowed before her splitting vision, but she went on and on, wearily, hopelessly. She could never win through.

Then, suddenly, the trim, vine-covered cottage was a shadowed white thing just before her. A great sob burst from her aching throat. Home! Never had the simple word been so fraught with meaning. She was running now, running with the last atoms of strength in her body. Nothing could harm her there, nothing. Aunt Celia would. . . .

She fumbled blindly at the latch gate. She had forgotten. Her aunt was gone for the weekend and would not be home until Monday morning. She would be alone in the little cottage, a prey to all the crawling, prowling Things of the night.

She flung the gate shut behind her. Her running feet were loud on the narrow gravel path. Her trembling hand reached mechanically for the door knob. It twisted, and the arched door opened silently into a well of darkness. With a cry, she staggered back. She had locked the door before she left for that fatal party. She was sure of that. What dreadful Thing was slinking in that suddenly clammy darkness, waiting for her unsuspecting entrance?

Her slender hand went dizzily to her brow. Perhaps she was mistaken; perhaps in the excitement of her departure she had forgotten to turn the key. Aunt Celia was the one who usually took care of those details.

She forced her leaden limbs over the threshold. Outside was hideous death, within was . . . .? Nothing happened. The cavern of the familiar room was nevertheless ominous with its very breathless silence. She bit her lip to force back the betraying breath; she fumbled slowly across the wall for the switch. The Delco unit whirred noisily in the cellar, and warm, blessed illumination sprang from the frosted bulbs.

Nothing was wrong, absolutely nothing. Every piece of the thrice-familiar furniture was in its ordered, meticulous place. Aunt Celia had *such* a passion for neatness. Sweet Aunt Celia—if only she were here to greet her, to take the lurking curse of solitude off the place!

Lucy locked the door, slammed the bolt, put the heavy chain into place. Now she was safe. Safe? With dreadful Things out there, possibly surrounding the house even now; with windows that could shatter under blows of stony fists? God! She could never last through the night.

Her arm too—it throbbed with a blinding pulse of its own. What had that monster done to her? She was afraid to look; it took infinite effort to bring her eyes down to the bareness of her left arm, just beneath the filmy shortness of her sleeve.

There, imbedded in an angry, swelling mound of inflamed flesh, was a round, dark, red hole. The room suddenly rocked before Lucy's darkened sight. That round red hole! A needle had been thrust into her arm, and then withdrawn! *Her blood had been taken by the Thing on the road!*

WHY? Why? In a shrieking corner of her brain, she knew why. But she must not admit it; she must not say it out aloud. She must get to the 'phone immediately; she must call for help!

Her half-mad eyes caught on something that lay flat and white on the floor. It was just over the door sill, as if it had been shoved through the tiny crack between door and floor. She stared at it with wide, fierce eyes. She had not seen it before. Had it been there all the time, while fright and hurry had clouded her vision? Or had some stealthy, unseen hand just now carefully edged it through the tiny space?

Writing was on it. Something cried aloud in her brain: "Don't read it! Destroy it; run to the 'phone; get help at once!" But even as it shrieked its warning, she knew that she *must* read those cryptic black marks, even if her life depended on it.

Slowly, stiffly, she bent and picked it up. The black-ink letters danced before her eyes in mocking blurs. They seemed to taunt her with the secret that they held. Teeth clenched, lips stiffly set, she forced her whirling brain to a slower pace. The letters cleared, sent their hideous message stabbing into her consciousness.

> Your blood has been tested. It is perfect. It is the inimitable ingredient. Prepare for our coming!"

The paper dropped from Lucy's suddenly nerveless fingers. She shrank against the wall, choking back the scream that tore at her throat; she stared at that oblong of paper as it slowly fluttered to the floor. The livid words etched themselves in letters of red across her brain.

Her blood—the inimitable ingredient!

Merciful God in Heaven! The very slogan on the label of *Sang de la Fille!* The secret ingredient which gave that ultimate taste to the cordial that was sweeping the world! Blood, that's what it was —blood of maidens, blended in a foul brew with alcohol and aromatic spices! With what monstrous impudence those vermilion-clad monsters who called themselves the Sect of Hermes had named their *liqueur,* chuckling horribly to themselves in the bowels of Devil's Mountain!

The world did not know, and flocked with avid thirst to this new and rare sensation. All day long, and every day, the huge trucks thundered into the hitherto sleepy valley, hurtled out again laden with cases of the squat, round bottles. The world ever clamored for more. Other *liqueurs,* other alcoholic drinks, were forgotten.

Elsie, Ruth, Flora, sacrificed, drained of blood, made into loathsome, shrunken corpses, so that this strange new taste could tickle the palate of unknowing drinkers. And she, Lucy Alcott, was next! *They had tested her blood, had found it perfect! Prepare for . . .!* Oh God! She must hurry; she must call for help!

The short steps to the wall-'phone in the hall were endless miles; the wait while a sleepy operator tried to make connection with David Cooper's home, was an eternity of hovering nightmares. Dave, her darling Dave! *He* had nothing to do with this; she had been hysterical, half-mad when she ran from him and her crowding fears. How happy she would be to hear his clear, thrilling voice on the wire. Over and over again she mumbled to herself what he would say: "Of course, darling. I'll be right over. Just don't you worry."

But why, in God's name, did it take so long? She would report the operator to the management. She was careless, inexcusably negligent. Didn't she know this was a matter of life and death?

But no! She was ringing; she could hear that strong, intermittent buzz. Dave must be sleeping, he must be. . . .?

"I'm sorry, Miss Alcott, but Mr. Cooper does not answer."

Click!

LUCY stared at the dead 'phone in her hand as if it were a shiny black beetle. It was impossible! It was . . .! Then she remembered. She herself had caused Dave to go wandering through the night, up the road into the wilder mountains, searching for her.

With a sob, she jiggled the 'phone again frantically. The sheriff! She must get the sheriff!

Thank God, he was in. He listened to her stumbling, hurtling words with cool, easily detectable scepticism.

"Of course, Miss Alcott," he soothed. "I'll be over in half an hour or so. It's ten miles from Monckton to Ellendale,

you know. Just keep the door locked until I come." She could hear his cheery whistling as he hung up.

She looked with shuddering eyes about her. Half an hour? She laughed, and was shocked to hear the strange timber of that laugh. Half an hour! Anything might happen in half an hour!

There must be something else she could do, someone else she could call for immediate help. Lucy tried to think. It was hard, with maggots crawling in her brain, with pain lancing her left arm, with every rustling wind outside a shrieking invitation to madness.

Of course! Why hadn't she thought of him before? Tom Steele! Good, faithful Tom. His home was not a quarter of a mile away; he could be at her side in minutes.

Whimpering with eagerness, she caught the 'phone off its cradle, gave his number. Tom *must* be home; he *must!*"

"Tom! Tom!" Her knees sagged with relief, almost pitched her headlong. How quickly he had answered.

"What is it?" He sounded sleepy. Then he roused. "Oh, Lucy, it's you! What's the matter?" There was sudden clarity, anxiety, in his usually gruff voice.

She was shrieking the words into the receiver. "Come over at once. They're after me—my blood! Please, *please* come!"

There was a clicking noise on the line, as if someone was trying to cut in; as if —someone was trying to hear.

"Hold everything," Tom cried. "I'll be over in five minutes. Get the sheriff, get Dave!"

"I—I have."

But he had already hung up. A great weight rolled off Lucy's heart. She could breathe again. Dear, faithful Tom! What a pity he was a lonely bachelor, grown old through the long years of his mother's illness.

In five minutes, he said. She walked back into the living room, light-headed with flooding relief from the terrible strain of the past hours. Tom would see that everything was all right. She even started to hum a little childish tune she remembered. And then she froze on a soprano note—froze into physical immobility as she reached the center of the room. *Someone, something, was moving in the cellar!*

Oh God! Were all her efforts in vain? It would take five minutes for Tom to get here, half an hour for the sheriff. In that time, she would be dead, a bloodless, horrible corpse. All the time she had been telephoning, that lurking Thing had been down in the cellar, waiting, waiting. . . .

Madness shrieked through her brain. She opened her mouth to scream. The sound made fiendish echoes in her ears. Then, without warning, the lights went out. The house was suddenly a tomb, a hollow cave of crowding shapes and red-glaring eyes and whispering noise.

She staggered blindly along, arm stiff-extended, trying to find her way to the door. The telephone rang, a quick, insistent burr. What good was it now; with the stealthy monster almost upon her?

Thump—thump—thump! Slow pounding of heavy boots, coming up the cellar stairs, coming for her!

She shrank against the wall, holding herself barely erect with spread hands. Her scalp was a prickling, crawling mass; her blood a roaring, seething rapids.

Thud—bump! It was in the room, feeling, feeling slowly around for her. Screams ached in her throat with unuttered sound. Her heart was a triphammer pounding on unyielding metal. He would hear that dreadful sound; he would find her. . . .

And all the while, the telephone buzzed angrily, insistently, trying to get her attention. Too late! No one could help her

any more. The unseen monster had stopped. Not a sound came from him. He was waiting for her to give herself away. Her reason hung on a frayed thread. Good Lord, couldn't he hear the pounding of her heart, the loud murmur of the blood in her veins?

The telephone stopped. It was tired, even as she was. Her head went round and round. Her limbs were numb and cold; they could not support her any more. Desperately she gripped at the flat smooth wall for better purchase, missed, and went stumbling.

A hideous laugh enveloped her. She screamed as a shroud went over her head, muffled her body. Something sweet, sickeningly sweet . . . . Oh God, she was drifting off!

CHAPTER FOUR

Prisoner of Dread

HOW her head ached! Round and round and round went the small, loose pieces in her skull. She tried to catch them, to piece them together. Somehow it was important, her fumbling senses knew that. But they eluded her grasp, went round and round continually. There was a sweet smell somewhere, but it was getting fainter. Another more pungent odor was beating it off, driving it away with sharp, acrid whips. Slowly her brain cleared, slowly the whirling fragments fell into ordered patterns. She opened her eyes.

For a moment, bewilderment seemed but a greater nightmare. Where was she? She had never seen this fantastic place before. Surely she was dreaming, or dead. She tried to force her throbbing body upright, but something held her back, plucked her down with slicing fingers. Her still vacant eyes looked dully at her wrists. They were bound with stout Manila hemp. The lashings went around her prone form, and out of sight beneath a table. Her dress was a thing of shreds and tatters, as if ripped from her in her strugglings. White, satiny skin shivered in the cold dampness.

The frigid draught of air was like ice water on her numbed senses. She looked wildly around. Rock met her eyes overhead, all around. Damp, spotted granite, dark grey, dripping with slimy beads of seeping moisture. A dull, red light cast bloody shadows on the rough-hewn walls, made them alive with gloating, crawling shapes.

Lucy moaned with horror. She was underground, immured in a clamping tomb of rock, bound helpless to a table. What was going to happen to her? Slow, inevitable death from hunger and thirst and the vermin that burrowed beneath the earth, never to be found until her bones were an unrecognizable, crumbling mass, or . . . .?

She twisted her head with agonized effort. The ropes cut cruelly into her slender neck, but she must see—she *must!*

The cavern was not large. Barrels lined the walls. Almost opposite her was a huge, gleaming, copper globe. From its rounded top issued curious whorls of shiny copper tubes that to her staring eyes seemed alive with sinuous motion, writhing like a nest of snakes. A huge pipe sprang from their midst, entered the slimy, solid rock, and disappeared.

A thin steam issued from a vent at the top of the copper globe, spread with fantastic, bloody shadows over the roof of the cavern. It assailed her quivering nostrils with sharp, spicy odors, mingled with strangely numbing fumes.

Realization flooded her with the sniffing of that flavor. Alcohol! Lucy strained against the ropes with a great scream. She knew now where she was. Better to be buried alive in a vault, with the everlasting dead for company, than in this cave with the shiny implements of man's industry about her.

She was in the underground passages, deep in the bowels of Devil's Mountain, which the men of the House of Hermes had hewn for the brewing of their hellish liquor. *Sang de la Fille!* Blood of the maiden! Then it was true, every shrieking word of it—the gossip that had been whispered in cryptic phrases through the village as if no one dared say it outright.

She had heard it, of course, as had Tom and the others. But it was a stealthy undercurrent, for the village had feared the seldom-seen sectarians and their giant leader. There had been no proof, no evidence on which to call in the law. Just rumors of which no one acknowledged the fathership.

But it was true! Lucy knew now they were damnably true, now that it was too late. Too late! The two simple words were pregnant with doom. She had been brought, under choloroform, to this secret, rock-hewn distillery of the fanatical sect, to be slaughtered like any sheep, to feel the life-blood welling from her throat, dripping into that huge copper globe— *the inimitable ingredient!* Her disordered brain conjured up a vision of David, her beloved, sipping with critical tongue the perfumed *liqueur,* smacking his lips over it, not knowing that the girl he mourned as lost was close to him, an essential part of what he drank.

SHRIEKING madness descended upon her. In a red haze, she felt her body whip against the confining thongs like an eel whose back has been broken. As if they came from a stranger, she heard the searing screams lash from her throat, smash into fragmentary echoes against the jutting rocks. Her body became a gridiron of spurting wounds, into which the solid hemp dug deeper and deeper, but she did not feel it. Stark terror made her insensible to hurt or pain.

A door banged open. Heavy boots echoed hollowly on the stony floor. Her screams died down to little whimperings as she forced wide, haunted eyes upon the figure that loomed over her.

The flickering red shadows, the duffusing steam, made him seem a giant in size. A long, scarlet robe enshrouded his form. Fierce, fanatical eyes glared out at her from under great shaggy eyebrows. A tangled mop of coarse, black hair fell round his shoulders, mingled with the curling, writhing strands of a huge, black beard that covered his face with its uncut luxuriance.

Lucy could not scream any more; her throat was a raw fire.

"Golas!" she whispered through parched lips. She had never seen the strange Head of the Sect face to face, except that night when a lost little girl, she had fled down the mountain from the sight of his scarlet figure and the sound of his thundering voice.

His mouth twisted and grinned evilly under the masking beard. Red worms of madness crawled in those glaring, shadowed eyes.

The man was mad, that was it. The religious fanaticism of the sect he had fathered had turned his addled brain. In his madness, he had stumbled on the blood baptism of the *liqueur* he had concocted to provide the House of Hermes with ample funds—and *she* was merely an ingredient. There was no mercy in those eyes, there could be no mercy in that mad, lusting brain. *There was no escape for Lucy!*

Slowly he raised his red-shrouded arm. A grave-cold hand slithered down her shrinking flesh. The worms danced evilly in his red-rimmed eyes. Was there no God in Heaven? Was there to be worse than mere death in store for her?

He saw the panic in her eyes, felt the convulsive movements of her body. His great beard waggled with the hoarse chuckle.

"So you're afraid of Golas?" he jeered. "Not every one is good enough for you, is he, Lucy Alcott?" His voice was a deep, bass rumble. Hate lanced from his mad eyes. "Well, take a last look at that body you think so lovely. Soon it will a thing of emptied flesh and bones. Your blood, the dainty red blood that flows in your veins, will give the last delicate flavor to *Sang de la Fille!*" His hideous laugh rang around the cavern. "What a stupid world! No one but myself knows the true reason for its name. The fools think it something similar to *Lachrymae Christi*, the Italian wine, *Tears of Christ*. But I, I know better! You, Lucy Alcott, will be the fourth of the stupid girls of this village whose blood runs in the sparkling *liqueur* that the world drinks and smacks its lips over." He threw back his head and laughed again and again. "Fools, *fools,* all of them!"

TERROR, such as she had never known before, sent red hot needles of agony lacing through Lucy's skull. Her blurred brain felt as though it would explode through the confining bone. Her blood was suddenly a moveless mass of ice. She gasped for air to fill her bursting lungs.

"You daren't do that, Golas!" she stammered with the desperation born of despair.

The man bent his shaggy face toward her. She recoiled against the ropes at the twisted, unutterable hatred in that bearded mask.

"I daren't?" he mouthed. "I dare everything. *Everything,* do you understand? The other girls, I simply cut their throats and hung them up like cattle to drain into the cordial. But *you,* my dear . . ." He paused and smacked his lips.

Oh God, what will he do to me? Oh dear God, let me die now, at once! I can't stand it any longer; I can't! The dry constriction of her throat was a tearing torture. If only she could scream—the very madness of the sound, the laceration of the muscles, would be relief.

"You," he went on with fiendish laughter, "I shall first amuse myself with. I shall skewer you on this iron hook overhead, and you shall swing like a gigantic pendulum through the air, while the blood rolls down your pretty white thighs and goes drip, drip, into the final distillation. What do you think of that, my dear?"

The bands that corded her throat gave way before the pouring ecstacy of her terror. It was no human sound that beat with desperate concussions against the enclosing rock; it was the last wail of a soul already lost. The bearded man grinned hideously at her. His eyes were deep slits of gloating madness.

"Scream all you want, Lucy Alcott. It won't do you any good. No one will ever hear you."

His scarlet-clad form seemed to increase to gigantic size as he moved toward the table. The long, clawed fingers which barely protruded from the flowing sleeves seemed already tight around her throat. Lucy could scream no more. Faint moans bubbled from her swollen lips.

He jerked at her head, snapped it against the ropes. Pain lanced through her body. A knife glittered in his hand, poised for the downward slash at her bonds.

What was that? A faint, far-off murmur grew steadily in volume until it became a confused tangle of many sounds. Through the solid rock it came, muffled, grinding, like the distant roar of many waterfalls.

The knife hesitated in the killer's hand, dropped back against his side. A startled look came into his glittering eyes; his beard waggled with a curious movement of its own. He stiffened, listened. The noise was a clamor now, as of voices shouting.

"So soon!" he mumbled. His voice seemed lost in the tangle of hair. "I didn't expect——" He paused, looked furtively at the moaning, lifeless girl on the table. "You can wait," he said hoarsely. "I must see this, I must—"

His heavy boots went thudding over the stone. His blood-red robes were a swirl of rushing movement as he vanished through the steamy haze behind the great copper retort. Something banged open in the wall. A huge flood of sound poured into the chamber, a great clamorous outcry that drowned the noise of his racing feet through long, subterranean passages.

THE fierce beat of sound crashed into Lucy's consciousness to bring awareness again to her numbed senses. What had happened? For one thing, Golas was gone, frightened away by the muted roar that was now a ghastly tumult. She had obtained a respite. But she knew, as she lay flat on her back, bound with cords that her unaided efforts could never loosen, that she was doomed. Soon, all too soon, that mad fanatic would return, would impale her tender body on huge tearing hooks, and complete the fiendish formula of his devil's brew.

But that noise! What was it? Why was it now so terribly loud? Golas had left the door open in the haste of his upward flight, and the rocky passages acted like sounding boards, to bring every least sound as it rose from the upper battlements of the House of Hermes.

There were shouts now, scuffling of heavy-booted feet, mad, indistinct confusion, voices shrill with fear, voices hoarse with frenzied threats.

Lucy listened, and a great hope surged through her frozen heart. The steel bands stopped pressing on her skull, the blood once more pumped warmly through her body.

The stronghold of the House of Hermes was being attacked!

The villagers had been roused by the culminating death of Flora Wells, by her own disappearance. Tom Steele had come to her house and found her gone. The telltale odor of chloroform would have lingered in the rooms. The sheriff had come, no longer sceptical. Dave—her heart constricted with fierce emotion at the thought of him—had been found and told what had happened.

Tom Steele, no longer restrained from voicing his suspicions, must have talked. What had been rumors became certainties. They had roused the village. Even now, grim, determined men, under the leadership of Dave and Tom and the sheriff, were storming the lair of the Sect, once and for all to determine the truth of the other girls' deaths; to rescue her.

Happy tears bathed her cheeks. She strained her ears to gather distinctness out of that welter of sound. Voices rose above the general tumult, faded before she could identify them. Once she thought she heard Dave's clear, masculine voice; another time, she was almost positive that Tom's deep ruffness had floated momentarily on the surface.

Almost she could hear the trample of many feet as they stormed up the hillside. Perhaps even now Dave was scrambling, panting upward through thick underbrush and over rock masses, directly overhead, not ten, twenty feet above her, unknowing that the girl he loved was a helpless prisoner beneath, doomed to a horrible, torturing death.

She would be rescued; she must. Her beloved would see to that; so would Tom Steele. He *was* a faithful, loyal friend.

The noise was increasing. The rock passages conducted the sounds inward with strange clarity; almost magnified them.

That shouting, shrieking blur must be the villagers storming to the attack. That nearer, cleared thudding meant the inmates of the House of Hermes—strange fanatics, members of a sect whose garbled religion was a hodgepodge of God knew what hideous rites. She heard their hoarse cries, strangled in the never-shorn beards that all affected, loud with alarm and startled fear.

Good! Good! Lucy cried insanely to herself. Let them suffer as they had wanted her to suffer, as Elsie and Ruth and Flora and who knew how many other innocent maidens had done. She was slightly light-headed, lying there in the red-shadowed cavern, inhaling the stupefying fumes of alcohol, sniffing the tart, wild tang of strange spices.

A sudden roar, more furious, more savage than any before, swept down the open tunnels, dinned in her ears like the mad surge of the sea. Lucy strained at her cords, listened with every ounce of her being. Up there, in that incomprehensible clamor, her fate was being decided. If only she knew what was happening, if only. . . .

The raging, howling clamor died suddenly, as if it had been a single thunderclap. Silence! Silence as of the grave! To Lucy that sudden stillness was more terrifying than any noise, no matter how hideous. Had they abandoned her, those villagers? Had Tom Steele—had Dave, the man in all the world who should have gone through Hell itself to find her— had they all slunk away and left her to horrible, tearing tortures? Were they suddenly cowards? A great sob tore at her throat, died stillborn.

What was that?

CHAPTER FIVE

Fall of the House of Hermes

OUT of the stillness of the tomb rose a voice, a great, deep, rumbling voice. It shook the very rock around her with its bass vibrations, it poured out in a flood of sound more penetrating, more frightful, than the whole hideous welter of a hundred shouting men.

"Halt where you are, every one of you!" it resounded. "It is I, Golas, Head of the House of Hermes, who command it!"

Lucy whimpered in her throat. Golas, who had been interrupted in his tortures of a poor defenseless girl, was trying to stop the advancing horde of determined, angry men, was trying to stop *her* Dave, Tom Steele, the sheriff, with *commands!* She laughed wildly and shrank from her own laughter. Oh Lord, she prayed, please don't let me go mad now—now that my beloved is coming to rescue me. Please!

Ah, there it came! Just what she had expected. That fierce answering cry of defiance. It was like the last great breaker crashing on the shore. Now they would come on, wave on wave, and blot those evil monstrosities from the face of the earth.

But high above the growls, the mingled cries, came the voice of Golas once again —a great blast of sound that pounded and beat down the other to the merest whisper.

"I warn you," he thundered. "Not another move, or on your own heads be it. What manner of madmen are ye? Why do you come storming and clamoring for our blood? We are peaceful folk, minding our own business, and asking only that ye mind your own. What do ye want with us?"

Lucy shivered with controllable spasms. The damnable, cozening villian! How dared he utter such lies, when *she* was here below, a prey to unimaginable tortures! But no! They would never believe him, they would never....

A lone voice answered, saying things that her straining, bursting eardrums could not hear. Golas laughed, deep and rumbling. Yes, the madman was actually laughing. Did he think he would fool Dave, Tom and the rest with that pseudo-hearty laughter?

"What manner of children are ye," Golas demanded, "to believe such lies, such stupid superstitions? Ye would hark back to the days of witchcraft, to burn innocent people who do not conform to your ways, on accusations that ye cannot prove."

Smooth cunning—the cunning of a madman! But Dave would see behind the fair phrases, would know how to answer them.

Ah, there it came. "Let us know what is in the formula then."

That was the sheriff; she recognized his cool, even tones. Strange though! It should have been Dave Cooper, who loved her, who was a lawyer and a leader of men, who made that very pertinent demand. In any event, Golas was stumped. He could not answer, he *dared* not. The whole secret lay in the blood that had dripped from round bodies, even as hers. Golas was through now.

See, there was silence, as if he were hesitating. In another instant ...

Like a cannon shot the voice of the giant boomed out. "That," he declared flatly, "is a secret. We cannot tell you that. Our livelihood, the continued existence of our Order, depends on the preciousness of our *liqueur.*"

A wave of exultation burned fiercely along the quivering length of the imprisoned girl. He had called others fools. He was the greater fool. For once, his mad cunning had deserted him. He could have mentioned—anything. They would not have known the difference. But she had forgotten. Tom Steele would have known. He was a distiller himself. Now the villagers would move forward.

There they came. She heard dimly the crunching of feet on the rubble above; she heard the gathering, full-throated roar of determined men. They were attacking. She strained feverishly at her bonds, shouting hysterically, urging the unseen men along, bathed in alternate flushes of heat and icy cold.

GOLAS' huge bass rose above the din. "For the last time," he shouted authoritatively, "I demand that you stop. We are armed, and we shall shoot. This is private property. You have no search warrant; go back and get one if you wish, Sheriff. But now get out before I count three. At *three* I shall order my brethern to fire.

"One . . . !"

Lucy shrieked with hysterical laughter. Search warrants indeed! Dave would know that by the time they returned, hours later, she would be dead; there would be no trace of anything. And Golas would mock at them with bland, secret smiles and strange gestures.

"Two . . . !"

All Lucy's faculties were contained in her straining ears. Was it possible, could it be . . . ? Was the noise, the clamor of righteous wrath, dying down to hesitant murmurs? Almost she could hear the indecisive shuffling of feet.

"Dave, Dave!" she shrieked. "I am down here. Help! Help!"

But of course he could not hear. Her voice had not the carrying power of Golas', or the throats of a hundred men. But Dave would not let her down. If he loved her as she loved him . . . . *Had?* She shrank from that word. Why had she said it? Because she would not love a coward, a man who backed down before threats when his beloved's life was involved.

"Three!"

It crashed out above a sudden stillness with hideous triumph. For a whole minute, she knew that her heart was not moving, that all her faculties were rigid with nightmare paralysis. What were they going to do?

Oh God! The invocation tore hope-lessly out of her throat. Her head sagged limply against the ropes. *They were going away*. That silence, broken only by the faintest of shuffling feet! The brave men of the village were crawling down the mountain. The sheriff was with them, and Tom Steele, and *Dave!*

It was impossible; it could not be! Her eyes glared wildly; her brain was a kaleidoscope of madness. They were abandoning her to Golas and the House of Hermes. Soon, the bearded giant would return. He would taunt her with their cowardice. He would approach her again with those hideous hands; he would take her slender body and impale it on sharp hooks. Even now he was . . . !

She stiffened in frantic fear. Behind her something was opening, slowly, cautiously. The creaking grew louder. They were coming for her. Her shriek was the borderline between sanity and madness.

"Lucy!"

Of course she was mad now. Her reason had definitely snapped. That was why she had heard her name called in accents that were Dave's.

There was a swift clatter of feet, a sobbing, frantic voice. Someone was bending over her, tearing at her bonds with bare fingers. She opened her eyes incredulously.

"Dave! Dave!" It was he, come to save her! It was no mirage, no apparition. There was suffering stamped on his keen, lithe features; there were the burnt-out embers of agony in the dark hollows of his eyes, but the unruly cowlick still stuck out, and his eyebrows arched in a pathetic attempt at his old-time grin.

"Lucy, darling," he was saying, as his fingers untied the ropes in trembling haste. "Thank God I found you. I didn't believe Golas had you; I couldn't. But I thought if you were here, if what they were saying was true, this would be the place. I knew of the secret entrance to this vault, and came by myself. I let the sheriff and the villagers do what they insisted on." His face went grim and hard as his eyes flicked over her poor, tortured body. "Golas and the House of Hermes will have to answer to *me* for this night's work!"

THE last strand was loose. He lifted her with strong, eager arms off the table. "Come on, darling. We'll get out and——"

"Look out behind you!" Lucy screamed. From her cradled position, she saw the wild shaggy face of Golas appear over his shoulder, the down-dropping of a wooden club.

It caught Dave on the back of his skull. There was a sickening thud. His eyes went blank, filmed over. He staggered and went headlong. Lucy fell with him, sobbing and screaming, rolling over and over.

In one great bound, the triumphant madman was upon her, held her in a grip of iron. Dave, her lover, lay horribly motionless on the stony floor.

"Got back just in time!" the scarlet figure rumbled in his beard with hoarse chuckles. "Your David Cooper won't bother us any more, my dear. So he knew the secret entrance from the hill! Well, he won't make any use of it now, will he?"

She beat weakly at the broad, shrouded chest above. "You've killed him; you've killed the man I love!"

"Sure! Why not?" he jeered. The blows of her fists were like brushing feathers to him. Hate boiled in his shadowed, sunken eyes. "I hate you all, everyone of you," he shouted suddenly. "I was different from Ellendale folk, and you mocked me. All of you. Don't think I didn't know it, that I didn't plan my revenge. And now, Lucy Alcott, I have won. I have fooled everyone. *Everyone!*"

The thick beard swept over her tender skin with rasping, tearing bristles. His great hands tightened around her.

Lucy drooped like a broken, wilted flower. There was no strength in her body; she had no further will to live. *Dave was dead.* Let her die too; she was weary, weary. . . .

The bearded figure, still chuckling, threw her body over his shoulder as if she were a sack. Her head drooped downward. He lurched forward toward the copper retort, to the hooks that were suspended overhead. In seconds, she would be a struggling butterfly, impaled on huge pins, gushing out her life blood to join the concoction that simmered and steamed below.

She was beyond mere fear. Terror had become so all-embracing that she felt nothing. Her eyes barely opened. Merciful God in Heaven! Was she delirious now? Dave, Dave who was dead, was crawling along the damp stone after them. His face was paper-white and streaked with blood. Gore welled slowly from a matted skull. His features were twisted with terrific agony; his teeth protruded with painful effort over his lower lip. His limbs seemed the broken legs of a fly in a spider web. But he kept inching his way along, fired by some grim, indomitable purpose.

Life coursed shudderingly again in Lucy's frozen body. Dave was still alive, incredibly so. She smothered the scream in her mouth, but it was too late.

Her captor had heard, and swung around. Dave's pain-swept eyes lifted. Astonishment spread over his blurred features; he opened his mouth and thick, formless words spewed forth. His limbs thrashed violently in a mighty effort to move faster.

The bearded giant let out a roar. "I thought I scotched you before, David Cooper. Well, this time——!"

He threw Lucy violently to the ground. Her bruised body crashed with a dreadful thud. Everything rocked and roared. She could not move; perhaps she never would be able to. Incongruously, something far-off, almost detached from her, annoyed her. It was something that had just occurred; yet she could not focus her blurred senses on the problem.

THEN shrieking horror enveloped her, made her forget everything else. Golas was standing over Dave. His great foot was uplifted, and the dark of his trousers showed beneath the robe. Dave writhed and tried to pull himself erect. His face was a mask of agony. But his legs dragged and dragged.

The foot was descending. In another second, it would crash into the agonized face beneath, would stamp out, with hideous thumps, the last vestige of life in the man she adored—making a hideous, pulped mass of his head.

She shrieked hopelessly, tonelessly.

Were those running feet? Was that the sound of men? She tried to raise her head. Hope for the last time thrilled her weary frame. She tried to shout and could not. From behind the great copper globe, from the door through which Golas had just emerged, poured a flood of men. Her head fell back at the sight of them, sick with hope deferred. Great shaggy men they were, clad in scarlet robes, with wild, streaming locks and huge beards. Reinforcements for their chief, for Golas, who was about to crush out the life of David Cooper.

The bearded figure's foot was almost down now. Then something cracked, sent reverberations around the room. The killer staggered, his descending foot slid aimlessly to one side, and he went down, like a riven oak, across the thrashing body of the man he was about to murder.

Lucy forced her eyes wide open, in-credulous. Who was that who bent over her, with a strange, gentle concern in his deep-set eyes? Why, it was Golas! It must be—the same long, black hair, the same beard, the same robe. But Golas was dead, killed by the smoking revolver in this dual apparition's hand. See, there he lay, a huddled blob of red!

"Don't you worry, lass," said the Head of the House of Hermes. "You're safe now; and so is Davey Cooper, our lawyer. I heard screams up above, after I shooed those silly folk away, and thought I'd come down to investigate."

Others of the Brotherhood had lifted Dave, had brought him to her side. They crept painfully into each other's arms.

"I knew it couldn't be Golas," Dave whispered. "But I couldn't talk the Sheriff and the others out of it. I really came to warn him of the proposed attack, and——" He hesitated and looked up at the grim, yet kindly face of the giant.

The man wagged his shaggy head. "It *did* look bad for us, didn't it?" he queried. "But let's see who it was who imperson-ated me; he's responsible for those poor girls' deaths, for spreading the rumors about the House of Hermes."

He strode over to the huddled figure, ripped at beard and hair. They came off in his hands in great clumps. Beneath, glaring up at the rocky ceiling with hatred that even death could not quench, was Tom Steele!

"It's really simple enough," Dave explained later. "He had brooded over his wasted youth and the fact that the girls of Ellendale mocked at him as an old, unwanted man until his mind gave way. With mad cunning, he plotted a horrible revenge. The opportunity came when Golas and his Brotherhood discovered their secret formula and started making *Sang de la Fille*." He grinned wanly. "I was their lawyer, darling, and they've been pretty good clients. Their success was phenomenal. As a matter of fact, Tom Steele's business went down steadily in the face of their competition. He made them a private offer of partnership, and they turned it down. He was on the verge of bankruptcy, and his madness turned on them as responsible for *that* misfortune. In the cunning of his twisted brain, he saw the opportunity to obtain a fiendish revenge on all those he fancied were his enemies.

"The name *Sang de la Fille* gave him the idea. *Blood of the Maiden*. As a matter of fact I had warned Golas against the use of such a name, but he liked it. Compared it to the Italian wine, *Lachrymae Christi, Tears of Christ,* said it gave a novel touch.

"STEELE spread all those rumors," Dave went on. "He killed the girls and threw their bodies on my lawn. Possibly because I was the Brotherhood's lawyer, and in that way affiliated with them. He attacked you on the road, took a hypodermic of blood. He had already broken into your house and left the message there. He wanted definite suspicion to fall on the Brotherhood. That's why he didn't kill you at once. While you were staggering toward home, he ran ahead and hid in the cellar. His make-up as Golas was donned—he knew you did not know Golas personally. Then he waited for you to telephone for help, as he knew you would. He wanted the village to know what had happened. He had tapped in on the wire in the celler in advance, so as to know exactly what was being said.

"When he heard you call him, he answered at once. That was his undoing. For the operator, ringing back to tell you there was no answer at his place, heard him talking. She listened in and became suspicious. She finally located me—I was still hunting the roads for you. I raced at once to your home. You were gone, but the note was on the floor, where Steele had carefully left it. Meanwhile the sheriff had arrived, and the village was aroused. They were beyond reasoning—Steele's poisonous rumors had prepared the ground—and they tried to storm this place. The rest you know, except that I still don't understand how Steele found out about the secret entrance."

Golas smiled in his beard. "It was at his suggestion that I built it. He told me months ago we might need a way to escape. He said the folk around here were talking ugly things about us."

Lucy shivered in her lover's arms. What vileness there was in the world! Then Dave's lips met hers hungrily, and she forgot her still-racked body, the miasma of horror she had been through. She was content. . . .

THE END

NEXT MONTH—THESE MASTERS OF EERIE, GRIPPING FICTION:

Nat Schachner ● Hugh B. Cave
Arthur J. Burks
John Knox ● H. M. Appel
Wyatt Blassingame
Robert Newman

JUNE TERROR TALES   **OUT APRIL 25th!**

DOOM FLOWERS

By H. M. Appel
(Author of "The Dead Must Eat," etc.)

As Fred Swift and Natalie, castaways on an island of the dead, listened to the boy Peter prattle innocently of the ghastly orgies performed by his cult-mad relatives—madness crawled in their brains and horror froze their blood. . . .

SCUDDING like a wind-whipped bird before the summer squall which had dismasted her, the small sloop, *Sea Gull*, wrecked itself upon the black, snag-toothed rocks of a gloomy island shore. Thus Fred Swift and Natalie, his bride of yesterday, after heading for the Straits of Mackinac on a honeymoon cruise, came to grief eight hours out of Manistique.

Half-drowned, they gazed forlornly down, from the cliff they had climbed, to where the broken ribs of their boat were visible, caught on the foam-flecked fangs of rock. In Swift's heart the grim feeling of uneasiness grew, and his arm tightened round the waist of the tall, brown-haired girl whose soaked sailor suit clung tightly to her lissom curves. Looking back toward the grey shapes of farm buildings dimly seen in the waning light, he said:

"This is Tokeners Island. I had hoped we might miss it and strike Beaver. God knows what sort of welcome awaits us here."

Natalie's wondering glance lifted to his troubled, stern-jawed face. "What do you mean? Surely, any one will offer shelter to people just escaped from death —and as narrowly as we've escaped it!"

"We'll soon find out," was his answer. Helping her over the rubble of rock toward the smoother slope of a pasture field, he added grimly: "Don't be startled by anything that happens. There are ugly tales afloat about this lonely speck of land. It lies well off the steamer lanes. Fishermen, venturing too near, have been warned away with rifleshots. One or two men, thought to have been driven ashore here, never reappeared.

"The place was purchased a few years ago by a queer sect who settled their several families upon it and have not been seen on the mainland since. They are members of an obscure religious cult called 'Tokeners.' But don't worry—" Swift managed a smile, flexed a powerful fist in mock threat. "I'll make them put us up for the night and give us a rowboat to get away in when the storm dies. See, the wind is falling now——"

Cattle were lowing dismally in the barnyard of the farm they presently ap-proached. Raising its bleak bulk a full three stories, the unpainted house seemed vacant, its uncurtained windows staring like dead eyes. But meager crops were growing in fields stretching away toward a dark grove of pines a half-mile distant.

They passed through the barnyard gate, started across the sodden ground. Abruptly, Natalie halted.

"Look, Fred!" Those cows—and horses —they have black crepe tied round their necks. Why, even the chickens!"

WIDE-EYED, Swift regarded the animals and fowls, with their funereal marks of mourning. "Some one must have died," he said.

"Maybe they're all dead," Natalie faltered. "Oh, I'm so frightened. I have a feeing that something awful has happened——"

"Nonsense!" he affirmed stoutly. "It's just a part of their odd religion. If they were all dead, who would have hung crepe over everything? See—like over there, on the barn door and the outbuildings."

They found black crepe on the house door, too. Nor did anyone answer their repeated knocks.

Entering, they found the lower rooms deserted. Passing out to a verandah beyond, they scanned the fields and farm buildings, searching for signs of human life.

"That shed over there!" exclaimed Natalie. "The chimney is smoking. There must be some one——"

Hurrying back toward a small building near the barn they heard a boy whistling cheerily. Through an open door then they saw him: a red-haired youngster, barefooted and clad in faded blue overalls. He was stoking a wood fire in a stove beneath a large iron kettle, and he looked up, startled, when they spoke.

"Where'd you come from? Wrecked your boat, I betcha! Now, won't there be some excitement? His bright eyes sparkled.

"What's your name?" Swift asked. "Where is everybody?"

"I'm Peter. The folks are back in the woods at the Soul Temple, taking care of Mother Chloe. Her soul withered, so she died. They've all gone now to get ready for the planting. I'm glad I ain't got no soul yet," he chattered. "Johnnie'll get hers—then he can die any time. I'll be the only one left that can't die without going to hell—except Warden Ludwig, of course. He'll never have a soul because he ain't got no relations to get one from."

Natalie looked at Fred, the color draining from her cheeks. "Let's go!" she whispered tensely. *"Anywhere—"*

He silenced her with a gesture, turned to the lad, who had picked up a long iron ladle and was stirring the brew from which rich, meaty odors emanated.

"Making soup?"

"Naw." The boy laughed. "Rendering tallow for the sprouting candles. Have to have them or Johnnie's soul from Mother Chloe won't grow. Then he'd die——"

As he stirred the steaming mess, examining ladlesful with boyish importance, the big perforated dipper brought to light a number of small, white bones. These he dumped into a bucket on the floor. Swift's eyes narrowed as he studied them. Suddenly Natalie uttered a quavering shriek of horror. The next dipperful had disclosed a baby's skull!

"Good God!" blurted Swift. He caught his swaying wife, who moaned, fingers pressed to her bloodless lips. "Boy! That —that thing—" He nodded toward it, mouth distorted. "Do you know what you're cooking?"

"Why, sure! It's Myra's. It died in spite of everything Father Abel could do, and it didn't have a soul yet, so it goes into the sprouting candles. That's what

happens to any of us that dies without a soul. We must give our cast-off bodies to help the others grow good strong souls."

"Oh," sobbed Natalie, "take me away from this hideous place. . . ."

SWIFT stood fascinated by the innocent demeanor of the boy at his gruesome task, wondering what madness, what horrible fanaticism, had taught him such nonchalance. The lad, sensing their revulsion, said cannily:

"Seems funny to you, I betcha. Father Abel says folks on the mainland don't understand about souls and heaven and hell. That's why he won't let none of us ever leave the island, why we don't have any boats at all. Of course, it's sorta too bad, what'll be happenin' to you——"

"What will happen?" Natalie's words rattled like shattered glass. "What will they do to us?"

"Oh, tain't so much what they'll do— because we all gotta die, some time. But I reckon you're afraid of going to hell. I'm not. Warden Ludwig says it ain't such a bad place. We got it all planned to have plenty of fun if I should die before somebody leaves me a soul."

"Do you mean," Swift demanded, "that they'll try to *kill us?*"

"Oh, they'll kill you! That is—unless you're related, then only one of you'll have to die. We need fat for temple candles, to keep the souls white."

Nauseated, supporting his cringing wife on his arm, Swift cried: "You mean, they'd murder us as a part of their damnable religion?"

"Better not let Father Abel hear you talk so!" The boy frowned warningly. "It's all according to the Black Book. Strangers can't live here without souls— nobody can, except the Soul Warden, old Ludwig. And we gotta have temple candles, don't we? To keep the other souls from dying. Warden Ludwig thinks that's why Mother Chloe's soul withered—because we run short of candles. We're burning only eight now—the last of them made out of two men who got washed ashore. And that ain't enough—there'd ought to be two for each soul."

"Were those men——" Natalie's question was a mere gasping whisper on her dry and trembling lips. "Were they washed ashore *alive?*"

"Oh, sure. But Father Abel fixed 'em, over there in the barn. Now you two, you're married, ain't you? You sorta act like it. Well, one of you will be all right. I heard Father Abel say that if ever two related ones came together, one could die to give the other a soul. It'll be you, I reckon——" He fixed his round, bright eyes on Swift. "Because then she could live and marry the Warden. He's been wanting a woman——"

Fred Swift felt his face bleach white with anger.

"Let any one dare touch her!" he raged. "How many people are there on this island?"

PETER closed the drafts of the stove, commenting: "I guess it's about cooked now. How many? Well, let's count 'em up. I never stopped to figure. There's Father Abel, the patriarch, and his wife, Mother Chloe—only now she's dead. Simon—he's my father and Abel is his'n—and Sarah, my ma. Johnnie is thirteen and I'm twelve, so he gets the first soul. Then there's Simon, father's cousin, and his wife, Myra. Ella belongs to them, and their last baby is in there——" He pointed to the bubbling pot. "Because it died without a soul, like I told you. That makes ten, don't it, counting the Warden? Or is it nine? Anyway, that's all of us, till somebody comes or they have some babies that don't get sick and die."

"When," grated Swift, "will your people return?" Outside, dusk was falling,

shadows thickening among the buildings. "Soon, I suppose?"

"Any minute now," the boy said cheerfully. "Then there'll be plenty of excitement. Father Abel wants to press out this tallow to make candles for tonight, when the sprouting time starts. Won't he be glad we're going to have more temple candles, too!"

"For God's sake," begged Natalie, hysterically. "Let us leave before it is too late."

"Wait." Swift held her tightly, spoke to the boy. "Doesn't a boat ever stop here? You must get supplies from somewhere—the things you can't make or grow."

"Sure—the boat comes twice a year. It's due tomorrow afternoon. But that'll be too late to do you any good," he sympathized, "because Father Abel will fix one of you tonight. But then, dying ain't so bad—not that way. One crack on the head and you'll never know it was an axe that hit you."

"Listen!" Natalie clutched her husband's arm in quivering terror. "What is it?"

Solemnly, welling out of the gathering gloom, they heard a sound of chanting. Staring through the doorway, Swift saw a procession of black-cowled figures approaching along a lane leading from the grove. Then, with a clash as of celestial cymbals, thunder clanged in the darkening sky and lightning painted the nightmarish scene with a ghastly glare. Following the wind's dying, storm clouds had piled deep above the island, and now a sudden torrent of rain obscured the macaber forms of the Tokeners.

Wheeling upon the boy, Swift exclaimed: "Sonny! You say I'm going to hell for want of a soul, and that maybe you'll go there, too. So let's be friends. Do me one favor—just for tonight. Don't tell them we're here! We were married only yesterday—" It seemed a queer business that he should be pleading with this serious-eyed youngster for reprieve on such grounds. "Can you understand that I want to be with her a little longer?"

"Sure. You love her, I betcha." Blushing, the lad nodded. "I like her, too. I won't tell—but don't you snitch on me neither, when they find you tomorrow. Father Abel would whip the devil out of me."

DRAGGING Natalie by the hand, Swift fled through the hissing rain, hid behind a corner of the barn until the chanting fanatics had passed.

"Buck up!" he encouraged. "We'll be safe enough in the dark, even though the boy tells. And tomorrow we'll find a way to leave, if we have to float off on a raft."

They saw a bulky figure coming from the house, a man whose bushy beard made his head seem grotesquely huge. He entered the shed and reappeared, carrying the steaming kettle, followed by the lad. Soon a light gleamed in kitchen windows. Swift said thankfully:

"The kid didn't give us away. Now, while they're making the soul candles, is our chance to escape unseen."

Natalie pleaded: "Let's go to the farthest end of the island. We can hide among the rocks——"

"You'll suffer," he said doubtfully. "This rain is cold. If we dared risk hiding in the barn——"

"No, no!" The terrified whisper gushed out of her constricted throat. "I don't mind the wet—I don't mind anything—except those ghouls who want our bodies."

"More than that," Swift muttered beneath his breath, "I mind the one who wants a woman——"

They reached the rugged shore. Occasional lightning flashes made them crouch close to earth, lest their presence be noted by watching eyes. Circling above the line of thundering breakers, they sought a cave or overhanging ledge. But they found the going dangerous in the dark. Their hope of shelter faded.

Swift said: "Our best chance is the grove. Among the trees it will be warmer, and we'll be more secure."

"Near the Soul Temple? Oh, no—" Natalie clung to him desperately. "Anywhere but there——"

"It will be best," he insisted. "Once we get beyond the temple we'll be safe, for they've no cause to wander farther."

The rain dwindled to a drizzle and the air was still. Overhead the sky was a black, close-hung canopy which seemed to shroud the very island in crepe to match the mourners' veils. Faint flickers of lightning broke the murky shadows beneath dripping trees, and Swift stumbled forward cautiously, leading Natalie through drenched underbrush and briars. After a period of painful progress, the girl sobbed:

"Why did we come here? I'm being scratched to ribbons, and my knee hurts where I bruised it on that last log."

He caught her up in his arms. "I'll carry you."

"Put me down. You can't! You'll fall and kill us both. Fred! What—" her teeth chattered with fright—"is that light?"

An illuminated square was visible through the trees. In Swift's embrace the girl was shivering with fear and chill. A night of such exposure might well end fatally. His jaw tightened and he started toward the building.

"Sometimes audacity is the better course. If they knew we were on the island, the last place they'd search would be the soul temple. It may be the best place to hide."

A vivid, nearby lightning flash left a photographic impression of the building upon the retina of his eye: a place that was windowless, squat, with ornate cornices and a roomy cupola on top. If they could gain access to its tower——

THE glazed door was closed. Swift peered through the glass. Within the low-ceilinged room, eight tall candles flared, throwing an eerie yellow light over two long tables which ranged near the side-walls. Beside each candle rose the pale green stalk of a curious flower. Some were blossoming, others not; each bloom a white or yellowish lily in the heart of which a crimson spot glowed red as blood. He saw that one plant was withered and black. Mother Chloe's?

On either side, above the tables, reared massive wooden crosses. At the farther end, upon a sable altar of rock, lay a thick black book fastened down with a silver chain. In the center of the floor, draped in somber crepe, stood a rude coffin on wooden horses. Beneath the shroud, Swift surmised, must lie the dead woman's body.

"There's a trapdoor in the ceiling," he said. "We've got to climb up there before they come. Get a grip on your nerves, dear, we'll soon be safely hidden."

Natalie swayed toward him, trembling. "You know best, but I'm afraid——"

They entered. Over the room hung a sickening odor, faintly putrid—the grisly smell of death. Swift's harassed glance searched shadowy corners for a ladder, found none. Then he saw two ends of scantling projecting from beneath the bier and knew that it had been used as a support for the coffin.

Impatiently, he swept the black shroud from the naked corpse of an elderly woman. Natalie turned her face aside, exclaiming:

"They've plugged her nose and ears and mouth with wax! You see! They haven't finished with their horrible rites——"

"The boy spoke of 'the planting'," Swift murmured. "He mentioned a 'sprouting time.' I don't quite understand——"

Hesitating, perplexed as to how he might remove the ladder without upsetting the coffin, he saw Natalie staring at the nearest table of flowers.

"A-a-h!" The cry was wrenched out of her throat. "Look where they're going!" She reeled as though about to faint.

Swift steadied her, then looked. And saw that each sickly plant stood rooted in the gaping mouth of a nude form sculptured in gleaming silver. Faithfully reproduced were the bodies of men and women, along with a child or two.

A ghastly thought moved his limbs hypnotically. With outstretched finger he touched the nearest silvered cheek, jerked his hand away. No metal there! Only dry, wasted flesh drawn tight over human bones. Actual corpses had been painted. The soul flowers fed upon dead blood and tissue!

Again he examined the body upon the bier, saw that each orifice had been tightly stopped with wax. He wondered why. And, seized in the sudden grip of fear, despairing of ever reaching the cupola above, he drew Natalie toward the only exit.

Abruptly, they froze in their tracks, as a rumbling voice chanted in the night outside.

"God save us!" moaned the girl. "We waited too long——"

"No way out," blurted Swift. "Natalie . . . under the table! We must hide——"

THE door swung open. Peering up carefully from their concealment, they saw a tall form enter. Gowned in black, cowled hood framing a vicious face, the man stamped across the floor carrying a bucket and brush. Candle-light gleamed on his yellow snags of teeth as he bent above the coffin, grinning. With swift strokes he began to silver the woman's corpse. As he painted he chanted—that he was Warden of Souls, the Companion of the Devil. Finished with his revolting task, he left off singing, began grumbling to himself:

"Time enough for a mass before they come, if I hurry. They'll be chanting——"

Snatching up a can of water, he drenched the roots of all soul flowers save one. Upon the last he looked with an expression of such utter malevolence that Natalie, watching, scarce repressed the moan of terror which rose to her distended lips.

Swiftly striding to one of the wooden crosses, the Soul Warden drew from a hidden niche behind it an oddly shaped blue bottle. Out of it he poured liquid upon the flower toward which his animosity was directed. Replacing the vial, he exerted his enormous strength to invert the cross. When he had succeeded, he prostrated himself before it, began droning the Mass of Saint Secaire. Tearing part of his garments aside, making a revolting exhibition of his body, the Soul Warden went through a sensual ritual that expressed the most degraded depths of carnal lust.

His mumbled words were a meaningless gibberish until Swift realized that he was reciting backwards some hellish propitiation of the Evil One. Rising, making the sign of the cross upon the earthen floor with his left foot outthrust behind him, the Warden laughed aloud, stood the cross in its proper position, and raucously exclaimed:

"By Saint Secaire I promise soon to send plenty of souls to deepest hell! Strike the old one dead this night, Satan, and all the others shall die, too!"

With cowled head cocked to one side, as though listening to secret voices in the night, he began to shudder and groan, to clap his great hands and stamp with booted feet. Faintly, above the noise of the rain, Swift heard the Tokeners chanting eerily.

The soul Warden heard it, too. He steadied himself, visibly seeking control of the growing frenzy which possessed him. Leaping toward a table, he snuffed one of the tapers, began to crunch it hungrily between his broken teeth.

Natalie could not restrain an instinctive cry of horror.

"He's *eating* them! Eating the fat of those murdered men——"

Swift's jolting oath evidenced his utter desperation. Crawling from beneath the table he sprang erect, faced the menacing shape which towered head and shoulders above him. The Soul Warden, with a howl of amazement, snatched up a length of metal pipe which had lain between the silvered corpses, whirled it about his head, aimed a killing stroke that Swift barely evaded.

"Run, Natalie! Anywhere outside——" Swift yelled to her even as he ducked.

But the girl stood paralyzed by fear. Swift leaped inside the flailing arms, drove blow after blow to the slavering mouth. The Soul Warden's huge hand clutched his throat, forced him to his knees with astonishing ease.

Natalie, roused by her husband's plight, moved galvanically. Springing upon the Warden's back she scratched at his eyes and cheeks, screaming like a Fury. The man shook himself like a great dog, flinging her aside. Then, with deliberate intent to kill, he held Swift at arm's length, raised the pipe, brought it down with smashing force.

Fred Swift moved his head instinctively. That movement saved his life. He caught a glancing blow instead of one that would have crushed his skull. Yet even that blow was enough to bring blank darkness flooding over his senses. He never heard Natalie's hopeless shriek, nor the Soul Warden's victorious laughter.

WHEN Swift's eyes opened, the lights seemed blurred. Dim figures standing about the room resembled black, unstable shades. A deep voice was preaching sonorously. Then his vision cleared, and he strove to move.

He found himself bound to a cross upon the wall. Opposite, similarly fastened, hung Natalie's limp body, her head drooping upon her chest. He wondered if she were dead, before the anguished rise and fall of her bosom reassured him.

Standing near, regarding her with lust-reddened eyes, was the gaunt figure of the Soul Warden. Kneeling in a semicircle before the altar were two young men and their wives. Beside the dead woman's bier stood one who must, Swift knew, be Father Abel, the patriarch. With grief-striken face upraised, grey beard floating like a cloud, his enormous hands outstretched in supplication, the man spoke on.

"You who have caused her soul to wither and die—receive her into the realms of bliss. And let Your beneficence aid the sprouting of that new soul which shall spring from her sealed lips as· a token of salvation for a poor child who now lives without the promise of eternal glory."

In more normal tones, Father Abel said: "Now, children—the Ritual of the Planting."

The kneeling couples rose, gathered about the bier. From an ancient teakwood case the patriarch drew a small, dry, bulbous root. While he intoned strange prayers, one of the women filled her cupped hands with moist earth from a bucket. The other deftly removed a plug of wax from the corpse's distended jaws.

"Quickly!" urged Father Abel, "lest the life force escape!"

Black dirt dropped into the yawning cavity. He planted the bulb, tamped the mold around it. Each of the two younger men flicked water upon the bit of soil with their fingers, then all began to chant a solemn dirge.

And then Fred Swift, struggling to free his bound wrists, half-strangled by the loop of rope around his neck, cursed horribly and redoubled his efforts. Across the room, behind the backs of the intent mourners, he could see the Soul Warden —pawing the sweet curves of Natalie's body, evil hands groping over her thighs and breasts!

The sublimated terror in her brown eyes, the piteous appeal in the look she flung him, tore at his heart, bred in his mind such a depth of despair as almost fogged his senses.

Pulling upon his right arm until the flesh of his wrist was rubbed loose from the bones and his joints cracked sickeningly, Swift worked one hand from beneath the ropes. It hung at his side, a numb and bleeding thing. Wondering if the tortured fingers would find strength to deal with other knots, he moved his arm back along a limb of the cross when the chanting ceased. He feared the Tokeners might discover the progress he had made.

Father Abel, in the manner of one closing a ceremony, spoke ringingly:

"Blessings on the new soul which shall be Johnnie's! Now, light the sprouting candle."

ONE of the younger men stepped forward with a slim, white taper newly moulded from the kettle which Peter had tended. He thrust it into a silver holder, stood it upon the shrunken breast of the corpse. When he touched flame to the wick, the mourners wailed:

"A soul for little Johnnie! We pray that it may not wither soon."

"But all must wither in the end," the patriarch responded. "And then must the body surely die. When my soul flower fades, I shall join Mother Chloe——"

He broke off, eyes bulging, stared at one of the corpse-fed plants.

"Ah, woe! woe! It has withered even now——" Clutching at his throat beneath the billowing beard, the old man staggered in his tracks, uttered a choking cry.

Startled mourners cast quick glances toward the flower which was his life token. The plant had blackened.

Father Abel swayed and fell. His limbs jerked spasmodically, then he lay inert. One of the others bent an ear to the old man's heart, shook his head, rose up commanding:

"Soul Warden! Bring wax quickly! We must save his life force to grow a soul for Peter!"

The Warden left off his beastly stroking of Natalie's cringing limbs and hurried into the night, grumbling.

"There's no more than enough left in the hollow oak," Swift heard him mutter.

From the doorway a shrill, childish voice called: "I don't want no soul! Then I'll die, too." Three small, haunted faces peered in at the fantastic scene.

Fred Swift, brain racing with a flashing chain of ideas, regarded the withered plant through narrowed eyes. His freed hand crept behind the cross at his back, and his groping fingers found a hidden niche. From it he drew forth a squat blue bottle. Removing the rubber cork with his teeth he smelled the pungent fumes of some acid.

Replacing it, he concealed the bottle behind the cross-arm, cried:

"You, there! Which one is the son of that *murdered man?* Do you want to know why the flower withered—why your father died?"

"What do you mean? What can a soulless unbeliever know of such things?" a young man cried.

Swift faced him intently. "You are Simon? I know that your father was murdered! Believing he would die when his life token withered, he fell dead when he saw it blackened there. The one who caused it, murdered him as surely as though he had used a gun."

"Who did this thing? Speak!" Simon approached the cross.

"I'll tell you—but only if you let us go free. Release my wife—unfasten these ropes on me. Then you shall know the truth."

The young man turned to the others, muttering:

"He may have proof of what I suspect. To let them go would be no sin—if they leave the island." Uncertainly, he asked: "What do you say, cousin?"

The other nodded. "We must have proof—" His voice broke queerly. "Or soon we all shall die!"

"You agree, then?" Swift exulted. "If I show you what happened, you'll let us go?"

Hard upon their assent he produced the bottle, held it toward Father Abel's son.

"Acid! Your ugly Soul Warden poured it on the roots of that flower. While we were hiding beneath the table. *I saw him do it!*"

A ROAR of bestial rage sounded from the doorway. The Soul Warden cried: "So you've found me out! Well, it only means sending your souls to the Devil in a quicker way!"

Simon stood the bottle of acid upon his mother's bier and looked toward his cousin meaningly. The Warden lumbered forward, snatched up the length of pipe with which he had beaten Swift.

The women screamed, darted toward the door. With savage cries he beat them into quivering insensibility. The younger men, shouting fiercely, leaped at him from two sides, aiming awkward blows at his hulking body. Fred Swift, with his free hand, tore at the ropes which bound his throat to the cross. He was desperately intent on breaking loose before the battle ended disastrously.

The Soul Warden, yelling like a maniac, brained the cousin with a single stroke. Simon proved more agile and in the whirling fight dodged round and round the coffin until, unexpectedly, Warden Ludwig gave the bier a push. It smashed against Simon's knees. As he stumbled and fell across the corpse of his mother, the metal club swung once more, caught him sickeningly against the skull, crushed it like an egg-shell.

Stretching his arms aloft with a piercing cry of triumph, the Warden grinned at Fred Swift, picked up the unbroken bottle from the floor, poured acid upon the roots of every soul flower.

"I'll wither them all!" he screamed. "I'll send them all to hell!"

Striding to Swift's side, he poured the remaining liquid upon the prisoner's bare neck. Swift groaned in agony as the acid burned like fire, raised a stench of cooking flesh.

"You'll get worse than that," the Soul Warden gloated. "I'll carve your body to bits to make candles for my black masses. But you can wait till I've had some fun with *her*." He leered at Natalie.

"Touch her, and I'll kill you!"

But even as Swift mouthed the words, he realized how futile was his threat. Twisting and squirming in his bonds, he pleaded: "Do anything you wish to me, but let her go. Haven't you done enough tonight to satisfy your master, Satan?"

"Ho!" bellowed the Soul Warden. "That one is never satisfied. Besides, I've myself to please. For a long time now I've schemed to possess this fine island, live here with my pick of their women. But that one—" Again his eyes sought the terror-striken girl. "She's younger

and prettier. So I killed the other two——"

Going over to Natalie, he ripped the clothing from her slender body, cast the shredded garments aside, pinched and squeezed her tender flesh.

"Oh, God! Let me die," she moaned. "Fred! Help me! This is worse than death——"

Swift tugged and tore at his neck rope with the might of a man gone mad. But he could not reach the knot. His bloodshot eyes turned away from the anguish of Natalie's face.

He saw a movement near the open door, glimpsed a small form crawling along the floor.

"Peter!" he gasped. "A knife—cut me loose——"

As the Soul Warden turned, the boy dodged out of sight behind the table. To allay the man's suspicion, Swift stormed: "If I had a knife, I'd cut your throat——"

"Yah! Yell your head off. I'll fix you when I get through with her."

TO Natalie, as he untied one of her arms, the Warden scoffed: "You won't last long. But it'll be fun while you do. And when you're dead, I'll plant a soul flower in your mouth and burn candles made of your husband's fat, to whiten the blossom. You'd ought to like that."

Peter, reaching out from his hiding place, seized the bloody length of pipe.

"He killed all my people. I'm gonna jump up and bust him a good one," he whispered.

"No, no!" gasped Swift. "He'd not even feel it. Take one of the candles— burn the ropes from my ankles——"

The lad jerked a taper from the lips of the nearest corpse, touched flame to the hemp as directed. Swift tore at his neck rope with frenzied violence, felt the strands part where acid had bitten deep into their fibers.

The Soul Warden, his sense of smell keenly attuned to the sickly, perfumed atmosphere of the temple, must have sniffed the odor of burning. He whirled with a growl in his throat.

Peter leaped up, waving the pipe. "I'll kill you, Ludwig!" he screamed shrilly. "I'll knock your head off——"

With a grunt of contempt the Soul Warden came over and slapped the rod aside. Clamping both hands upon the slender neck, slowly and cruelly he began to throttle the child.

Natalie, still bound by an arm and both feet, shrieked a prayer for mercy. Swift, with one wrist manacled to the cross, swung his free arm outward, hooked his fingers in the Warden's collar. Snatching the man off balance, he hugged him against his chest and swung up both legs to fasten a scissors-hold around the fellow's loins.

The Soul Warden dropped Peter, gouged at Swift's eyes, lunged backward. Swift's lashed arm stretched, his shoulder cracked till he thought it was dislocated. But despite the agonizing pain, he did not release his desperate hold.

Sobbing, Peter struggled to his feet, found the iron bludgeon and swung it with all his boyish strength. It caught the Soul Warden behind the ear with sufficient force to knock him sprawling. Swift fumbled with the knot which held his aching wrist. As it loosened, the killer rose and sprang upon him with a demoniacal scream of hatred.

In their rolling, threshing fight, the Soul Warden's uncanny strength told

quickly. Swift lay upon his back, the other astride his middle. With one hand clamped across his face, pinning his head to the floor, the Warden bared yellow fangs and grated:

"I'll tear out your throat!"

Swift's groping fingers touched the pipe which Peter had dropped. Seizing it with both hands he thrust upward suddenly, putting all of his waning strength into the blow. A jagged end struck the Soul Warden at the juncture of neck and chin, ripped through flesh, brought red blood spurting. The man reared back with a gurgling cry, toppled, and wallowed in his own gore. Swift jumped to his feet. With merciless blows he beat at that mad fiend's body beneath him—until it was little more than a bloody, dead mess.

Young Peter crawled from his refuge under the table, spurned the dead hulk with his toe. For a second he stood staring at the naked girl.

"I'll get her some of ma's clothes," he said dismally. "Then I've got to find where Ella and Johnnie are hiding. You two can leave tomorrow, but I don't know what we kids will do—with everybody dead and us all alone."

"I know what you'll do," Fred Swift exclaimed, as he released Natalie and held her close. "We'll look after you three as if you were our very own. Without your aid, laddie . . ."

He shuddered. Then, gathering his wife in his arms, calling to the children to follow, he strode out of that hideous temple toward the bleak house, where they could find shelter until a boat came to carry them away from this island of withered souls.

TERROR TALES—THE MAGAZINE OF THRILLING, EERIE FICTION!

PRIESTESS

By Paul Ernst

(Author of "Flesh Feeder," etc.)

A Novelette of Eerie Fear

THE wild sea pounded at the base of the cliff on the edge of which my house was set. Its grim chorus filled the air, and mingled with the wail of the wind that drove the tons of water.

The gale whistled and moaned through the bare, black branches of the trees on the cliff-top. The trees tossed their limbs against the drab gray of the sky with a rattling protest of strained wood. The shutters at my windows slatted, and the window-panes shook as if unseen hands clawed at them.

But I heard little of the storm. I lay in my bedroom on the landward side of the house and only dimly saw the black lace at the window-pane formed of the criss-crossing tree branches that writhed and tossed outside.

I was very ill. I knew that because I was seeing the face again. And I did not see the face unless I was near death.

It had not always been that way. Years ago, when I was a child, I used to see that same face often in ordinary dreams. Dreams? Nightmares, I mean.

It was always the same. The black night would seem to thicken and grow blacker around me. It would fill with murmuring voices—coming from God knew where

OF DEATH

It was hauntingly beautiful, that shimmering green face which promised him delights unutterable—and a doom which meant eternal soul-bondage to a creature more devilish than devine!

and saying God knows what. Then the thick, black air would grow silent, as if all the murmuring voices were stilled in waiting for something to happen. It would tingle as though charged with electricity; and as it tingled, I would feel an icy chill touch my spine.

After ages of time, while I lay in the unnatural darkness, a green speck would appear far over the rim of dark distance. It would grow brighter, like a lurid, green star, and it would begin to approach me slowly.

I could see it grow as I lay there in the night. I could see it advance toward me, smoothly, soundlessly, like something moving in suspension from an overhead rail. And I would wish with all my heart that I could cover my eyes with my hands and shut out the sight. For I knew what that sight would be. But I could never move my body; and if I shut my eyes, it did no good, because the green star seemed able to send its rays through my closed eyelids so that I was forced to observe it.

Ages of time, which yet fled like seconds during the approach of the green speck. Finally it would be as big as an orange, and then I could begin to make it out more clearly.

It was a face—a green face, shining in the luminous dark like a nightmare moon.

Swiftly, smoothly, soundlessly the face would come closer to me, ever closer. And as it neared my eyes unwillingly saw its ominous loveliness with growing clarity.

It was a gloriously beautiful face. The eyes were set wide apart under a low, wide sweep of forehead. The nose was straight and regal, with the eyebrows reaching from it over the eyes with the graceful curve of a bird's wings. The mouth was voluptuous, seductive, languorous.

Yes, it was rarely beautiful. Even as a child I knew that. But at the same time, it was somehow so menacing and so dreadful, that the sight of it chilled my blood. Hidden in its green, luminous beauty were suggestions of evil and cruelty that made my heart falter, though I could not actually trace those suggestions in any feature or expression.

Gloriously beautiful, hideously menacing and covetous was the green face. . . .

Closer it would move. Ever closer. And I would lay in a sweat of terror

watching its approach, unable to move or cover my eyes. Finally it would stop, within a yard of my face, with its emerald eyes staring unblinkingly into my eyes, and its long, green hair streaming out behind it as though in a wind, in graceful undulations like the green grasses of the sea on the breast of the waves.

That was all. The face would appear in the blackness, come closer and closer to me, and then hang suspended within a yard of me while the green eyes watched, stared, and the full, green lips parted a little in avid expectation of . . .

What? I couldn't guess.

That was all. But it is impossible to put into words the icy horror that lovely, terrible face inspired in me. I would lay there in a cold sweat, heart hammering in my ears, a taste of blood in my mouth, till at last I could stand it no longer and I would scream in the night till someone came to comfort me.

I grew very familiar with that face. All through childhood I had the recurring nightmare, and no one could ever explain it. I had seen no face like that in any child's books. Needless to say, I had never seen anything like it in life!

But from somewhere, somehow, that face came to me again and again, slowly growing as it neared me in the nightmare dark, till I screamed in horror and it fled away.

With adolescence, the face left me for a time. I had got so I feared to sleep lest the green face appear. But it came less and less often till at length I saw it no more and its vision remained only in memory.

THEN on the battlefield, after I had not seen it for ten long years—I saw it again!

We were going over the top, walking with that slow, steady, awful walk behind the barrage of our guns. The night was hideous with star-shells and exploding shrapnel. And I saw a faint, green flare in the blackness before me.

I knew at once what it was. Every quivering fiber of me whispered what it was. *The face!*

It swam soundlessly, smoothly toward me as I walked like an automaton. It approached within a yard, and then moved as I moved so that ever the same distance was between me and it.

A hell of sound and bursting flares around us. But I was no longer conscious of them, nor was I conscious of the scarred ground my feet stumbled over. All I could see was the face, suddenly appearing again from the nightmares of childhood.

The lips moved, and a message impinged on my brain.

"Straight ahead. Keep straight ahead. Follow me."

My body strove to obey the command, as muscles in a hypnotic trance move only to the will of the hypnotist. But my mind chilled with primal, instinctive fear and the sense that death was leaning very close.

I did not go straight ahead. I closed to the left as much as I dared.

And eight men at my right suddenly disappeared while I reeled and fell into the crater left by a hidden mine.

After that, I saw the green face again. It was not now, as it had been in my childhood, at frequent intervals. It was only rarely that the face appeared. But the very rarity of the appearances soon caused me more torture than the frequency of them in childhood.

For I soon realized that now I saw the green face only when I was at the point of death! In illness or accident, let death lean close—and the face appeared in thickening blackness and came smoothly, soundlessly toward me with emerald eyes glowing and seductive, green lips half-parted.

The last time I had seen the face had been when I was driving swiftly along a narrow road toward a bridge approach. It had appeared as always like a green star far off. But this time it had fairly rushed at me, hair streaming out behind, eyes eager, mouth straining a little in hellish expectancy.

I slammed on the brakes, shivering and sweating—and stopped my car within inches of a hundred foot drop where the old bridge had fallen a few moments before.

That time the face had been convulsed with fury and—yes, there was no mistaking it—disappointment. The emerald eyes had flashed balefully. The lips had drawn back from sharp, small teeth. The face had faded back into the distance with soundless wails of baffled rage that rasped on my inner ears.

Appearing always when I was at the point of death, always with lips half parted in a frenzy of eagerness! Fading back into what ever black land from which it had come, shrieking with soundless disappointment when I did not die!

My green goddess of death, I called the face from that time on, and a great deal of my thoughts were claimed by it after that narrow escape.

There is much about which man does not know the answer. There is much that he will never know. And it seemed to me the green face fitted into the category of the unknowable but horribly real

Were there black worlds on the rim of the world we know, peopled by things constantly with us but, as a rule, unconscious of us as we were unconscious of them? Was the forever unseen owner of the green face a denizen of one of these regions? Had a connection been formed between us, somehow, when I was a child, that had allowed my green goddess of death to appear partially to my mortal gaze?

The more I thought about it, the more I was sure that something like that was the case. For that face, though invisible to others, was very real to me. I knew every line of its terrible beauty. I could not—*I could not*—have imagined it! Its visitations were actual.

But, assuming for the moment that that wild theory was true, what was to be the end? I thought I could guess.

The green goddess had marked me for her own, but I must die to be within her reach. From her unknowable world over the rim of our comprehension, she watched me, and when I was near death, she came to me—and beckoned me on as the sirens used to beckon men to destruction!

For I come now to a manifestation of the green face's appearance that makes me shiver even as I tell it. Each time it appeared after the night on the battlefield, *it tried to lure me into following it!*

It appeared as it always had, a green speck in the thick blackness that grew into the horribly familiar face as it neared me. But after that night in France, when it receded from me again, it beckoned with eyes and lips and demoniac will for me to rise and follow it! I must fight with myself as with another person to keep from complying with the unspoken command. And I must fight down another desire: The terrific, soul-shaking desire to kiss those voluptuous green lips!

The green face was waiting tirelessly for me to die. It wanted me to die; it lurked ever watching for my death. And it wanted to hasten that death by a kiss of its lips. For I knew, without knowing how I knew, that a kiss from those green lips would be a kiss of death for me.

And yet, even knowing that, I found it always more difficult to keep from follow-ing the face, and pressing my mouth to its mouth, when it appeared. . . .

Do these thoughts of mine seem tenuous and illogical? They wouldn't if you had even seen the green face!

The face belonged to a very real being, existing in a very real place, even though being and place were beyond our common-sense understanding. I *knew* that. My green goddess of death! Waiting just over the horizon of comprehension for me to die and be delivered over to her! Always near when death was near—avid to hasten death with a kiss of her sinister, lovely lips!

And now I was seeing the face again as I lay in the bedroom on the landward side of my house and saw with dim eyes how the tree branches outside my window made moving, black lace against the pane. . . .

CHAPTER TWO

Into the Dark

THERE it was! There! A glowing green speck in the distance, slowly advancing toward me!

Gradually it came nearer, soundlessly, steadily, like a mask hanging on an unseen cord which some one above was moving forward. Nothing under it, no body or support of any kind—just the green face glowing in the darkness and slowly growing in size as it neared me!

I cowered in the bed, trying to raise my hands to shut out the sight of it, and being, as always, unable to. I hated the face—and loved it. I feared it—and yearned for it!

The face of my green goddess . . . beautiful beyond words . . . terrible beyond description. . . .

It was very close now, not ten feet away. In all its beauty and its terror, it glowed in the dimness. Eyes like flashing emeralds. Lips as seductive as the lips of Cleopatra—and cruel as an executioner's sword.

Now the face was so near that by stretching out my hand I could have touched it.

I panted in a paralysis of fear and longing. The emerald eyes stared deeply into mine. The green lips moved with a message of strange, unutterable things. The face was soundlessly calling to me again, beckoning me with lips and eyes to follow it back to the caves of blackness from which it had come.

Its soft, green glare dazzled my eyes. The full, green lips were within inches of my own, half parted, avid. . . .

I swayed toward them—moved convulsively back, and screamed aloud in the blackness.

The face slowly receded into the distance. But it did not disappear entirely. It remained far off, a green speck, watching me and bidding its time.

A hand clutched mine. I breathed deeply and clung to it. As I clung, the phosphorescent, green speck faded still farther away and the dimness lightened a little around me. I looked up.

I saw a different face now. This was a normal face, lovely but with no menace or evil in it. The face of Elaine Boland, the girl I was to marry—if I lived.

Her dark, brown eyes were filled with compassion and fears for me. Her forehead was wrinkled a little under its smooth sweep of chestnut hair. Her cheeks were white and drawn. But she smiled a little as I looked at her.

"Feeling better?" she murmured, pressing my hand again.

I nodded, taking pleasure even in my extremity in the deep beauty of her eyes and the silky sheen of her hair. This was the girl I loved. The green goddess? Even as she was not human, so the emotions of overwhelming desire—and of loathing and repulsion—which she inspired, were not human emotions. Elaine was life for me; the green goddess was death.

I looked past her and saw two figures near the window. One was a man, pompous looking, with a van Dyke beard, dressed in a wrinkled, brown suit. The doctor, I realized dimly. Elaine had called him when she arrived to find me raving light-headedly with an infected throat which I had done nothing about until too late.

The other figure was that of a quiet-faced, middle-aged woman in nurse's uniform. As far as I knew I had not seen her before, though I knew she must have been here for some time.

The nurse leaned toward the window, looked out and down the road. The doctor snapped the face of his old-fashioned watch open and shut impatiently, looking every few seconds at the time.

"It ought to have come before now," I heard him mutter. "I don't know what's keeping it. I want this man in the hospital as soon as I can get him there."

The nurse stood still closer to the window. "There's something moving, off by the intersection. That might be the ambulance. . . ."

The two of them faded from view as my eyes dulled again. I stared at the face of Elaine. I tried to see only her face—but the other began growing from a green speck into a face again, and kept floating between Elaine's countenance and my own, with eyes and lips beckoning me to follow it. . . .

WHERE? I could not imagine. But I knew it would be some place of shadowy horror. I shuddered as the green lips moved, and I actually thought to hear the words: "Follow me! Follow! I am your destiny, and your goal!"

Elaine pressed close to me. I felt her lips on my forehead.

"What is it?" she whispered. And for a moment her face and hers alone showed clear. "What is the matter? Your eyes—they seem to see frightful things."

My lips moved stiffly. "Face. The green face. Death. . . .!"

The words, forced with difficulty through my swollen throat, were broken croakings in the room.

The nurse turned. "He's delirious again."

The doctor pressed to the window pane. "That's the ambulance, all right," he said. "Stay here please, Miss Boland. The nurse and I will go to the door and see that the ambulance is ready for him."

Dimly I heard them leave the room. I was alone with Elaine.

"Face!" I whispered hoarsely again. "Keep the green face from me." My fingers clenched frantically over hers. The face was growing clear and distinct again.

"What is it?" cried Elaine softly, her eyes anguished. "Oh, what is it?"

I wanted to tell her all about the green goddess of death who lurked on the rim of our world waiting for me to die, willing me to leave life and come to her. I wanted to tell her of the green lips, and of my fascinated desire to press my lips to them in a kiss I knew spelled death.

But I could say nothing. I could only lie panting there, fingers clenched around Elaine's hand as once, when the green face showed clear, I had been wont to clutch my mother's hand when she came in answer to my nightmare screams.

Elaine! Perhaps she could save me. Perhaps she could guard me from the ominously eager, green face—and from the struggles of desire within myself. For more than ever was I impelled to follow the face, and I sensed that *this* time, unless some life-saving accident intervened, I would do so!

My senses were swirling again. Around me the air was thickening and growing blacker. And in it the green face began to grow more brightly, more seductively than it ever had before, like a green star shining from black caverns of evil.

"Elaine," I tried to call. "Elaine!"

Only she could protect me from the obscenely beautiful green goddess whose face alone was visible to me. Only she could fight off the influence of this other-worldly creature that lurked on the rim of the world—waiting, like a lovely ghoul, for me to die.

Despair filled me. I could not cry out to Elaine. And I felt the touch of her hand growing weaker. A sense of irrevocable doom filled me. For I felt that, this time, my goddess of death would win; this time, I would not be able to overcome her lure for me, but would follow her even as she silently commanded.

As though sensing my thoughts and seeing my weakness, the green face rushed more swiftly toward me. And now the lips were smiling and the eyes were green gems of triumph.

It rushed till it was within a foot of my face and its green glare dazzled me. And I stared at it in appalled fascination while chaos tore at my mind.

Now the green face was so lovely that it drew at my soul. Now it was so horrible that my heart froze. Yet I was forced to look at it, through eyes closed or open, as men were forced to gaze at Medusa's head though every instinct of life urged otherwise.

Like a tangible thing I felt the desire to crush the green parted lips to mine—and die.

"Elaine!" Once more I tried to cry out, but could not. And after that I tried no longer; for now I knew myself no more able to fight against my deathly desire. I *must* take death with a kiss of those lips. I *must* follow the green face to whatever region of dread and darkness it yearned to lead me.

IN A trance, knowing that I must not do this thing but unable to stop myself, I gathered my muscles to rise. The green face receded slowly from me, then halted, plainly waiting for me to follow. I sat up.

Hands thrust wildly against my chest. A pleading voice rang in my ears. Dimly I saw Elaine's face close to mine. But through it and drowning it in its green glare the face of my green goddess of death shone clear, with its smiling lips promising unutterable things.

I struck aside the pleading, clutching hands and stood up. My illness seemed to fall from me like a mantle. I was strong and well—more vibrantly so than I had even been before.

I took a step forward.

Sobbing, crying out, Elaine clasped her arms around my body in her effort to hold me back. And that perplexed me a little, for I knew she could not have seen the green face—no one could but me—and I could not imagine how she could have guessed that she was about to lose me forever.

But my perplexity was quite apart from my desire, now steady with the calmness of fatality, to follow that green face and claim at last the promise from the full, green lips. I jerked Elaine's arms from me and held them away. My eyes were averted from her face. I could see only the green face of the goddess luring me to follow.

I walked toward it. . . .

Elaine stumbled after me, clutching at my shoulders, crying out to me to stop. The evilly beautiful, green face faded faster into black vistas before me. I tried to quicken my pace to keep up with it, and felt my shoulders gripped more despairingly by Elaine.

I turned and struck her in the face.

I saw blood trickle from her lips, saw the lips themselves puff out. I heard a piteous, low cry come from them. But though the cry cut me to the heart, it could not stop me. I had to follow the deathly, green face. Elaine fell back a step and I hurried forward.

It was dark, but the darkness seemed ominously alive. It seemed to hold within it some black luminosity that allowed me to see even with closed eyes. And the things I saw were things to stagger the mind, though they could not stop my progress through the blackness after the receding green face.

CHAPTER THREE

The Monster

SO DARK. . . . But I could see as though dim moonlight illuminated my steps—and I wished that I could not see at all!

Very soon my feet left the figured carpet of my room. Or, rather, the carpet seemed to fade slowly and its place to be taken by a smooth, rocky surface loosely strewn with fragments of shale.

Under my tread, the lose shale twisted and turned so that I was constantly on the verge of falling yet never fell. And as the fragments turned, they scratched against their rock bed with small shrill sounds like the squeaks of dying, small animals.

Among the shale fragments tiny things crawled and scuttled. They seemed to fear me, yet be impelled to attack me. Their myriad legs stung my bare flesh as they crawled over my feet, and their teeth left marks though they did not pierce the skin. I stamped at them and they squashed pulpily under my feet, turning to blobs of heavy moisture under my tread.

So dark. . . . But I could faintly see the things beginning to appear as I stumbled in blind haste after the green face. Equally faintly I could hear Elaine's voice, far behind me, as she reeled after me in the fainting darkness. A far off, feeble voice, stopping me not at all in my determination this time to follow the face to wherever it willed. Much more clearly I could hear the unspoken message from the green lips: "Follow me! I am your destiny...!"

I followed, even faster, stumbling in my trancelike haste. After me came Elaine. Constantly I heard her wild calls to me from the blackness behind. But I paid no heed.

The face! I must hasten and catch up. Something whispered to me that at last I would see the body beneath the face, and at last drain the ultimate, perilous sweetness from the green lips.

So desperately were my eyes glued to the green face ever receding before me like a will-o'-the-wisp that I saw little of the wild land into which I was hastening. But I saw enough to blanch my cheeks and make the long, chill shudders of stark fear crawl up my spine.

It was a gray and ghostly place. Tufts of sparse grey stuff like coarse grass grew here and there, seemingly sprouting from the solid rock. Among this grass crawled figures that were like figments of a disordered mind, now visible, now fading from my gaze when I tried to see them more clearly, as faint stars fade when eyes are turned directly on them and reappear when the gaze is directed away and only the corners of the eyes catch their dim light.

Now as I staggered blindly through the luminous dark, I sensed Things pacing me silently on either side. I could never quite see the Things. I could only perceive their outlines feebly now and then against the distant, black horizon, miles off, where it met the luminous, black sky.

They moved with sluggish ease beside me, slowing as I slowed, moving more swiftly as I increased my pace, as dolphins trail a ship at sea. They had no definite shape and no definite features. They were simply amorphous Things that flowed over the loose shale like primeval blobs of protosplasm, without eyes or senses of any kind, yet knowing I was an alien there and knowing what it was I followed. And knife-thrusts of fear stabbed my brain in the presence of the Things, because I sensed that if ever they attacked me I would be overwhelmed in living, suffocating ooze.

Still I stumbled forward, ever forward. And no cry of fear came from my numb lips; only the pleading call: "Wait! Wait!" to the green face. For the dread that surpassed all other fears in my brain was that the face would mockingly fade from my view and leave me to stagger alone and lost in that black, ghastly place.

I felt the rocky, shale-strewn floor grow softer to my feet and I looked down. The shale fragments were rapidly disappearing as I fled, and the rock surface was beginning to be covered thinly with muck. The ooze was deathly cold to my bare flesh. It was clammy, chill—yet seemed somehow as alive as the Things that paced beside me with their wavering outlines now unseen and now mistily clear against the immensely distant horizon ....

DEEPER and deeper I sank into the muck as I went forward after the smoothly receding face. Finally I was slogging through it knee-deep. And in its depths I could feel crawling life that coiled weakly around my legs and squirmed as it was trodden under my bare feet.

But still the only cry that burst from my lips as I lunged forward through the clinging slime was: "Wait! Wait!"

And like an echo from Elaine, struggling in the nightmare blackness far behind, came the same wild cry, "Wait! Oh, God, wait!"

The squirming, icy ooze grew shallower, became ankle deep and then was but a thin carpet under my cringing feet. And then, suddenly, without warning, I found myself at the edge of a steep cliff.

I stared down and down into the deepening shades of blackness below, and felt the mad desire to hurl myself into those shades. But as I shuddered on the brink, with whimpering cries tearing from my lips as I watched the green speck recede in the blackness below, my bare feet felt the first of a series of niches cut in the rock and leading down, and I plunged down them.

The rock of the cliff was as grey as rotten jade; rock that must have been ancient when the world was young. The niches crumbled under my feet so that with each step, it seemed that I must slip and flash down to death in the darkness below. But I never quite slipped though I hurried downward with insane recklessness.

Far below, in the distance, the beautiful, terrible face faded constantly back into deepening darkness; while from far behind sounded the wild, faint voice of Elaine: "Wait! Oh, God, wait for me!"

The steps in the face of the rotten jade cliff took odd turns. They crisscrossed at queer angles that left me breathless as I followed the turns. They seemed to have uncanny capacity to reduce distance and compress space. For though the long climb down seemed to stretch for miles before me, I found myself nearing the bottom in an unbelievably short time, with the green face nearer now, and with Elaine's voice almost lost behind.

But at the bottom of the niches I found my way barred.

A monstrous thing stood there, squarely in the path. A thing vaguely like a

human being, yet hideously unlike any mortal shape. For it was reptilian in semblance, with lizard claws for hands, and with dully gleaming scales covering arms and legs and torso. But a wholly human head was set on the thick, scaled neck; and the lips of this head muttered: "He is mad. I must protect him from himself, for he is mad."

I crept warily toward the fearsome lizard thing, and it crouched in the path with its talon hands spread wide to stop me. I charged it, shouting, but its cold, scaly hands caught me and threw me back.

Twice more I tried, and twice more I was thrown back, so I saw that I would have to be clever and kill this thing.

And now, in its guile, the monster came slowly toward me and its head took on the semblance of one I had seen before. The face, with its cold, slit eyes, became the face of the doctor with its van Dyke beard. But I recognized the deception and was only enraged by it, for I knew I had left the doctor far behind in my house at the edge of the sea.

"He is mad," the thing mouthed, as though to itself. "I must stop him, but I must not hurt him."

"Perhaps I am mad," I croaked, coming craftily nearer. "Perhaps you are right and I should stop here."

But as I spoke I stooped and fumbled along the rock at my feet. And my questing fingers found a rock fragment. It was worn smooth to the touch, and was hollow, rather like a vase, my fingers told me. But I paid little attention to its shape, being preoccupied only with its satisfying weight and the thought of the destruction it could wreak.

I threw the missile at the head with the van Dyke beard. It struck fair on the lying cheek, and I saw the flesh of the cheek open like a red, uncurling flower with streaming crimson petals. And then I had bounded over the prostrate lizard thing and was racing along the path again with the green face far, far ahead of me.

I toiled through the luminous blackness with legs that seemed made of lead. And now the shadowy Things no longer paced me, I saw. They had stayed on the plateau high above, as if afraid to try the long descent down the rotten jade cliff.

As I ran I screamed to the green face: "Wait! Wait!"

And far behind sounded Elaine's sobbing voice: "Wait! God, wait!" And I marvelled at the strength of a love that had made her toil down the breakneck cliff behind us—but knew that I should sacrifice her too should she try to stand between me and my green goddess of death.

CHAPTER FOUR

The Pit

I RAN across a limitless plain in the live, black night. As I ran, I gained a little on the face, and I kept that gain in my mind and tried to look at nothing but the guiding speck before me. For now in the quivering blackness all around me things mewled and whimpered, and reason whispered that I dare not look at these things or my sanity would totter. And now and then they would bump against my legs, soft and pulpy; but always I kept my eyes resolutely on the green speck.

And again, after endless distances had been covered, I found myself at the edge of a descent. But this descent was not down the face of a cliff; it was a black, down-slanting shaft.

Without a pause, I hurtled down the shaft, for the green face shone far ahead and down it, and I knew without question that my path lay there.

Down and away I raced, feeling rough steps beneath my feet but disregarding them and running as if there had been no steps but only a smooth slant. Down and away, with the face moving soundlessly, smoothly far ahead of me.

The slant debouched at last into a cavern so immense that it was almost impossible to see the walls far to the right and left. Glittering specks in its vaulted roof looked like the stars of night. And as I hurried down the cavern, it grew yet larger till I could not know whether its far walls still enclosed me or whether I had come out to limitless space once more.

Warm air suddenly beat against my face, and I stopped. A cry burst from my lips. Now, between me and the distant green face, there yawned at last a barrier that seemed impossible of passing.

The smooth rock ended in a gulf so wide that I could scarcely see the other side, and so deep that the hot blasts of air beating up from its black depths seemed to come from the core of the earth itself.

I cried out with all my strength to the green face to wait, but it would not wait. While I stood on the edge of the awful chasm, it still receded on and on in the distance before me. Was this the end? Was I finally to be deserted by the face, and left to perish here in utter blackness?

I ran up and down the brink of the gulf, imploring the face to halt, pleading for help across the chasm. And at last I saw a way across. But such a way!

Stretching across the gulf, almost imperceptible in the grim blackness. was a thing that at first I took to be a bridge of rope, like a rope ladder, dipping far down in the center, and with transverse strands appearing all to fragile to hold my weight.

But the fragility of the bridge was not

its most fearsome feature. It was alive, formed of living, serpentine forms.

The two parallel rounds that stretched from edge to edge of the terrific abyss, were slowly expanding and contracting, expanding and contracting, shortening the down-drooping arc of the bridge and lengthening it again as they moved in steady, blind pulsation. And the small, weak looking rungs between the parallel supports were moving too, lengthening and shortening, as if continually on the verge of loosening their holds upon the longer, larger serpents and sliding down to the bottom of the gulf.

Was this my only way across to the other side where I might again take up my blind, mad chase—this bridge of living, serpent things?

I raved and screamed in the cruel darkness, but I started with bare feet along the living rope ladder, feeling each squirming movement of each live rung with terrified and quivering flesh.

I moved out from the edge of the abyss on the living bridge, trying to keep my appalled eyes from looking downward, where the vision reached and reached till the mind grew dizzy with sheer distance. And as I moved, with each step, the live rung I had just left loosened its hold at either end on the parallel serpent lengths and fell, squirming crazily, into the depths. So as I went I barely reached each succeeding rung as the last fell into black space behind me.

BUT now the main supporting lengths were moving with quickening anger, writhing like endless blind worms as they tried to shake me loose and send me plunging into the hot depths beneath. And at length, when I was nearly across, the twin supports parted with a soft grating hiss like that of rotten yarn being pulled asunder.

I swung with the short fragment against the cliff wall which was my goal. Now the bridge fragment was a ladder, with the longed-for brink of the chasm straight above my head. I climbed up the ladder; but even as I climbed, the parallel lengths stretched and thinned, so that as I ascended rung after rung of the hideous thing, I still made no progress up the face of the cliff.

After ages of labor that left me grasping for breath and swimming in unearthly exhaustion, I crawled over the brink and lay for awhile before getting up to reel after the green face.

The face! I must not lose sight of it! I got up—

And I shrieked curses that came from the depths of my sickened soul. For as I stood there I saw, farther off in the dimness, the end of the chasm I had crossed with such infinite weariness. I could have gone around instead of crossing with such nightmare futility of effort.

Staggering, blaspheming, I started again the frantic pursuit, through endless leagues of darkness, of that alluring green face.

And now at last the luminous darkness through which I had fought my way for so long grew brighter with a greenish brightness. The light came from ahead of me, and I saw that the luring green speck had at last stopped its pitiless retreat and was waiting for me. Waiting, waiting. . . .

Long had that green face haunted me; long had these full green lips tantalized me with their ominous beauty. Now, at last, I was going to keep a rendezvous with my green goddess of death! And this time I was coming to her instead of lying in an icy sweat while she came closer, ever closer, to me.

The green speck was growing larger as I approached it. The greenish brightness seemed to be radiating out from it, and washing back again till the face became the focal point for all the light.

As I stumbled nearer, exhausted by the long, eerie trip, I saw that I was approaching the shore of an endless green sea. Slow combers rose in the water's depths, like the flat, wide heads of serpents, and bent to crash against each other as they neared the shore. And the roar of their crashing combined into many voices. But all the voices reiterated one thing:

"He is mad! Stop him! He is mad!"

And I raved in answer to the deep, roaring voices. "I am not mad. Ask *her! She* will tell you!"

At the edge of the green sea, the green face hung like a glorious, but evil, mask, suspended on an unseen cord. And light from the sea gathered in it, and light from the brightening, greenish air. The face smiled, with the lips moist and panting and the eyes green wells of cruel desire.

I stopped a score of feet away from the face. A rendezvous! A meeting here by the green sea with death! For I knew that, with a kiss of those green lips, I would die convinced that I had known the ultimate of hell's pleasure.

The green lips moved, and I thought I heard words. "You are here. At last you are here!"

I STEPPED forward again, stopped, knowing once more that old chaotic feeling of being torn between horror and desire. And as I paused there, with the green face motionless and dangerously smiling only a few feet away, I heard faint steps far behind.

They were uneven steps, pitiful steps —the steps of Elaine, who had followed me around the torrid pit, even to the shore of this ghastly sea. But I closed my ears to the broken pleading of their rhythm, and gazed only at the green face. "Darling," I muttered.

And from far behind came the wild call: "Darling. . . ."

The green lips smiled more languorously yet; for my green goddess knew that she had won in spite of the stumbling girl in the darkness behind. And now my heart almost stopped, and then it raced so hard that I could scarcely breathe.

Under the green face, with the green sea as a background, the faintest conceivable suggestion of a throat was appearing.

In all these years, I had seen only the face of my death goddess with never a hint of the body; only a face, like a suspended mask glowing in the night. Now at last, it seemed, I was to see the rest of her. And I shuddered so that I could hardly stand as I paused there in the glow of the face—a ghostly zephyr blowing its pale, green hair out behind it.

What form would appear? What was I to see, at last, before I tasted the kiss of death? The body of a monster? Of a demon? Or a lovely woman-shape?

By now I knew definitely, with a knowledge confirmed, that there *were* other worlds than ours, impinging on our known world, and that these worlds were populated by real things. My green goddess was an actual being, living in an actual place—a region into which I had penetrated. She was a real being, *but what kind of a being?*

The face seemed human save for its inward, green glow; a beautiful though horrible countenance. But what sort of substance and form was under it? Something to stagger the imagination? Something on which a man could not gaze and live?

With a feeling of icy terror that made all other terrors endured before seem mild, I watched the slow materialization of the body belonging to the green face. The throat was all visible now, and it was slender and lovely—though sinuous with a suggestion of serpentine grace. Lithe shoulders began to appear, and under them full, firm breasts.

As the body slowly grew into visible being beneath the face I had seen so often, I knew for awhile a surcease of my terror—then felt it surge back with renewed force.

The body of my death goddess was a woman's body. But it was so beautiful that it was horrible. My senses swam as I gazed at her. For man was never meant to see such uncanny loveliness.

Gorgeous as a perfect statue in greenish bronze, nude save for a green sash around her lithe waist, the goddess stood before me, revealed at last in all her diabolical allure.

She stood on a low mound of the green sea-sand, straight and graceful, arms spread wide at her sides, head back a little, emerald eyes watching me while an enigmatic, covetous smile shaped her full lips.

In a dream, in a trance, I took a few faltering steps toward her. And then Elaine's voice sounded very near, and I wrenched my eyes away from the sinister beauty of the green goddess and looked behind. . . .

ELAINE was stumbling toward me over the loose, green sand. She was sobbing, dishevelled. Her long, dark hair was loose and hanging nearly to her waist. She staggered rather than walked, and her face was drawn with fatigue and fright. Her body was naked from the waist up, where her garments had been ripped from her. She had been attacked, I thought dimly, by the Things on the high plateau. Or perhaps the monster at the foot of the cliff had ripped her clothes away.

"Wait!" she sobbed, as she stumbled toward me over the yielding sand. She stared toward the green goddess with eyes that were wide with horror. "Wait!"

I turned back toward the green figure standing on the green mound like an incarnation of hell's triumph. The figure had not moved. It simply stood there, arms stretched wide, emerald eyes glinting with sure victory.

Elaine half fell against me, her arms encircling me.

"Wait! Don't move! Don't go forward. It's death if you do!"

I moved impatiently, angrily in the circle of her arms. I knew it was death to go forward. I knew that the touch of the perfect lips on the green face would spell the end for me. But I had known that from the start, and cared not at all.

"No, no!" wept Elaine, as I tried to put her from me. "Oh, if only I were stronger! If only I had help!"

I gripped her shoulders and pushed at them. "Let me go! The green goddess. . . . I must go to her!"

She held me more frenziedly. "You must not! It is death!" And then she stood back suddenly, freeing me. But it was not a move of surrender. "It is death to go to your green goddess! Death! Death! Come to me instead. If you love me, come."

I hesitated there in the green sea sand. But it was not a pause of indecision, for I knew that I was going at last to the embrace of the owner of the green face. It was only that I wanted to hurt Elaine as little as possible.

As I hesitated, Elaine stood straight, arms stretched wide in simulation of the pose of the green one. Her eyes sought mine.

"See," she said, color like flame mounting in her cheeks as my gaze swept over her half-naked body. "See! I am as beautiful as she is. And I love you more than she. I would save you—she would beckon you on to death. Come to me!"

I looked at her, and then at the creature on the mound, with her body like a glorious statue in bronze that has greened with time. And the green one still said nothing, still only stared at me with mocking emerald eyes in which at long last was the sure knowledge of victory.

I moved from Elaine toward the green one.

Elaine cried out despairingly, a last time, and stumbled through the sand to stand between me and the green goddess.

"Do not look at her! Look at me! Am I not as lovely as she? And she is death for you—while I am life!"

I raised my clenched fists, and she did not move. Her hands clutched at me.

I struck her down, and stepped over her body as it lay in the green sand of the seashore. Stepped over her and went to my rendezvous with death.

Now soft, soundless laughter moved the green lips. The outstretched arms curved a little toward me. The green goddess waited on the low mound. Nothing was between us any more. I had removed the last barrier in striking down Elaine. I was hers.

I walked up the sharp rise of the mound with leaden feet. And the green one waited, laughing softly. I reached the low crest and stood there, near enough to touch her.

Death to embrace her. Death . . . .

MY arms went out. My hands seized the green body, and my fingers closed, savagely, brutally. The green one stood still, laughing soundlessly, lips a green lure.

I sought to put my arms around her, and she stepped back. Raving, delirious, I grasped at her, and the green sash tore loose in my hand.

And now I had her in my embrace. My arms strained her form to mine. My lips were only inches from her lips. I had but to press forward a little more, and our mouths would join.

And the green one laughed soundlessly, while her gem-like eyes were terrible in their triumph.

Strange madness filled my brain, and I was strong with a god's strength, yet terrified almost beyond endurance. But gradually the terror died and left only the strength. Her eyes pierced my heart. Her lips promised unearthly, inhuman things . . .

I pressed forward to take death with her kiss . . . .

The green sea combers seemed suddenly to rear higher, while their booming voices roared in my ears.

"Get him! Hold him! He is mad!"

I pressed far forward—but felt demoniac hands clawing at me. They grasped my shoulders and arms and held me back, while the green sea combers boomed: "Hold him! Hold him, for God's sake! He is mad!"

And now the emerald eyes were flashing with all the fury of hell denied, and the green lips were writhing in maniac anger as they mouthed wild words. And the fair body was fading in my clasp.

The green goddess was receding from me. In a frenzy, I lunged to follow her.

But the demoniac hands held me back.

I fought there on the green seashore with the strength the touch of the gorgeous green body had given me. I lashed out with my fists, and felt them grind home against the unseen bodies behind the clutching hands. And I felt some of the hands loosen and heard groans, but always other hands gripped me in their places, and always there were enough to hold me from taking another step forward after my screaming, retreating goddess.

I tore at the hands, but they were implacable. I screamed at the invisible beings the hands were joined to, but over my screams roared the booming voices of the sea. "For God's sake hold him! He's mad! One more step . . . ."

Abruptly, I felt a sharp sting, like the sting of a serpent's fang, and the god's strength that had been mine began to flow from me like water. And I cried there beside the green sea, because I knew that I was beaten and I could no longer follow the green face and the body I had at last seen revealed beneath it.

The sting of the serpent's fang ached intolerably, and through the tiny puncture it had made, my strength drained till I would have fallen save for the clutch of the hands on my arms and shoulders. And as my weakness grew, the dread region I was in changed hue and tone.

The green sea became less green, faded more and more, till it was a dull gray sea whose combers roared and pounded but spoke no word. The greenish sky faded to drab gray, with clouds scudding across it like gray ghosts. And the mound of green sand on which I had stood was becoming hard and angular, and painful to my bare feet.

With dimming eyes I looked up and around. I saw a face under a white cap on the peak of which was the red cross of an ambulance driver. And there was the white, frightened face of the nurse, and the face, somehow gashed from temple to chin, of the doctor. And behind the doctor, crying and shuddering, was Elaine with her clothes half stripped from her and her lips puffed and bruised.

And I was standing, not on a mound of green sea sand, but on the broad sill of my basement window, with the rocks of the ocean shore eighty feet below me.

The ambulance driver said: "One more step. . . ."

Then I saw the doctor peer into my eyes, nod a little, and relax his grip.

"He'll do now," he said. "He'll sleep for at least six hours. Thank God we caught him before he'd fallen. But he nearly killed the lot of us first . . . ."

I felt that I was being carried somewhere, and my eyes closed in a sleep that was like a little death. . . .

YES, they can explain it beautifully— the doctors and the few friends to whom I have told this story. They know precisely what happened.

The green face, of course, has been a dream figment from the start. I never really saw that, much less a fiendishly lovely, green body beneath it.

As for my struggle through the luminous black night of an other-world, a child could follow it step by step, they say.

The niches cut down the face of the rotten jade cliff were the steps of the stairway from the second to the first floor of my house. The monster at the foot of them was the doctor, summoned by Elaine's cries and trying to overpower me. The final descent was into the basement. The pit, from the depths of which infernal heat had risen, was simply the pit in which my furnace rests. Out of the basement window on the cliff side of my house, from which I had nearly jumped to my death, I had seen the prosaic ocean and thought it green.

A real being owning the lovely, terrible green face? Coming from some real place to claim me when death struck? Nonsense! Delirium!

Yes, yes, of course. . . .

But no one has ever yet been able to explain the tiny teeth marks on my ankles and feet when they caught me in the window and no one has ever yet been able to explain the gossamer green sash, of curious weave and intricate design, which they almost had to break my fingers to take from my clenched hand when they finally got me to the hospital. . . . .

THE END

KEEPERS OF THE

By Arthur J. Burks
(Author of "Eater of Souls," etc.)

Sitting before their empty plates in that ghastly banquet hall, what strange fare did those weird men await? Why did they stare at Darda, Jay Dode's lovely model, with haunted, hungry eyes?

THERE was something about the place, either in the black drape or in the oddly furtive, almost sinister, aspect of the diners which frightened Darda from the moment of our entry.

I couldn't be sure myself exactly what it was. I think at first I was too much engrossed in Darda to take note of anything. This, to me, was just another strange place to eat. Darda and I always

BLACK TAVERN

A Novelette of Evil Passions

selected the out of the way, peculiar places.

A man in a long overcoat and a broad brimmed, floppy black hat had slipped a card to us on the icy, wintry street. The address on it had brought us here.

Darda, my one and only model, whose exquisite beauty I tried to give to the world in my painting, gasped as her eyes played over the people in the place.

"They all look hungry," she whispered to me.

"They probably are," I said, grinning. "Isn't that usually why people come to restaurants?"

"But I don't mean that kind of hunger," she said, with a little frown. "It's another sort of hunger, Jay. I feel as though every last man here—and you will note that I am the only woman—is hungry for me!

I can't explain it, but it makes me flinch inside me, as from the caress of little razor blades against my flesh."

She tried to smile at her own dramatic simile, then went on, more serious than ever. "Even the men with their backs to us, who haven't looked at us at all, seem to be watching me, and hungering for me. I feel their hunger reaching out for me, as with invisible tentacles, from the backs of their skulls."

I confess it gave me a turn. It made me look away from gorgeous Darda for the first time.

There must have been twenty men in the long room. They were sitting one to a table—the tables were really small for two—and all were facing the same way. Ahead of them was a long black drape which reached all along the wall.

That drape was funereal. To my vivid imagination, coupled with the indefinable fear expressed by Darda, its black length masked all sorts of sudden terrors, only now born in my brain.

Why did all these men stare at the drape? Why did they, on occasion, turn and look fleetingly at Darda and—I thought—lick their lips as though with ghastly expectancy?

My heart began to hammer with a rising dread.

Of all the people here, only Darda and I were eating!

The others merely sat and stared at the black drape, with now and then one of those furtive glances toward us.

If they ate, what was the manner of their eating?

Darda had felt it first, had expressed it in that one word, "hunger," and she hadn't meant hunger for food! What sort of food, then? Of what ghastly viands did these strange men partake?

I studied them, trying to remember my Lombroso and the study of character by the face. I picked out types. And each one, as I recognized it, gave me more of a start than before. There were fauns, satyrs. There was Hermes of the winged feet. There were Eros, Narcissus. The likeness grew in my mind as if with sudden, unexpected explosions.

"For Heaven's sake, Darda," I said, "what is this? A dream? Am I Jay Dode—and are you Darda, my model?"

"I don't know anything," she answered, "except that I am more afraid than I have ever been in my life. Let's get out of here!"

We rose and fled from the tavern of the black drape as from a place accursed, and I swear that the intangible hunger of the habitues followed us like an emanation from some dank, evil tarn, followed us even to our studios.

When Darda had gone to her own quarters I did what I always did when I was alone. I crossed the floor to each of my canvases in turn, tossed aside the cloths which covered them. While Darda was present she eclipsed my best effort, so that there was no need of replicas for her. When she was absent they were all I had. I lived with them, slept a dreamless sleep while they watched me in the night.

I studied again the newest canvas but one. I had almost attained, here, the thing I had been seeking—a perfect likeness of Darda. If I ever got the likeness perfectly, I knew, the figure would step out of the canvas and smile at me. Which was, of course, absurd. But don't think there was any madness in me. It was only a worshipful reverence.

I started toward the next canvas—and then stopped short. It wasn't where I had placed it.

"That's funny," I said, "where did it go? Did I move it before we went out to that tavern?"

I shook my head at that. Absent-mindedness was an artistic characteristic I did nct permit myself. I dislike "temperament."

Something had happened. Someone had been here while we were out, and because Darda had come into the room with me I hadn't thought of looking toward the canvas on which we had last been working. Darda hadn't looked at it either, else she would have missed it.

I raced from one canvas to the cther. I had them everywhere. Against the corners, hanging on the walls, leaning against chairs. My association with Darda had lasted almost a year. The canvases were all nudes. And when I had finished uncovering them all—growing wilder and more amazed as each succeeding canvas was still not the one I sought—Darda's pale counterpart looked out at me from a score of places.

But out of the latest canvas, no!

Not that it would have, anyhow, for the fancy had come to me to leave the head to the very last in that one, to cast the mounded breasts with their tips that were like strawberries, to paint the mounds and curves undistracted by the eyes of her. . . .

Should I disturb Darda? Panting, somehow afraid, I sat down on the edge of my couch to try and figure out what had happened. Had the landlord taken the painting? Nonsense! I owed him nothing, had paid my rent for several months in advance, a most unusual gesture in the Village.

I wouldn't go to Darda with this, not yet at least. She needed sleep for her beauty's sake. I admitted that when I was taken out of myself, as I now was. Had a thief broken in? Why had he taken that one canvas and none other? The thing that hurt me the most was that if a thief had taken it, if *anyone* had taken it, someone saw the glory of Darda who had no right to it whatever.

It almost drove me mad.

I lifted my eyes to the nearest of the canvases. Maybe my excitement had done it, I don't know, but for a moment I had a frightful scare. I looked into the eyes of Darda in that canvas, unable to believe what I saw. It was the head and shoulders of a man holding his coat lapels close about his face, whose head was topped by a black hat with an unusually wide brim!

The hallucination—it could have been no more than that—was gone the instant I saw it. And I knew why it had come. Subconsciously I had been thinking of the tavern where we had supped, reliving our contact with it, from the man who had given us the brown card to the strange people in the place.

FRIGHTENED, almost expecting to see the faces of the different habitues of the place in the other canvases of Darda, I snapped a quick glance at each in turn—and sighed with relief.

There was an easy explanation for what I thought I had seen. The tavern and its people had impressed me deeply, but I was so possessed by the glory of Darda that other impressions had to force themselves through. That was all, and it explained why I had seen the head of the man of the brown card where the glowing face of Darda should have been.

"Well, there's no use doing anything before morning," I decided at last. "I'll find that canvas, wherever it is, and destroy it, no matter who has it. They shall not keep it to look at. I shall make another. Who knows, maybe it's an act of Fate, a hint that if I start again I may achieve the end I aim at!"

I undressed. I looked for a long time at the various canvases, then turned out the light over my bed. Under the covers I was conscious of the wind which whistled like banshees outside, of the screaching of the "L," of the blasting of motor horns and sirens.

I shut these out in the usual way, by staring at the center of my study, where subdued lights from outside came through the window to form a big rectangle on the floor. Tonight, as always, by sheer imagery, I brought all of my Dardas forth from their canvases, to pose for me in the gentle light. What would she do, say and think if she knew how it was with me? That here, alone, I had, not one Darda, but all the Dardas I had created on canvas?

Yet all of them together, I knew, still amounted to but the palest carbon copy of the original.

My eyelids started to close.

Behind them I saw all the habitues of the tavern where we had supped. But the impressions of all the Dardas were still there, too, so that I saw them together. I didn't realize for several moments what my imagination had done for me; that in piling one sensation upon another, I had brought both of them together.

And the resultant picture left me almost mad!

All the Dardas had been dancing silently in the room, in the midst of the dim light. Thus I saw them as I dozed. Then I saw the men of the tavern, among the Dardas. There was the man with the pointed ears and the slanted eyes, the man with the assymetrical face, the man with the pointed chin and the hooked nose. There were Mephistopheles, the Satyr, the Faun, Narcissus and Eros, as, mentally, there in the tavern, I had dubbed the various strange ones.

In my sleep-waking dream they all came into that lighted space, too, and danced with Darda. But Darda was nude! Their hands touched her and she did not seem to mind. Then I noticed that all of them, too, were nude, and that their hands, their legs, their gross torsos, touched each of my Dardas in turn.

So stunned was I by this impossibility —hating myself because even in my dreams this should seem to be impossible —I could not even drag my eyes open for a moment.

I saw them embrace her. I saw them posture in a dance which spoke of lustful love. I saw red lips pressed against hers, saw her put her gorgeous arms behind the shoulders of the Satyr or the Faun, her hands against the back of his head, forcing his lips harder against hers—with their bodies undulated together, slowly, meaningly.

I sprang to my feet with a scream of terror that this could be possible, even in a dream. No man had ever touched Darda so. No man would while I lived. It would never occur to her even to think of such a contact.

Perspiration beaded my whole body when I stood erect on the floor. And, erect, I found only the many canvases, peering at me through the dim light.

"Thank God," I whispered. "Thank God! Oh, thank God!"

I couldn't stop saying it. It kept going through my head, out over my lips, time and again, as though I had no will to stop it.

I WANTED with all my heart to dash out into the hall, run down to her door, bang against it, never stop until I had seen her face again. But she would think me mad.

And almost, I was. It was, of course, the fact that my latest canvas was missing, which caused my strange aberrations. So that I fought with all my will to keep from running out into the hall, screaming, going to Darda.

I knew I would have been welcome, for she would never have dreamed that I would come to her in any way but with that in my heart which had been there since I had first seen her—save that the feeling had grown with each speeding second we had spent together

"It's only the food I ate," I told myself. "I should never eat lobster, should have known better. And all those queer people, the icy wind, the missing canvas. Yet who in the world could have taken it?"

I harked back to the waiter who had called me by my name because he had had my landlord point me out to him and name me. Had the landlord also shown him my studio? Had he dared show my paintings to anyone, even himself?

I started to telephone. Then I looked at my watch. It was two o'clock in the morning.

I managed to laugh at my own vague fears.

Nothing could be wrong with Darda, of course, I tried to reassure myself.

I turned out the light again, started to lie down. But, God Almighty! I could not. I would never sleep. I would never be able to do anything but quake as with the ague until I had seen Darda again, knew that she was all right.

I turned the light on once more. My hand trembled as I felt the light-chain. Then I stared at myself in the mirror. My lips were flabby with incomprehensible fear. My eyes were as wild as those of a maniac.

"Let her think me crazy," I told myself finally. "I've got to know."

I dressed. Maybe ordinary clothing would restore me to sanity. Maybe. . . .

But the clothing did no good. I think I put it on because, though most of the time I saw Darda unclothed, she had never seen me any way but covered.

I went out into the hall—and gasped. The lights were turned off. But of course! I knew it all the time. The landlord saved electricity after he was sure all his tenants were in. And yet the blackness of the hall reminded me so vividly, so forcefully of the black drapes in the tavern—damn

that tavern! Why should it keep returning to my mind?—that I shivered.

I dashed down the hall. I knew exactly where Darda's door was. Lord knows I had traversed this way times enough.

I found the door. I knocked on it softly. I put my ear to the panels to hear her breathing. Soft as it was I could always hear it—perhaps because it was Darda's, and I was so keenly conscious of everything about her.

Was that why I had wakened?

It came to me like a thunderclap—even as I realized that I didn't hear her breathing. It wasn't a matter of bad food and lasting impressions, than, but of the thread of feeling which stretched between me and Darda, between—I hoped—Darda and me.

Darda wasn't in that room!

I knew it instantly. But I must be sure. I might have the wrong door in spite of my certainty.

There was no mistake. It was her door.

I hammered on it, calling her name:

"Darda! Darda!"

There was no answer of any kind. In others rooms I heard men and women stirring, then cursing my noise. But to Hell with them! I gave them no thought. I hammered again, terror mounting until I was already half mad with it.

I tried the lock. The door could not be opened that way. I had no key. I raised my voice, shouting for the landlord. But without even waiting until he could arrive, thankful for my power which now, in my terror, was that of three men—I stepped back and hurled myself against the door. It crashed in with a noise that rocked like an explosion, that shook the very house itself.

I fell into darkness. On hands and knees, panting, I felt for a bed. I found it. I rose, ran my hands over it. It was rumpled, had been roughly folded back. Darda had gone to bed, had risen again, was gone.

I struck a match, looked about, my fear rising until it was a ringing in my ears. Beside the bed was a rumpled black hat with a broad floppy brim.

CHAPTER TWO

The Fiend With the Lancet

SO, THE dozing nightmare I had had had meant something! Darda had been calling me. But from where?

The hat of the broad floppy brim seemed to tell me that. The memory of the tavern came flooding back, especially its habitues who, in the dream, had danced with the Galateas from my canvases of Darda. Darda's mind had sent me a message. Her mind had been filled with *them,* and she had sent them to me.

Was the rest of the nightmare real? Was Darda being fondled by those men? If she were . . .

Great God!

And the picture of her, the last I had done. You will remember that I said I had left the head to the last, which meant that the figure on the canvas had no head at all? That meant—Mother of Christ!— that it had been taken because of the body of Darda, because of the breasts which were so lovely, because of the legs that were perfect, the thighs that were white marble columns aglow with life.

And those men . . .

What were they?

I crumpled that hat again in my hands. If its owner had been there I would have crumpled him in the same manner, hurled him from me with every bone in his body broken. Its presence told me that Darda had been taken from here against her will, certainly with a gag in her mouth else she would have called to me—and she would

have called and I would have heard her even across the sea of sleep, where her thoughts had reached me anyhow, to show me the ghastly travesty of that nightmare dance.

I dashed out, down the stairs.

The lights were on now. People were shouting at me from a dozen doors, calling me vile names I scarcely heard.

On the stairs I met Matin Lowe, the landlord and owner, in his night garments, his hair tousled, his eyes heavy with sleep. He was coming up to meet me with an ugly automatic in his hand. He aimed it at me before he recognized me. But no bullet would have stopped me now.

He lowered the weapon as I grabbed him by the shoulder.

"Quick," I croaked. "Why did you tell the tavern keeper my name? Why did he ask you?"

"Tavern keeper?" he quavered. "I know no tavern keeper who does not already know your name."

"I mean the tavern of the long black drape, and the habitues there who are so strange."

Did I imagine it, or did his eyelids droop a little, his breath still for a moment? But of course I did.

His eyes opened again, very wide. "Tavern of the black drape?" he said. "You'd better wake up, Dode. You're walking in your sleep. I never heard of such a place. What's the name of it?"

"It has no name, only a number." I told him the number.

Again his eyes were veiled for a moment. "I've heard things," he said, "about a strange new cult, out of Egypt. People do say . . ."

"This isn't a cult," I said. I shook him until his teeth rattled. "This is a tavern, with a black drape all along one wall. Only men go there."

"The cult is supposed to be for men

who are very rich," he said. "It is a ritual, like the Black Mass, only more hellish."

I GRABBED him by the throat, forgetting his automatic. He could have put it against me and pulled the trigger and I wouldn't have felt the smash of the bullet. He didn't think to fire.

"Who took my painting?" I demanded next. "Who took it, I tell you?"

"A man came, with a note from you. I gave the picture to him. Your note said to."

"How did you know it was a note from me? "You've never seen my writing."

"I didn't know, but I thought . . . God, have I made a mistake, Mr. Dode?"

"You made a mistake which may cost you your life when I get back." I snarled.

I hurled myself at the door. Outside, I realized I was garbed in light clothing. The wind cut through me like a knife, seemed to congeal my palm against the steel of the automatic. But I didn't know these things except subconsciously. How long had Darda been gone? I looked along the street toward the door of that tavern. I saw the tin sign swinging in the wind. I even heard the doleful sound it made as it swung.

Then I was running toward it, running at top speed. The faster I ran the faster I needed to run. Seconds were precious, for now I knew that the dance I had seen, somehow sent to me from the mind of Darda, was approximately real. It could not be entirely real of course, for there was but one Darda, while in the dream there had been all the Dardas I had created. I remembered as I ran, something I had once said to Darda:

"If you sent me a message that you needed me, even from beyond the grave, I would rise from my own grave to answer!"

She had smiled then. Now I was sure she had remembered and sent the message—*from beyond the grave?* Dear God, no, not that!

I reached the tavern door. Black—the name I had given to our waiter there—had said the place closed at twelve o'clock. It was now after two. Of course I was being foolish. The proprietor might call officers, have me arrested. If an officer saw me now, with an automatic tightly gripped in my right hand, he would have taken me in—if he had lived to make the arrest.

There was the door, and the knocker. Gripping my automatic in my right hand, I worked the knocker with my left.

Only echoes came to me out of the depths of the tavern, beyond the door of which I knew the ebon drape hung motionless, masking God knew what mysteries.

No answer.

I banged on the door with the muzzle of my automatic. I shouted a name. I shouted Darda's name; I shouted for our waiter of the evening, Black. Still no answer. Heavy and powerful as I was, I could never crash this door. No use trying. I looked to my right, seeking a window, but there was no window.

And then, inside, I heard the rhythmic sound of heavy footfalls. The door opened, on a man I had never seen before. Like my landlord, he wore a sleeping garment, and his eyes were heavy with sleep.

I started to push past him. His eyes widened when he saw the automatic. But he didn't fear it. He thrust his hands against my chest.

"Are you crazy?" he said. "Where are you going?"

"Into this damned tavern!" I snapped. "Get out of my way!"

"Tavern?" he repeated. "Tavern? Got kicked out, eh? I *thought* they used dope in there. It's next door, fool. Look and see."

He pointed to my left. I hadn't seen it

before, not even tonight when I had come here with Darda, but the door I now faced was a replica of that door to the left, even to the shape of the knocker—cast as a lion on the rampage.

The explanation was simple. Builders often duplicated houses which stood side by side—and I seldom noticed anything at all when I was with Darda.

Now I was too wild with anxiety to notice anything.

I DIDN'T apologize. I stepped to the second door, clanged the knocker. The man at the other door closed it with a disgusted bang. I waited anew, cursing myself for my blindness which had caused so much delay when very seconds were precious.

I heard a rustling sound inside. It came to me clearly in spite of the shrieking of the wind, perhaps because I listened so strainedly that the wind was shut out for me. The door started to open. I didn't wait to see the face of the ugly one who had met us here before. There couldn't be any *other* doors this close; this had to be right, and I was wasting no more time.

I stepped into darkness.

The door clanged shut behind me, and I was still in darkness, a darkness so deep and velvety that it could be felt, almost tasted. But I was in the right place, I knew, for all sound from outside was erased with the clanging of that door as though it had never been.

I shouted for Black. The echoes smote me in the face. I had a sense of being in a narrow, confined space.

I shifted my automatic to my left hand, fumbled with my right. My fingers came in contact with cloth—and when I knew the texture of it I knew its color, too! It was velvet. That black drape had had the sheen of velvet in the tavern's light.

But this drape was to my right!

Good God, that other door had been right, after all, and I had been sent to the second door, and was in behind the ebony drape!

Why, in God's Name?

I hurled myself straight forward, but I didn't get far. Many hands grabbed me. Many bodies flung themselves on me. I knew that if they were not nude they were nearly so—men by the rough feel of them and their strength. They ripped off my clothing as they held me, stripping me to the waist. Then they hurled me through a curtain, into a lighted space of vast dimensions, surrounded by funeral black.

Straight ahead of me was Darda, in the hands of the figure I had likened to Mephistopheles!

She was nude.

He held her with one hand. His other hand held a surgeon's lancet.

TERROR held me speechless and motionless. For moments I was like a man suddenly turned to stone. There was Darda, gazed upon by a man other than myself for the first time, and he held a lancet in his hand, poised over her right breast. Never since I had known her had Darda been so beautiful.

She stood on tiptoe, her shoulders back, her arms from just above her elbows hidden behind her torso. Her head was tilted back, and her black cloud of hair hung behind her. So gorgeous, she was, as to make one's throat ache, one's heart stand still.

But never for Mephistopheles!

"Darda! Darda!" I cried.

She did not answer. No quiver of her flesh told that she even heard me. It was as though she had been poised there in stone, or as though she had been the perfect painting I had striven so long to fashion.

Mephistopheles looked straight at me without shifting the position of the lancet.

"Ah, Jay Dode," he said softly, "you are late in coming!"

So, I had been expected all along then? They had been waiting for me to come. But why? I tried to place his voice, because it did not seem to come from where I saw the man, though his face and form were so clearly shown I could have read the words on his lips if I had not heard them. The words seemed to come from everywhere.

I poised for the attack.

"The banquet," said the satanic one, "should be titled: 'The Feast of Dode and Darda!' There is euphony there, Dode, which you as an artist should appreciate. Dode and Darda. Dode and Darda. It has a pretty sound, has it not?"

"How dare you use that name," I heard my voice croaking. "*My* name, for her?"

"The feasters of Thebes," he answered, "dare anything. Underlings do as they are bidden, as you will do, Dode, in the feast of Dode and Darda. Dode and Darda. It has a sweet sound on the tongue, so that I have difficulty in making an end of saying it. But the feast must begin, Dode."

What did he mean by "feast?" What, in Heaven's name, were the "feasters of Thebes?"

I didn't need an automatic for this man —though I was amazed to discover that my unknown, invisible, naked enemies had sent me into this lighted space with the automatic thrust into my belt. The feel of its barrel was still cold against my flesh. I hadn't put the weapon there myself, so it must have been given to me for a purpose! What could the purpose be?

I should doubtless find out, when and if I found cause to use the weapon.

I HURLED myself forward, straight at Mephistopheles. Even as I did so he shifted the lancet, so that he held it delicately between thumb and forefinger. He turned to his left and bowed, as though he were a magician about to perform some feat of legerdemain. He had all the self-confidence of a master of that craft.

I turned to my right, to see the audience to which he bowed. But I saw no audience. I saw instead the nude figure of Darda—to my *right* now, poised as I have just described, motionless.

Amazed, I looked forward again, and there she was. I sighed with relief. *These* were paintings, then! There could never be two of Darda in the flesh, and that this was her I was positive, even while mentally I took off my hat to a painter obviously more skilled than I.

Or had more of my paintings been taken? Of course not. I had counted them all and had missed but one.

There was one inescapable conclusion then, which twisted my heart into a knot and left it bloodless and cold: Darda had been posing for some other painter than I. I couldn't believe it possible.

Then, ahead of me, I saw Darda move. She moved so little that only an eye as sure for detail as mine would have seen it. I saw her throat move as she swallowed. The Darda directly ahead of me, at least this Darda was a living woman!

And the lancet now, to which Mephistopheles was giving his whole attention, was poised above the flesh just under her left breast. He made a quick motion. I saw the crawling and twisting of the soft snowy flesh under the lancet's tip, and after the stroke of the lancet, a streak of crimson!

The streak widened, grew. It became a thick streak, a band. And now the lower edge of the band was ragged. It was blood, and it was running down her flesh.

No painting, this. It was Darda herself who had flinched to the touch of the lancet.

I whirled to look at the painting to my

right. There, upon it, was the same broad band, ragged at the base! Even as I stared in disbelief, a drop detached itself from the broad band and fell, to make a red ellipse on the white flesh of her stomach. I whirled back, sick and dizzy, to see the selfsame drop on the first Darda!

But the first Darda, I was sure, was the real Darda. I did not understand the apparent reality of the second one—but I meant to discover its meaning!

I dashed straight ahead, hand outflung like talons to clutch the throat of Mephistopheles. Even now he was extending the lancet across her body, leaning forward so that for a moment his body, as nude as Darda's, blotted out her left breast— leaning forward to repeat under her right one the fearful stroke I had just witnessed. I knew he planned the same act, for the movement was the same.

"Don't, damn you to Hell!" I yelled. "I'll twist your head from your body!"

He paid me no heed whatever.

The lancet moved. Again the thin streak of crimson appeared in the midst of the writhing flesh, grew to a broad band which widened, grew ragged at the base, and finally loosed a single globule, which fell almost precisely beside the first!

A master artist, in his line, this man, his work of horror so perfect that he could write his dreadful genius in blood on a living victim. Darda was the canvas on which he wrote, Darda's flesh that which crawled under the stroke so fearful in its delicate precision.

I think I screamed, but Mephistopheles did not notice. Now I thought I knew why Darda's head was back. She thus looked up to heaven so that her eyes should not see the gross animality of the body of Mephistopheles. There could be no other reason. She could not deny her body to the torturer, but she could withdraw herself, send forth her soul. Already tonight she had done that, and I had re-

ceived her message, terror-distorted—it had brought me here to see in grim reality the personification of my nightmare.

"Darda! Darda! It's Dode! Fight against him! Fight! Fight!"

She did not seem to hear me. Perhaps her senses were dulled by the pain of the lancet. For she made no answer. Only her throat moved a little, as though, in pain and agony, she swallowed. My God, what was being done to Darda?

THOUGHTS were lightning swift. I was still moving toward Darda and her captor at full speed. In a second now I would have his neck between my palms. I would lift him up and break his back against the floor with one mighty swing. My hands were about touch him. I could already feel his flesh under them.

And then, with an awful crash, like a sledgehammer blow on the jaw, I collided with something I had not seen before.

It was like slamming into a solid wall. My hands struck it first. My knuckles bent back, forcing my taloned fingers into fists. My forearms bent back in their turn. My arms came back against my body, and I struck with all my length against that invisible obstruction.

I looked, not at Darda, but myself, and it blotted out both Darda and Mephistopheles. My face was a mad horror. I had bitten my lips through and they dripped red blood upon my chest. I saw the automatic aslant in my belt. I saw my torso ridged with muscle as I strained to reach for the captor of Darda.

Then I knew and screamed!

Twisting itself into a maniacal, almost fiendish expression, my own replica opened its bloody mouth, the very teeth of it red, and screamed back at me. So it seemed, perhaps, because of the echoes.

I had collided full force, with a mirror which seemed to blend with the floor at my feet, the ceiling above me, hidden in blackness so deep I could not pierce it. I looked up to make sure—and knew that the ceiling was of black velvet.

Again I saw the madman that was myself, and again I screamed. My own apparition frightened me, so that I whirled from the mirror, for fear I would go entirely mad—I who was already so near to madness. I whirled, I say, and looked at a very galaxy of Dardas!

Off to my right I saw her, in serried ranks, stretching away to infinity. To my left she was again, countless numbers of her, stretching away and away, so many of her that at the end, all the Dardas seemed to blend together into one, the last ones blurred and almost unrecognizable as Darda. They would not have been recognizable at all except for one thing: each of her replicas had the broad band under the breast, ragged at its lower edge, and the two drops of blood, apparently exactly in line, along the white flesh of her stomach!

As I stared, forcing myself by a sheer effort of will to keep my hands from darting to my hair and pulling wildly, madly, another two drops fell, one from each of the slanted wounds under Darda's breasts! What a master artist was the wielder of the lancet!

I stood there, forcing myself to be calm. I knew even then that only in utter calmness would I ever be able to deliver Darda from this torture.

I tried to reason things out. All about me, behind me, before me, to right and left, were the replicas of Darda, more of her than I could ever transfer to canvas, though I worked until the very end of time.

One of these, I told myself, must truly be the real Darda. But which? Countless thousands were the reflections from mirrors. Only one was the figure, so hellishly placed, of Darda herself.

I must find that one, out of the myriad,

and pull her free of Mephistopheles—of whom there were as many replicas as there were of Darda—even as I had to come to grips with that man—come to grips and kill him!

But how could I know which?

I hurled myself at the closest. And I was thrown to the floor by the terrific impact, my nose broken. I staggered up, my face close against the mirror—unrecognizable now because all my face was a mask of blood.

As I watched Mephistopheles shifted his attention to Darda's shoulder.

CHAPTER THREE

Satan's Labyrinth

ONCE, as a lad in school, I had placed two mirrors on edge so that they formed two sides of a triangle. Between them, near the open end, I had set a waxen candle, aflame. Standing back I had looked down what had seemed to be an endless row of candles.

Yet I knew there was but one.

Darda was the candle. But how many were the mirrors, and how hellishly placed? There must be a way to know, to start with one figure and estimate just where the figure stood whose reflection caused all the others—the reflection of Mephistopheles and of Darda.

I must be cool, must figure this thing out for Darda's safety.

I didn't, then, hear the sound which came from somewhere outside this devil's labyrinth, a rising tide of it—like a pagan paean of rejoicing, of thanksgiving. I heard a roaring in my ears, and knew that it was only my own blood, rushing like molten fire through my heart and soul. Only that, nothing more, for I knew no other sounds could come to me from outside.

I knew because the closing of the outer

door had erased the sound of the "L" train, and the shrieking of the wintry winds from the cold bosom of the Hudson.

No, I made the sounds, all of them now, for Mephistopheles did not speak again. He was too busy with the shoulder of Darda. As I watched he shaped, in the hollow or her right shoulder—or was it her left?—a small cross, also etched in blood.

I know now, looking back, that I would have, but for my frenzy, found her more quickly than I did. Obviously, if Mephistopheles used his right hand with the lancet, then all the reflections would show him using the left. All I had to do was seek out the figure which used only the right!

But where to find it in all that myriad of figures? Besides, I did not think of it. I am bowed with shame as I remember that the thought did not occur to me, so that, instead, I hurled myself against mirror after mirror, like a blue-bottle fly smashing against a window-pane. And as I did so I kept shouting:

"Darda! Darda!"

But never once did she answer. Nor did Mephistopheles look up, deign to speak. All the sound I heard—which I thought to be my own blood pounding in my ears—was that distant roaring, like the sea across the sands, or like a distant choir singing.

I smashed against a mirror and fell. And now when I rose to all fours, like a dog which has been beaten, and stared at myself—I stared at a veritable madman.

My hair, dank and stringy, was almost hiding my eyes. Through the lattice of it I saw my eyes like caverns filled with the lights of Hell.

I stared at my own reflection and laughed. How awful was my laughter, cracked with terror and pain. . . .

And how strangely it was followed by the distant roaring of sound, as though the far choir shouted its approval or delight, or as though a mightier wave had broken across the shingle I had imagined.

I got to my feet again.

"I might touch all the Dardas, grasp at every Mephisto," I told myself, "if I were fast enough on my feet, if I did not stop to breathe, if I stopped myself when I touched a mirror, so that I did not hurl myself back with the force of my own striking. Obviously they do not intend to kill her at once. Maybe, in the end, I shall reach her before she dies of the torture. I only wish that the roaring of my blood in my ears would cease, so that I might hear the voice of Darda if she calls."

That was it. I would try that.

I find it impossible now to select words that will describe the terror and the pain which followed. I caromed against one mirror, slewed off against another. It was as though all of them, one after the other, closed in tightly against me as soon as I had struck one and fell back.

Now and again my reflection in this or that one blotted out both Darda and Mephisto, and my face was a horror which grew and grew. I looked, near the last, as though I had been beaten with a sledge-hammer—and had refused to die because, so long as Darda remained in the hands of the man with the lancet, I could not.

Over Darda's stomach there now was a patchwork of red stains, where globules had fallen from the cicatrices under her breasts.

There was a cross of red on her right shoulder, another on her left.

And now, from each of these, exactly and perfectly, a drop fell upon the curve of her right hip and her left.

I screamed again, only to discover that scarcely once had I ceased from screaming. Realizing this I made an end for a moment to listen. I thought in that ghastly heart-beat of time that I could hear the striking on white flesh of the red globules. But that of course was absurd.

Yet I did hear the roaring sound.

PANTING, so that my breath rasped like a file from my lungs and throat, I stopped, back against the last mirror which had added to the horror of my face, and listened to that roaring of sound, now like the beating, in slow, perfect rhythm, of a myriad of wings.

I stared at the nearest, or what seemed to be the nearest, figure of Darda. Her posture had not changed. Yet there was a subtle difference somehow. I grasped at that difference to avoid utter insanity, trying to see wherein the difference lay.

Down near the floor, between her feet, seen because the weight of her pain had caused her knees to part a little as though she would have sunk to the floor upon them, I saw yet another smudge of white —an expanse of flesh that was never as white as the flesh of Darda.

I stared at it, and knew why her hands were still behind her, so tightly pressed against her back, as though behind her she twisted and untwisted her clasped hands in an ecstasy of agony. That additional expanse of flesh was the knee of a man.

That man, I knew, held her arms imprisoned, kept her from falling either forward or backward. And I knew, too, why her head was thrown back, her hair hanging so straightly downward.

Behind her, where he would have remained invisible to the end but for the moving apart of her knees, a man stood and held her hands tightly imprisoned, pulling her head back with one hand clutched tightly in her hair!

So I had two men to slay instead of one!

I began again.

I ranted, raved, swore. I even cursed Darda herself because her beauty had brought us both to all this torture. For, however great her torture must have been, my own was greater still. Yet only because I knew how deeply, tragically, she must be suffering.

To have that marvelous flesh so redly marred! To feel the searing eyes of other men upon her! To feel the touch of that knife! To know the horror of a stranger's hands against her body and in her hair.

No wonder her throat moved as she swallowed her pain!

"Darda! Darda!"

My croaking call to her drowned out the roaring sound which I still did not identify. If I *had* identified it then, it would have driven me even closer to madness than I was.

She did not answer. Now I knew it was because her head was drawn so tightly back.

Now, all at once, when I paused again as it suddenly came to me about the *one* right hand or the *one* left hand holding the lancet, which I might have picked out from among all the reflections as that which was not a reflection at all—Mephistopheles suddenly looked at me and smiled. His eyes were alight with a feverish frenzy, as though he had been a devotee drunk with his devotions. His lips were tremulous with it.

He bowed to me.

Then he bowed to his left again.

And the roaring sound, more like chanting than ever before, rose again, as though the choir of my fancy had applauded, in song, his ghastly artistry.

That *must* have been it, for he bowed again and again, and his smile was filled with pride and satisfaction. He knew how well he had done, how greatly he merited the applause, if applause it were.

And it must have been, for amid the roaring I heard a soft sound, many sided, as of palms patting against wood. Once, in a restaurant far away, it had been the custom for all habitues to pat the tables like that when they wished for something, or when a newcomer came to dine or sup.

Did the sound come from the tavern?

Where *was* the tavern? It hadn't been like this when Darda and I had supped last night, this morning—when *had* it been?

I THINK I must have guessed the truth then; that I was behind the ebony drape—and that the habitues of the tavern, whose presence I had not guessed at, *were still as Darda and I had left them!*

Only now they were worshipers at a shrine which had first been built in— where?

Thebes?

Whither was my madness leading me?

I whirled again to look at Darda and Mephisto.

But Mephisto had vanished from all the mirrors, and only Darda remained, standing still with her hands behind her, her head flung back, her hair drawn straight and tightly down.

What was to happen next?

Would to God I could wipe out the memory of it! But the truth in all its horror must be told.

Now in place of Mephisto appeared . . .

The man whose chin almost touched his nose. His skinny, horrid body was a bag of bones, his hands were bony things, skeletons save for the thin white skin which covered them.

He cackled with laughter and said: 'Pretty! Pretty! Pretty!"

And then he put his bony arms around Darda, and pressed his awful lips, which made me think of the beak of an octopus, against Darda's flesh—against the wounds under her breasts, against the red crosses on her shoulders, against her neck.

And where he touched her neck, once on either side, he left the shape of his lips in crimson.

And all the while that sea of sound outside went on, rising, increasing, the patting sound of applause rolling loudly forth.

The awful old man looked at me and cackled, with the light of his eyes I had seen it in the eyes of Mephisto.

I raised my automatic, which had remained with me through it all, leveled it straight at the old man and pulled the trigger. If, now, I aimed straight at the true Darda and her torturer, and slew her, I would at least release her from this hell on earth.

But all I did was break a mirror—all I did was that, and—God in Heaven—afterward I watched other habitues of the tavern take their places in succession beside Darda, to touch her, to fondle her— to claw her with their nails, strike her with whips of wire . . . .

Absolutely crazy with the sacrilege of it, I emptied my automatic, first at one mirror, then at another—ending by hurling the useless weapon at still another. And after each shot, and after the weapon itself had been hurled, showers of glass fell in this Satan's labyrinth as the mirrors broke apart and crashed to the floor.

But there were *still* other mirrors, and I *still* had not found Darda

I hurled myself at the nearest of the broken glasses, looked through the jagged hole a bullet had made in its center, at him whom I had called the Satyr in my mind—looked through, like a maniac peering between the bars of his cell.

And through that ragged mirror, the next moment, I saw the greatest horror of them all. A horror which laughed at at me, with laughter like the roaring of the sea across a beach!

With only that laugh, the strength I had dissipated came back to me. **My** agonies were forgotten. I hurled myself forward, through the broken mirror which, with countless others like it, had tricked me almost to my death.

Again my hands were like talons, strong to rend and slay.

CHAPTER FOUR

The Feasters of Thebes

THEY sat as Darda and I had seen them when we supped tonight—or last night? All looked intently in one direction. The tavern was the same. There were the same people, with the same waiters in attendance on the habitues.

But now, waiters and habitues were strangely garbed—in togas from ancient Rome, or the cloaks of old Phoenicians or Egyptians. The clothes were of white, above which the awful faces of the men were like ugly wounds. Also, I noticed that now, instead of chairs, the habitues reclined on luxurious couches; instead of tables there were tabourets, upon which ranged an array of the most gorgeous foods.

Every face was turned in my direction. Last night the habitues had all looked toward the long black drape. Now, I knew, the black drape had been removed, or rolled up, like a curtain in a mighty theater, so that the habitues could watch as they dined.

But what did they watch?

I didn't seek far for the answer to that! They watched the torture of Darda, *and the torture of Jay Dode as he tried to release Darda!*

Like performers in an arena, Darda and I had been, for the delectation of these men who, for tonight, imagined themselves kings and rulers in—Thebes?

Their mouths moved as they ate of their food. They smacked their lips over wine as red as blood. Waiters filled the glasses as quickly as they were emptied—and the watchers never blinked their eyes, so intent were they on what we were doing.

For while Darda and I had not been able to see because of the mirrors, these people of the tavern had been able to look through the backs of the mirrors at us! I knew there were mirrors like that, which men had made for man's amusement. Here the keeper of the tavern had turned them to ghastly purpose.

No wonder no women came to that tavern—save only those who were intended to come!

Scouts for this group had seen Darda. The brown card had been the next step. And it had been intended for me to follow her, to bash my brains senselessly against the mirrors—as part of the awful ritual of these men who imagined themselves feasting in Thebes!

What a ghastly pagan cult, if this were true. I tried to think back, in that infinitesmal heartbeat of time before I went through the broken mirror, to books I had read about the ancient feasts of rulers. Snatches of them came to me, oddments from varied reading.

" . . . a woman walked on her hands among a forest of knives, whose blades would have slain her had she fallen. . . ."

" . . . a woman sought to curry favor with the masters by amusing them . . . she fought another woman, a knife in either hand, slowly but surely killing her, a stroke at a time with the blades. . . ."

" . . . all during the feast a beautiful girl slave moaned amid the laughter of her lords. Crucified head downward against the wall, it took her all the many hours of the feast to die . . ."

" . . . one woman inspired her lords to laughter by her challenge to three sturdy, masculine slaves. . . "

So, here in this tavern, money had made

it possible for men to fancy themselves beyond modern law, beyond the law of God, beyond everything except their lusts for power, exemplified in this torture play with their victims both men and women! And the women must be fair, the men powerful enough not to die too soon!

Here, indeed, Darda was safe from the usual sacrilege men might visit upon a beautiful woman in their power.

But what a horror they set in the place of that sacrilege!

I WOULD make an end of it. I could not find Darda. But here, somewhere amid the feasters, was one who must know which of the many Dardas was mine. Mine, did I say? Yes, mine! Now I knew something which it had taken this horror to show me. There was something earthy, after all, in what I felt for Darda.

She was my woman, my mate. And I would hold her against the world.

The waiter who had served us tonight saw me through the hole in the mirror. He could have seen only my eyes, but I saw his face go white as he stared at me, straight ahead. I stepped back and crashed through.

The waiter started away from me, stumbling backward, his hands lifted as though he would protect his head.

The habitues, as though they thought this, too, were part of the ghastly entertainment for which they paid, laughed in glee as the gory apparition which was Jay Dode crashed a second time into their tavern—or should one say their banquet hall in ancient Thebes?

I gave Black no time to defend himself.

"This one," I whispered inside me, "knows the secret of the mirrors. I shall spare his life. But these others . . ."

I was mad, no doubt about that. For, as I jumped to the attack I thought of how Christ himself, whip in hand, had lashed the moneychangers from His temple. My cause was as righteous as His had been, and His strength must have been in me as I set about my task of mercy and justice.

I struck Black on the side of the head. He crashed to the floor so hard that for a moment I thought I had slain him. The habitues laughed.

I stood between two of the couches of the "rulers." I stooped, my arms flung wide. I caught the two by the backs of their garments. Heavy, sodden with food and drink, they were difficult to lift. But I lifted them because my arms were strong to punish.

I swung them, even as I lifted, so that they faced each other. I brought their heads together with all the strength at my command. The sound was music in my ears. I heard myself croaking:

"Does this seem a part of your banquet, O rulers in Thebes? You are strong—like most rulers!—to witness the torture of others, while you feast and drink. But are you strong to bear?"

I hurled the two from me, to right and left. I leaped the couch of one of them, my own blood dripping redly upon it. I must have been a crimson horror indeed as I sprang, for the two upon whom I next fastened my hands—which were as red with blood as my face and my torso—squealed like frightened rabbits, or like mice caught in a trap.

They squealed but once. I gave them no time for more. As I cracked their skulls—so that never again should these two, at least, look upon the glory of Darda—I looked at the sprawled body of Black on the floor, making sure that he did not regain consciousness and escape me in the end, since he was my key to the true shape of Darda the glorious—now glorious no longer because the hands of vandals had been heavy upon her.

Only in my memory of her, it came to

me—an added torture as I worked out my own justice—would I ever be able to transfer my ideal of her to canvas . . . if, even, I ever again essayed the use of brush and paint.

"No living man, until tonight," I heard myself shouting, "ever looked upon *her*. No man who has done so *shall* live!"

THEY squealed at that. They staggered from their couches, heavy with drink, tried to escape me. I saw madness growing in the eyes of many, who must have been near to madness already, else they never would have been "feasters in Thebes."

I overtook them, struck them behind the heads, alongside the jaws, watched them go crashing down to the floor. I laughed as they fell—and as I stayed aware of Black, that he should not escape me.

They scuttled for safety.

" . . . out of the temple they go," I told myself, "out of the temple . . . out of the temple . . ."

One thought of the door. He screamed, and others followed. I pursued. I saw a whip, tip of it red with blood. The Faun had been the last to use it. I caught it up, flung it down again. The blood of Darda was too precious, even for this. But was it? What better than her blood to mete the ends of justice? I caught it up, and like a superman wielded it.

I drove the last of the feasters out into the street in their white garments, out into the wintry wind from the Hudson, now colder than the breath from the oldest glacier. And they went, and were glad to escape. They hadn't died, those who went; not in body at least, but I knew by what I saw in their eyes, as they looked back over their shoulders, that the minds of some of them had died a little, which might be even worse than death itself.

Then I turned back to Black.

I jerked him to his feet. I drove him through the broken place in the mirror. The man who held Darda up, with her head back, had not deserted his post.

"Tell me, Black!" I said.

His fear gave voice as he told me. I think he somehow warned the man who held Darda—the man with the assymetrical face. That one leaped away from her. I released Black long enough to catch him, to crush in his face with the hardest blow I had ever delivered, ever would deliver again. Darda fell face downward on the floor.

I dropped beside her, turned her over, sought to cure her pain with kisses. I kissed the marks upon her, held her tightly. Her lips opened, finally. So did her eyes. They looked into mine as my lips touched hers for the first time. Her arms trembled as they went around me. I lifted my head, because I could feel her lips against mine, shaping words:

"I do not mind, really, Jay," she was saying. "Really I do not mind, if the result of all the terror has finally taught you *this!*"

From Black I forced the headless canvas he had stolen through his minion, the man in the broad brimmed hat. The feasters had seen the face of Darda, many times. They had needed the canvas to show them the glory that only I had seen.

Back at my studio, just before dawn, I turned all my paintings to the wall. Neither I nor Darda mentioned the room down the hall, for now, in a Oneness which terror had given us, which mundane law would truly arrange for us when doctors had done for Darda what even my love could not do, we had need for my studio only, and no need at all for the many pale Dardas.

THE END

—TWICE A MONTH—

—*April 1st Issue*—	—*April 15th Issue*—
A feature-length novel of a man who was born to outlawry!	A human, moving novel of a man's fight for honor!
GUNPOWDER HERITAGE	**BADLANDS ORPHAN**
by Oliver King	by Walt Coburn
—*Three Western Novelettes*—	—*Three Old West Novelettes*—
The Rolling R Rides to Glory	**Heir to Glory Range**
by Walt Coburn	by Ray Nafziger
Guns for a Nester!	**The Soul of Salado**
by Harry F. Olmsted	by Harry F. Olmsted
The Whistler's Gallows-Trap	**Bought with Gunsmoke**
by E. B. Mann	by John Colohan
—*Three Short Stories by*—	—*Three Short Stories by*—
Bart Cassidy	**Bart Cassidy**
John G. Pearsol	**Miles Overholt**
George Armin Shaftel	**George Armin Shaftel**
—*and*—	—*and*—
Other Features!	**Other Features!**
On Sale Now!	*On Sale . . . . March 29th*

  "STORIES THAT BRING THE OLD WEST BACK TO LIFE!"

GRAVEYARD GUARDIAN

By
Robert C. Blackmon
(Author of "Moon Mania," etc.)

What mad, half-human monster leered at Roy Barnes in that noisesome abode of the dead? What relationship did it bear to the Gravedigger, the Sheriff, and the girl Roy loved so desperately? And worst of all, what grisly doom overshadowed all those imprisoned there in that ancient bastille of despair?

THE SOUND was strangely muffled, as though dulled by the furry blackness on either side of Roy Barnes' slowly moving coupe; and the car's headlights, a livid finger in the cool, moist night, made hulking things of the low brush beside the narrow dirt road. A slight smile touched Roy's fine-cut, sensitive lips. Some farmer with a shotgun, he murmured, blazing away at a 'coon, or——

His long fingers tightened on the steering wheel, his wiry body stiffened against the leather back of the coupe seat. Not a shotgun—the sound was too flat for that. More likely a pistol, an automatic. Yet— farmers around Sheridan would hardly own an automatic. They——

A short laugh pushed to his lips and he relaxed, a frown marring his high forehead. He had more important things to worry about. For instance—the problem of how much he could save out of the three hundred he'd get for clerking through these three summer months in Uncle David Barnes' general store in Sheridan. He'd need every cent of it. And more—much more. An M. D. sheepskin costs plenty, and he was just in his second year.

Roy stared through the windshield, scarcely seeing the rutted dirt road. Determination gleamed in his blue eyes. He'd make it. Three hundred from Uncle David, back to school until that ran out, then another job. That was the way to do it!

A curve loomed ahead and Roy automatically turned the wheel. The headlights swung, silvered the road around the curve. Suddenly, his drawn breath made a sharp sound in the coupe, and Roy's wiry legs tautened as his feet jammed brake and clutch. The coupe shuddered to a halt. Roy's left fist twisted the door handle and he hit the running board, dropped to the dust of the road.

Less than fifty feet ahead and squarely in the headlights a slim-bodied girl knelt in the center of the road, leaning over a furry, black shape. She looked up, brown eyes strangely large in a small, oval face framed by curly, jet-black hair. Her mouth, small and red against the smooth white of her skin, was drawn in a frightened O.

She pushed to her feet, brushed dust from the front of her simply cut dress with one slim hand.

"My—my dog—" Her voice was soft, throaty. "He ran away. I came after him and—and found him with this dirty bone. I was trying to take it away from him when you came around the curve and——"

But Roy didn't hear the rest. A cold prickle started along the back of his neck, spread to his scalp. The quickening beat of his pulse sent blood throbbing to his temples. His mouth felt suddenly dry, cold.

The girl, as she talked, had extended one hand toward him. And grasped in the slim fingers was a femoral—a green-stained human bone!

——"and I'm going to lock him up to teach him not to run away," she finished.

SHE tossed the bone into the brush at the side of the road. The shaggy black dog followed its flight with bright, eager eyes. But when he started after it, the girl called him back at once. "Goliath!" The abrupt sharpness of her cry made Roy jump. "Come back this instant!" she added. Then she turned to Roy, smiling demurely as the dog crouched whimpering at her feet. "You—you don't remember me, do you, Roy Barnes? I'm Edna Lang. I was just a kid when you left—pigtails, and all that. I heard your Uncle David say you were coming back for a while. I—I'm glad to see you."

"Why—Edna Lang!" Ray stalked forward, grasped the slim fingers she offered —and tried to forget that they'd held a moss-scabbed human bone a moment ago. "I'd never have known you. I—uh— Listen, is there a cemetery anywhere near here?"

Edna Lang's chiding laugh rang clear in the cool air. "You've forgotten Sheridan, as well as me!" she cried merrily. "The old Stockade where they buried the Yankee prisoners during the Civil War isn't over three hundred yards away. Over there." She pointed off to the right. Her dark eyes were gleaming in the coupe headlights. "And old Frank Diggs is still caretaker, and he still stays drunk, as he did when we used to pitch rocks against his house to make him swear. I don't go to the Stockade now." Her small face went grave. "It—it's supposed to be haunted—or something." Then her lips flashed into another quick smile. "It's been nice to see you, Roy. You—must come to see me while you're here. Now, I've got to go. Come on, Goliath."

"How about going with me in the coupe. I can——" Roy started.

"No, thanks. It's just a little way by the path." Edna Lang started toward the side of the road. Goliath followed.

"But Edna! You'll have to pass the stockade. I——"

"I won't go near it. Come on, Goliath. I'll see you at the store in the morning, Roy. Good night!"

The next instant she was swallowed by the darkness to the right of the road. Roy could hear the patter of her feet die away, the sharp barking of the dog. After that the silence was unbroken.

Slowly, thoughtfully, he went back to his coupe. From the door pocket he got a flashlight, and strode toward the spot where Edna had tossed the bone. A short search disclosed it, lying there in the brush. By the light of the flash he examined the thing.

It was a *femur*, all right. Still moist and moldy. It had evidently been buried a long time. The dog had——

A sudden thought flashed into his mind. The Stockade! The bone had come from the grave of a Union soldier. Frank Diggs was too drunk and lazy to take care of the graves. The dog had found a grave partly open and had unearthed the bone.

Roy strode back to the coupe, placed the bone on the floor-boards, started to get in the car. And then, his foot already on the running board, he stopped. His pose was that of a statue, but every nerve in his wiry body was jangling with abrupt shock.

A shrill, terror-filled scream had cut through the night. It fairly knifed through the pumping blood in his ears. It was the cry of a woman faced by some ghastly horror.

Edna Lang!

Roy left the running board in a flashing leap, plunged into the brush at the right of the road. Dimly, he was aware of branches whipping his face, tugging at his clothing. Yet the mad ringing of that scream shrilled in his ears, forced him on toward the Stockade. A briar clawed at his ankle, raked the skin through his socks. He kicked himself free, pushed on, his flashlight making a racing white spot ahead of him.

He reached the Stockade, where his light washed a scanty stubble of grey headstones. He swung it farther, and it spotted a towering shape which sent horror-chilled blood coursing through his veins.

THE thing had the general shape of a man, yet all human resemblance stopped there. It was tall, at least six feet, and jutting from what should have been a face was a ghastly, beaklike thing now slimy with blood. It had no eyes, but behind the horrible beak was a tangled mass of greyish hair. Its hands, shapeless, dead white things dripping with blood, were raised in a half-defensive gesture. Its body was a queer black hulk.

In that first quick flash Roy saw the body over which the *thing* was standing—

the body of a man. The corpse's chest was bared, and a horrible mass of blood marred the white skin. Roy went abruptly sick as he saw the dead man's chest was but a deep-gouged hole of raw flesh.

Then he saw Edna Lang. The girl was sprawled upon the ground some distance to his right, near an open grave.

He had time for no more than a look. The towering thing made a queer, gurgling sound, whirled, and galloped off into the darkness.

Roy sprinted after it, following the noise it made as it tore through the thick brush. But in a moment he missed the sound of the thing's retreat. He stopped, listening. And the mad pounding of blood in his ears blocked out everything.

Nerves jerking, he turned, strode back to the Stockade. But when he reached it —once again he froze motionless. Hard muscle knotted at the angles of his jaws, goose-pimples of horror broke out all over his rigid body. Somewhere in the darkness ahead something was gnawing and crunching bones!

Pressing a stiff finger to the flashlight switch, Roy shot the beam toward the sound. Relief spread a warm glow through his body. For picked out in the shaft of light, was Edna Lang's dog Goliath. The animal crouched over something on the ground, worrying it and now growling softly.

Roy strode to Edna. He breathed easier only when he was sure she was uninjured.

The girl lay slightly on her side. One slim hand rested on the warm swell of her young breasts. Her small face seemed drawn with terror. Even as Roy looked, her lips moved, though he couldn't make out anything she said. Her eyes fluttered, opened—and a frightened cry burst from her throat.

"Take it easy, dear." Roy's deep voice carried the soothing quality of a future physician. "Just lie still. Everything is all right." He pressed her cold hand reassuringly.

"I—Goliath ran away again—" Her voice broke. Then she went on more calmly. "He came toward the Stockade and I followed, then I saw that—terrible —" Her smooth shoulders jerked spasmodically.

"Just keep quiet." Ray patted her hand. "You're perfectly safe now. You stay right here. I'll be back in a moment."

He pushed to his feet, stalked to the body of the man. The corpse lay upon its back, its sightless, horror-filled eyes staring up at the blackened sky. The lips were drawn, slightly parted; thin trickles of blood streaked the corners of the mouth.

The body looked to be that of man of about forty-five, slightly built. It was clad in rough, stained trousers and a faded blue shirt. The shirt had been ripped down to the waist, baring the chest. And that chest had been pierced by a fist-sized hole.

ROY gritted his teeth, against a surging wave of nausea which threatened to engulf him.

The hole in the corpse's chest was just the right shape and size to have been made by the ghastly beak of the thing he had seen. And the thing's beak had been foul with blood!

A queer mixture of horror and fear seeped into Roy's tensed mind. Mad thoughts stirred in his brain.

Was the thing some ghastly monster which ripped open the graves of the dead, to feast upon . . . ? Cold reason pushed the thought away. The graves in the Stockade were the tombs of soldiers killed by wounds and disease while imprisoned in the building which had once stood upon this spot. And *their* bodies had wasted to moldering bones by now—bones like the one Edna had taken from Goliath. While the man who lay at his feet had been dead not over a half-hour!

His forehead creased by a deep, puzzled frown, Roy swung the light toward Goliath, then strode toward the animal.

It crouched over a jumble of green-clotted human bones. Alongside, a roughly rectangular hole exhaled the musty reek of new-turned earth. Roy could see instantly that the place was a recently disturbed grave. He swung the light toward the hole, and the bright flash of a small metal object upon the ground caught his eye. He picked the article up, held it in the light—and his lips tightened grimly.

The metal object was an empty brass cartridge case, fitting, perhaps, a 7.65 millimeter Luger automatic. The metal was bright; in fact the case had the sulphuric smell of burned powder still clinging to it. It had been fired recently, within the hour!

Roy's blue eyes narrowed and he grunted softly. So the sound he'd heard *had* been an automatic, fired in the Stockade!

He dropped the empty shell in his coat pocket, stepped toward the dog. "Goliath," he rapped, "get away from those bones!"

The dog crouched lower, growled. Roy stabbed downward with a long-fingered hand, grasped the scruff of the dog's neck, lifted him from the ground. Goliath's growl changed abruptly to a whimper.

"Roy!" Edna Lang had gotten to her feet. "There—there's something—moving—coming toward—" She darted to his side, gripped his arm. He could feel her slim hands trembling with fright.

Something moved in the darkness behind her. A tall shape loomed in the gloom.

Chill sweat beaded Roy's forehead. Stiff-muscled, he swung the flashlight toward the unknown, stalking shape.

Impaled in the bright spot of light was a tall, bony figure. Close-set, bright eyes gleamed from a weathered face. Gnarled fists gripped a double-barreled shotgun in front of a narrow chest.

Roy recognized the man instantly. It was Sheriff Carl Hedge.

Hedge's shotgun swung toward the light. "Swing that damn' thing!" he rumbled. "And don't make no funny moves. I got you covered. What you——"

"Hold everything, Sheriff. This is Roy Barnes and Edna Lang." Roy turned the flashlight upon himself and the girl. "Edna came in here after her dog. She saw a terrible, beak-faced thing and screamed. I ran up here, saw the thing——"

"Beak-faced—Thing?" Sheriff Hedge grounded the butt of his shotgun, jammed a gnarled fist on his hip. "What you mean —a bird?"

RAPIDLY Roy explained. When he told of the corpse. Sheriff Hedge strode to the body, looked down as Roy held the light.

"Gus Harper! Why, Gus an' me've been friends for twenty years or more." The Sheriff turned a pair of gleaming eyes to Roy. "You been studyin' for to be a Doctor. . . What killed him?"

"The chest wound, I guess. Unless—" Roy's long fingers slid into his coat pocket, touched the empty automatic shell—"it was this. I found this shell on the ground a moment ago. It's been fired recently. I believe I heard the very shot about a half-hour ago. Perhaps——"

"Reckon you're mistaken." Sheriff Hedge took the shell, turned it over. "Nobody'd want to shoot Gus, then dig a hole like that in his chest with him already dead."

He pushed the empty shell into the pocket of his corduroy trousers. "I been hearin' things 'bout this Stockade cemetery bein' haunted or somethin'. 'Lowed it was all talk, but—" He shook his grizzled head slowly. "Reckon that beak-faced thing done it. I'll get a posse an' comb this——"

In the darkness, off to the left, a twig snapped.

Roy spun, his flashlight beam sweeping toward the sound.

A gaunt figure reared at the edge of the Stockade cemetery. A tall, bony man. His long arms dropped straight from bony shoulders to end in big, shapeless hands which swung near the baggy knees of his wrinkled trousers. His lined face, pierced by the twin bright spots of his eyes but with a large, flabby mouth, was surmounted by a tangled mass of greyish hair.

Roy's quick-drawn breath sucked through set teeth. The beak-faced thing he'd seen in the Stockade a few minutes ago had had hair just like this wild, greyish mop.

"It—it's Frank Diggs!" Edna Lang's sharp whisper sounded almost in Roy's ear, and he could feel the girl's slight figure press against him.

"What you doin' here?" Diggs walked toward them, moving with a queerly shuffling gait. "Nobody ain't supposed to be in here at night. You got to get out. I'm the caretaker an' I got orders to—" He saw Sheriff Hedge and stopped, blinking owlishly. "Hy'de, Sheriff. What——"

Roy and Hedge explained. Diggs' toothless gums showed almost black against the light as his flabby mouth sagged open. He looked at the corpse, picked nervously at his ragged clothing, the while he eyed both Roy and Hedge suspiciously.

"I ain't got nothin' to do with this, Sheriff," he whined. "You—you got to get him out of here. This here cemetery's Government property an'—" His voice

went shrill, cracked. "By God, I don't believe either one of you! There ain't no ha'nts in here—ain't never been! There ain't no beak-faced thing! You're lyin', all of you! You been adiggin' in my graves! By God, I——"

"I'll take Edna home, Sheriff," broke in Roy. "You'll find me at Uncle David's store."

"Go ahead, Roy."

Sheriff Hedge gripped Diggs' bony arm. "You, Frank," he rumbled, "get back to your shack and stay there until I come for you. I'm takin' charge of this. I'm raisin' a posse and combin' this whole valley for that beak-faced thing that killed Gus. When I find it——"

"You ain't gonna find it!" Diggs screeched. His flabby lips writhed over his toothless gums. "There ain't no such thing!"

DAVID BARNES sat in a sagging chair near the rear of the Barnes' General Store. His gray eyes twinkled as he looked at Roy, sitting near him.

"So you saw little Edna Lang, eh? Took her home, eh?" He chuckled deep in his thin chest, sucked vigorously on his foul black pipe. "Guess you two was so excited in the Stockade you don't know what you saw, excepting maybe Gus. You just——"

"I tell you I saw the thing." Roy leaned forward tensely. "I heard the shot, and I found that empty cartridge case. I'd swear it had been fired within a half-hour. Gus Harper hadn't been dead a half-hour, I'd say. That hole in his chest was——"

"Maybe the hole looked bigger, somehow." David Barnes' thin lips tightened about his pipe-stem as he eyed Roy steadily.

"No, I don't think so." Roy smiled mirthlessly. "I've seen enough dead men, Uncle David, not to be stampeded by a little blood. I'm positive that I saw the beak-faced creature. Edna saw it, too. I'm positive——"

"Your great-grandmother was positive once too often, Roy," David Barnes broke in mildly. "Guess you've heard all about it. Anyway, when the Yankees came through here, they broke into your great-grandmother Amanda Barnes' home, and a rat-faced, peg-legged Yankee soldier caught her trying to hide a small silver box that contained twelve diamonds she'd pried out of their settings in rings and brooches. The stones ranged from two to five carats apiece. Amanda was trying to save them to help tide the family over Reconstruction days. She wouldn't give the silver box up, and the peg-legged Yankee killed her. Then he took the stones anyway." Barnes, puffing slowly, fell silent.

"I've heard about my great-grandmother, Uncle David." Roy's voice went soft. "Positive or not—she must have been a courageous woman. But to get back to tonight. That Luger shell——"

"Luger?" David Barnes snapped erect. "Why, Frank Diggs used to have one of them German Lugers! I've seen it. He——"

"By George!" Roy jerked to his feet. "Sheriff Hedge ought to know that! I left him at the Stockade. Only take me a few minutes to run out there and tell him. I'm going to! I'll be back in a few minutes, Uncle David!"

Leaving the store, Roy headed for his coupe.

PARKING his car near where he'd seen Edna Lang, Roy left the machine and headed toward the Stockade, flashlight in hand.

The night seemed darker, cooler—and somehow more threatening. Thoughts of Frank Diggs possessing a Luger automatic had driven the idea of the beak-faced creature from Roy's mind, but now a mental picture of the ghastly thing was becoming clearer and clearer as he neared the Stockade.

A night-bird fluttered in the trees off to the right. His pulse quickened. Chilling thoughts beat in his brain. Perhaps Diggs had fired the Luger in the cemetery in the last day or two and had left the empty shell on the ground. Perhaps the beak-faced thing——

Roy stopped abruptly. Cold sweat bathed his body. His stiff fingers switched off the flashlight and he stood motionless, listening.

Somewhere from the darkness ahead had come a weird, moaning cry. It welled louder, louder—then chopped short on a choking sob. It stopped.

The smothering blackness seemed to press closer about Roy, to touch his eyeballs, his lips with cold, dead fingers. Clamoring blood filled his ears with a mad cacophony of sound, so that he had to fight to keep back the chilling blast of terror which swelled within him.

The beak-faced horror might be lurking in the nearest shadow, waiting to plunge its bloody fangs into his chest, rip his vitals out. Roy's lungs went cold, tight. But he pushed on toward the Stockade. His lips were grim, his muscles taut.

Nearing the cemetery, he saw a dim glow of light ahead. He slowed his pace, crept forward silently, and reached the first grey headstone.

In front of him, fifty feet away, the dim glow seemed to be coming from the earth. Then he saw what it was. The light was coming from the mouth of rectangular hole in the ground. Raw, piled dirt made an oblong mound beside the hole.

Then the full significance of the sight bit into Roy's brain. The rectangular hole was an open grave! The light was coming from the earthy maw of a tomb!

Roy stared, scarcely breathing. Something was moving in the light. Something moved—and a ghastly shape rose from that grave. Outlined against the glow, Roy could make out a shapeless black body, huge, dead white hands, a tangled mass of greyish hair—and a pointed, blood-smeared beak where there should have been a face. The thing rising from the open tomb was the beak-faced horror!

Mad thoughts tumbled in Roy's mind; the clammy fingers of a nameless, stunning terror gripped him. Instinctively, he chocked back the cry rising to his stiff lips. Diggs was wrong—there *was* a beak-faced monster!

The ghastly thing crawled from the grave, spewing low, throaty sounds, sounds of gloating triumph. It seemed to be clutching something in one dead white hand. The other hand, from which the light was coming, was screened from Roy's eyes by the shapeless black bulk of the body.

The thing seemed to glide over the ground and the light made a crawling splotch of brilliance on the ground before it. Then the light struck a shape sprawled upon the ground, and Roy's breath stuck in his suddenly tight throat.

The shape was human. Its chest was bared, and the flesh of the chest was a raw, bloody horror. The beak-faced thing had claimed another victim—and that victim looked like Sheriff Hedge!

Roy ground his teeth together, to control his jerking nerves.

The gliding thing had turned and was moving in another direction, its light creeping before it. Eyes glued to the moving glow, Roy stared, body stiff and tense. Then the light touched another figure upon the ground, and pounding blood threatened to burst its veins and flood his brain. The moving light had spotted the figure of a girl . . . Edna Lang!

AS the beak-faced creature neared the prone girl, a black, furry shape darted from her side, flung itself upon the advancing horror. Roy heard a short, angry bark, a chesty growl. The leaping black thing was Goliath, Edna's dog.

The shapeless arm of the beak-faced thing swept in a vicious arc. Steel flashed in the dim light. The meaty thud of a blow sounded. Goliath yelped once, and dropped to the ground.

The ghastly monster leaned over Edna. Its dead white hands reached for her and Roy, frozen stiff with horror, saw a crimson drop detach from the dead white fingers, spatter on the white skin of Edna's throat.

Something seemed to explode within his brain then and he felt his body jerk erect, heard strange, roaring sounds burst from his lips. He plunged forward, racing for the beak-faced monstrosity.

It whirled, and something whizzed past Roy's head. He caught the gleam of red-misted steel, plunged on. The thing seemed to squirm, pawing at its black body, then a searing flash of fire blossomed out. Roy felt a tearing pain strike his left arm, heard a deafening roar. Then he crashed into the beak-faced creature.

His pawing right fist scraped cloth, backed by hard muscles. He lashed out again, banged into flesh-cushioned bone. A hollow grunt sounded.

Roy tried to strike with his left fist, and found he couldn't raise the arm. It seemed queerly dead, powerless. He smashed out with his right again, felt something crush, give way under the blow. A cold, slimy something exploded against his mouth and he felt the hot spurt of blood over his chin, the numbness of smashed lips. He felt himself falling, the hard ground against his back. A smothering weight dropped down upon him.

The light had fallen to the ground, and in its dim glow, Roy could see the thing above him—a tangled mass of greyish hair, a long, pointed beak slimed with blood. The sharp bill lowered, touched his face, and Roy smashed out with the desperation of sheer terror.

His fist banged hard flesh. A throaty roar of pain boomed above him. He thought dully—then he *could* hurt the thing!

Cold, slimy hands clawed his throat, tightened until a red mist crawled before his eyes. His lungs swelled to the point of bursting and he tore with agony-maddened fingers at the hands about his throat. They loosened momentarily and he dragged searing air into his chest, felt strength flow like heady wine into his veins. Something banged his forehead, blasted lights within his skull, and that throttling pressure gripped his throat again.

Roy twisted his body frantically, tried to throw the weight off his chest, clawed with his right hand at the shapeless, rubbery things tightening about his throat. Congested blood hammered at his brain, strength ebbed from his muscles as water through a sieve. He twisted weakly, winced as his injured left arm was wrenched. But the resulting pain momentarily pushed back the crawling blackness which threatened to engulf him.

He thrust out with his right arm, hoping to get leverage to turn his body, break the grip about his throat. His clawing fingers touched cold steel. Forcing his hand to grasp, his dimming senses recognized the object he clutched to be a gun—specifically, an automatic. Raising its ton-like weight with a racking effort, he swung weakly at the black bulk above him.

Steel thudded on bone, and a bellow of rage came from above him. He struck again, blindly. The pressure left his throat, but slimy fingers gripped his right wrist, twisted the gun. He gripped the weapon with all his might, tried to swing it again. A savage movement tore the automatic from his hand. But even in the moment of losing it, the weapon exploded, almost deafening him with its roaring blast.

A mad scream of agony shrilled in Roy's ears and he felt the weight upon his chest shift, topple. The black figure dropped down upon him, squirming, groaning, and something warm dribbled upon his cheek, streaked across his jaw.

SUCKING cold air into his burning lungs, he pushed the moaning figure aside, staggered to his feet. He gritted his teeth as the movement twisted his left arm.

The light lay upon the ground ten feet away. He stumbled toward it, saw it was a flashlight.

Picking it up, he staggered toward Edna Lang's slim form, lying nearby. At the second step his foot struck a small object upon the ground. He swung the light down, and stared dully. It looked like a small grey box. Moaning as the action set his left arm to throbbing, he leaned over, grasped the thing.

It felt cold, metallic to his fingers. He shifted the flashlight under his right armpit, clamped it tight, held the box in its white glare. Dully, his eyes made out the box's ornate outlines, noted the tracery of engraving upon its top. A—M—A—N—D—A. He spelled the letters out slowly. B—A—R——

God! What he held was the silver box Amanda Barnes had given her life to protect! His great-grandmother's . . .

Dazedly, Roy fumbled at the small metal container, got the lid loose. His eyes blinked as the earth-stained interior blazed with a fiery glory of reds, blues, greens: a flaming rainbow of color. The little silver box was filled with precious stones!

Moving feverishly, he snapped the box shut, jammed it in his coat pocket, stumbled toward Edna. The girl was beginning to stir. Her eyes opened. Seeing that she was all right, he turned, went back to the beak-faced creature.

It was, he saw now, a man. The beak was a crushed wreck of paper, wire and string. Roy pulled it from the thing's head. The greyish mop of hair came with the beak and revealed the pain-contorted features of—Sheriff Carl Hedge!

The tall law officer was moaning, mumbling words. Roy dropped to his knees, bent close.

"——I had to shoot Gus—He caught me—knew about—the box." Hedge's lips writhed with agony as he tried to raise his hand to his head. Roy saw that his hands were encased in blood-smeared white rubber gloves . . . and then the purpose in wearing those rubber sheaths flashed into his mind.

"You opened Gus's chest to get the bullet!" he rapped. "You knew the bullet could be traced to the Luger. How you got the gun——"

"I bought it—off Frank two years ago." A bloody froth rose to the Sheriff's lips. "Heard David Barnes tell—Amanda—many times—Got to figuring—tracing diamond story——Found peg-legged Yankee was buried in Stockade—Nobody knew his name—anything about stones —Had to open——"

"You had to keep opening graves until you found the peg-legged Yankee soldier." Things clicked into place in Roy's mind. "The beak and haunt yarns were to scare off investigators. You found the peg-leg's grave tonight, after I left. And——"

"And peg-leg rotted away—The box was hidden in leg—Buried him with wooden leg and—Oh, God!"

The Sheriff stiffened, and the next instant went sickeningly limp.

ROY pushed to his feet. Swinging the light, he spotted the corpse he had seen while crouching at the edge of the Stockade. It was Frank Diggs. The cemetery caretaker, he decided, had come back, caught Hedge, and the Sheriff had shot him, then opened his chest too, to extract the damning bullet.

Roy heard a movement behind him, turned. Edna Lang had gotten to her feet. He stumbled to her.

"Roy!" she sobbed, "Goliath ran away again. I followed him to the Stockade —and—the terrible——"

Roy shoved his good right arm about her shoulders, pulled her quivering figure to him.

"I know. I know what happened, Edna dear," he said softly, and that soothing note of the future physician was in his quiet voice, despite the throbbing ache of his left arm. "Everything is all right now. I'll get my M. D. three months sooner now and—well—I know you've got the nerve to be a Doctor's wife!"

TWO BIG NOVELS!

Nat Schachner and Hugh B. Cave write *two* exciting, blood-chilling feature-length novels in the June issue of

 ## TERROR TALES   *Out April 25th!*

THE BLACK CHAPEL

S O NOW we are gathered here once more, my friends, the devoted followers of that most alluring and fascinating deity, Fear. Just as our forefathers, in the vanished, time-obscured past, congregated to worship the unintelligible forces of a malignant, malevolent nature, so are we come here to bow our heads while the last haunting chords of the Fearsome Goddess' swan song echo and reëcho eerily from wall to dark wall of this Black Chapel. It is a fitting requiem to the soul-gripping nightmare holiday we have just celebrated.

We have stood with Laura Standish, in *Chains of the Living Dead,* inside that desolate cabin, overshadowed by the roaring, evil façade of Superstition Mountain. With her, we looked into the terror-filled night at the mindless, soulless creatures who were linked together in chains of madness.

We have been at John Murdock's shoulder when he first felt the loathsome presence depicted in that *Portrait of Evil,* taking possession of him. We too crouched in that horrible crypt of murder while, axe in hand, he prepared—all unwillingly—for an evil thing beyond the understanding of normal man.

Side by side with Lucy Alcott when she fled screaming through the night—fleeing from the ghastly menace of *The Devil's Brewers*—we also were running.

When Fred Swift and Natalie listened to little Peter prattle innocently of his cult-mad kin, we listened too. When they saw the repulsively beautiful *Doom Flowers* growing from ancient Chloe's dirt-packed mouth, we also beheld the gruesome sight.

In Priestess of Death, we followed, breathless and awed, as the narrator raced on his mad journey to a rendezvous with the green-faced lure—a rendezvous with death!

And when Jay Dode struggled with the *Keepers of the Black Tavern,* frenzied that his beautiful Darda was being made the victim of a Roman holiday, we too, were there.

Finally, with Roy Barnes, we invaded that place of mouldering corpses, to find a beaked horror acting as a *Graveyard Guardian!*

So have we come at last to the end of this month's adventuring into the Realm of Fear. Now in truth can we join in a final lusty chant to conclude our eerie service.

For months, now, TERROR TALES readers have been clamoring for a place in which to express themselves. Here are some few of the many letters we have received.

Terror, Plus!

Editor, *Terror Tales:*

This is the first time I have ever written to the editor of a magazine, but the excellence of TERROR TALES impels me to do so.

American magazines arrive much later here, and so I have just finished reading the January issue. But I must say that it is supreme. It gives me a real chill, and the stories are marvelously well written, too. *When Love Went Mad!* by Mr. Zagat was a masterpiece of eerie fiction. I have resolved never to miss any of this writer's stories if it is humanly possible for me to do otherwise.

May I assure you of many devoted readers on this side of the pond who are avid TERROR TALES fans, among whom, one of the most ardent is

Yours very sincerely,
Leonard Thistlethwaite,
London, England.

Likes Cave!

Dear Editor:

I am laying down my February TERROR TALES to write you about Hugh B. Cave's masterpiece, *Enslaved to Satan.* I have been reading TERROR TALES long enough to expect to find outstanding stories in its pages—but this novel leaves me absolutely breathless with excitement.

There have been times when Mr. Cave has not done as well as this, but all is forgiven now. Anyone who can write a gripping, marrow-chilling story like this one, has my vote every time.

I like all the others too—Zagat, Cummings, Edson, and Blackmon. They're fine indeed, but *Enslaved to Satan* is the best story I *ever* read!

Jimmy Clarke,
Houston, Texas.

A Zagat fan.

To the Editor:

Well, Arthur Leo Zagat has sure done it again! Here I thought that *When Love Went Mad!* in the January issue was about as good as a story could be, and along comes *Riverfront Horror* in the February and knocks that for a loop of Chinese ash-cans.

This Zagat guy does something with words that makes my innards crawl up and down my spine—and boy oh boy! maybe you think I don't eat it up!

I've been reading TERROR TALES from the first issue, without skipping one, and I'll keep on, too, if you continue to have these knockouts, even if the mag comes out every week. And how's that for an idea, Mr. Ed? How about having a copy of TERROR TALES, all fresh and blood-chilling, on the stands every week?

Russell Eddy,
Denver, Colo.

A Sad Story!

Dear Mister Editor:

I am only now learning to read the English. As a result for that, I am reading all those interesting things which I can come over.

Imagine my great happiness it makes not many days ago when I found an example of your TERROR TALES at a periodical-selling-depot. Immediately I purchased for myself an edition, and read it with the greatest of joy.

Then, it makes a few days later, I was compositioning an exercise for my master of English, a North American gentleman who lives in this place. I had the opportunity to employ the word: ghoul. My teacher called to me after the class and questioned me of where I had learned such a word.

I told him veraciously, and he commanded that I should bring the example to the school the day after that day. I obeyed humbly, and can you imagine the happening?

My master has taken my edition away from me, and this evening when I was comming to leave the school, on passing his classroom, there was he, reading the magazine with much eagerness.

Luis Alborada,
Quinta, Nicaragua.

A Big Novelette of the French Foreign Legion

FOOLS FOR GLORY

by Georges Surdez

In the April 1st issue of

Twice a Month  15c

ALSO—THESE STIRRING STORIES: CHAMP, a story of the prize ring, by Eddy Orcutt. SAILOR OF FORTUNE, a story of deep waters, by Jacland Marmur. THE WOODS RUNNER, a serial of Indian days, by Hugh Pendexter. WAY FOR HIS EXCELLENCY, a story of the Spanish Main, by Arthur D. Howden Smith. RIVETS, a story of the bridge builders, by R. R. Lee and others—also *Camp-Fire, Ask Adventure.*

 The April 1st issue of *Adventure* is on sale March 15th

YOU CAN'T BEAT OUR PRICES

And we defy anyone to excel our quality. Every standard brand tire reconstructed by our modern method is positively guaranteed to give full 12 months' service under the severest road conditions. This guarantee is backed by our entire financial resources.

Buy Now Before Prices Advance!

SAVE ON TIRES

BALLOON TIRES

Size	Rim	Tires	Tubes
29 x 4.40—21		$2.15	$0.85
29 x 4.50—20		2.35	.85
30 x 4.50—21		2.40	.85
28 x 4.75—19		2.45	.95
29 x 4.75—20		2.50	.95
29 x 5.00—19		2.85	1.05
30 x 5.00—20		2.85	1.05
32 x 5.00—22		3.65	1.05
27 x 5.25—17		2.90	1.15
28 x 5.25—18		2.90	1.15
29 x 5.25—19		2.95	1.15
30 x 5.25—20		2.95	1.15
31 x 5.25—21		3.25	1.15
27 x 5.50—17		3.35	1.15
28 x 5.50—18		3.35	1.15
29 x 5.50—19		3.35	1.15
30 x 5.50—20		3.35	1.15
.. x 6.00—16		3.75	1.45
29 x 6.00—17		3.40	1.15
30 x 6.00—18		3.40	1.15
31 x 6.00—19		3.40	1.15
32 x 6.00—20		3.45	1.25
33 x 6.00—21		3.65	1.25
29 x 6.50—17		3.45	1.35
30 x 6.50—18		3.50	1.35
31 x 6.50—19		3.60	1.35
32 x 6.50—20		3.75	1.35
31 x 7.00—17		3.95	1.55
34 x 7.00—20		4.60	1.65
35 x 7.00—21		4.60	1.65

REGULAR CORD TIRES

Size	Tires	Tubes
30 x 3	$2.25	$0.65
30 x 3½	2.35	.75
31 x 4	2.95	.85
32 x 4	2.95	.85
33 x 4	2.95	.85
34 x 4	3.25	.85
32 x 3½	2.70	.80
32 x 4½	3.35	1.15
33 x 4½	3.45	1.15
34 x 4½	3.45	1.15
30 x 5	3.65	1.35
33 x 5	3.75	1.45
35 x 5	3.95	1.55

TRUCK BALLOONS

Size	Tires	Tubes
6.00—20	$3.75	1.65
6.50—20	4.45	1.95
7.00—20	5.95	2.95
7.50—20	6.95	3.75
8.25—20	8.95	4.95
9.00—20	10.95	5.65
9.75—20	13.95	6.45

HEAVY DUTY TRUCKS

Size	Tires	Tubes
30 x 5	$4.25	$1.95
34 x 5	4.25	2.00
32 x 6	7.95	2.75
36 x 6	9.95	3.95
34 x 7	10.95	3.95
38 x 7	10.95	3.95
36 x 8	12.45	4.25
40 x 8	15.95	4.95

ALL OTHER TRUCK SIZES

ALL TUBES ARE GUARANTEED BRAND NEW

Send Only $1 Deposit on each tire. (On each Truck Tire send a $4 deposit.) We ship balance C. O. D., 5 per cent discount for full cash with order. Any tire failing to give 12 months' service will be replaced at half price.

GREAT LAKES TIRE COMPANY, Dept. 789
4014 SOUTH STATE STREET,   CHICAGO, ILL.

Remember

12 MONTHS WRITTEN GUARANTEE BOND WITH EVERY TIRE

WE WANT DEALERS

www.ingramcontent.com/pod-product-compliance
Lightning Source LLC
Chambersburg PA
CBHW080913020726
47502CB00008B/2446